Also available from Unsung Stories

OUT OF THE DARKNESS

EDITED BY DAN COXON

UNSUNG
STORIES

Published by Unsung Stories

3 Rosslyn Road
London E17 9EU, United Kingdom

www.unsungstories.co.uk

First edition published in 2021
First impression

Hardback ISBN: 978-1-912658-12-1
Paperback ISBN: 978-1-912658-11-4
ePub ISBN: 978-1-912658-13-8

Edited by Dan Coxon
Proofreading by Jonathan Oliver
Cover design by Vince Haig
Text design by Cox Design Limited
Typesetting by Vince Haig

Printed in the UK by TJ Books Ltd, Padstow, Cornwall

CONTENTS

INTRODUCTION

When I first started work on this book, at the back end of 2019, mental health was a hot topic in the media. According to some estimates, one in four people in the UK will experience mental health issues every year, ranging from schizophrenia to mild depression. On a global scale, that figure rises to 792 million. Even more worrying is the fact that over 70 per cent of people suffering from mental health problems receive no treatment at all. Pile these statistics on top of one another, and that's a whole heap of suffering.

As someone who suffers from depression, the news articles were more than just another media storm. My depression began at some point in my teens (which is not unusual: it's estimated that 75 per cent of mental illness starts before the age of eighteen), but it wasn't officially diagnosed until I was forty. Up to that point I had self-medicated with alcohol, periodically falling into bouts of severe depression and self-destructive behaviour. In short, I struggled – and at the time, I didn't know why, or what to do about it. As mental health increasingly entered the public discourse, and as I began to find my own way out of that long, dark tunnel, I wanted to contribute something to the discussion. This book felt like the natural response.

Then the Covid-19 pandemic hit.

If Britain – and the world – was suffering a mental health crisis before, then it has been doubled by the effects of the lockdown and the virus itself. The coronavirus struck a blow not only to our physical health, but also to our mental wellbeing, as loved ones died, jobs were lost, social interactions were limited and the ever-present dangers of living a normal life multiplied exponentially. People who had never experienced anxiety attacks before found themselves nervous at the prospect of leaving the house; those who stayed at home found themselves isolated and scared. The Centre for Mental Health has estimated that 10 million people will need mental health support in the UK as a direct consequence of Covid-19, with a staggering 1.5 million of those being under eighteen. Fuelled by the pandemic, what was a worrying swell in mental health issues has become a tsunami.

Clearly a single book isn't going to fix the problem (and a book of horror stories, at that). The treatment of mental illness needs to be ongoing, and dealt with at a governmental level. But this anthology of stories now seems more relevant than ever.

Horror and dark fantasy are often portrayed in the media – in their usual simplistic terms – as the cause of mental illness. Every time a violent crime is linked to a horror movie, they appear to rub their hands with glee. But my own experience – and the experience of many of those who read and write horror stories – is markedly different. I've had numerous conversations with horror writers who have suffered mental health issues, and have found solace and comfort in the genre. By exploring the dark recesses of the human psyche, these stories help illuminate and make sense of the world for those suffering from mental illness – a world of anxiety, and despair, and fear. It's by shining a light on these emotions that horror can help us understand and deal with our own issues. There is also a strong community surrounding the genre, both online and in person at book launches and conventions, that can offer support and help battle isolation. Those of us who missed Stokercon and Fantasycon this year due to the pandemic can testify that our mental health has taken a battering because of it.

I'm not suggesting that horror might be a cure for mental illness. To do so would be as simplistic as the arguments that aim to vilify it. But when I first conceived of this book, it struck me that an above average number of people in the genre community suffer from mental health issues, and it would be to everyone's benefit to bring the discussion of those issues out into the light. Acknowledging the problem is often the first step on the road to wellness.

The stories collected here all deal with mental health in some way, and many are written by people who have first-hand experience of the challenges mental illness can present. They tackle the topics of anxiety, depression, obsessive–compulsive disorder and other issues, as well as the pressures mental illness can place on family members and friends – sometimes obliquely, sometimes head-on. At times that can make for challenging reading, but the authors have all actively engaged with the central philosophy of this book: that with support and open discussion, those who are suffering from mental health problems can move out of the darkness and into the light. In addition, all the authors involved are donating their fees and royalties to Together for Mental Wellbeing, and I will also be adding my fees to that donation, supporting the charity in helping people with mental health issues on their journey towards better mental wellbeing and independent lives. Just by buying this book, you've already made a small difference.

If nothing else, I hope these stories help you talk to your friends and loved ones in a different way about your and their issues, and that the horror genre will begin to openly discuss mental health in a positive and engaged way. In the words of Bob Hoskins, it's good to talk. The conversation starts here.

Dan Coxon, April 2021

ABOUT THE CHARITY

Together for Mental Wellbeing is a national charity supporting people who experience mental distress to lead fulfilling and independent lives.

We value people as experts in what works best for them, and each individual we work alongside influences and shapes the support that they and others receive from us.

Founded in 1879 – making us the UK's oldest mental health charity – today we work with approximately 4,500 people every month, at around 70 locations across England.

What makes us stand out is that we put people at the centre of their own support – they set their own goals and are in control of how we work alongside them to achieve these. We ensure that the people we work alongside lead the way, not just in their own support but in decisions at every level of our organisation.

We see beyond diagnoses and approach people as whole individuals with a range of circumstances and needs: social, emotional, physical, spiritual and economic. We focus on people's strengths and believe everyone can – and should – be supported to live the life they want to lead.

Our services include:

SUPPORT IN THE COMMUNITY
Each person we support sets the goals they want to achieve and we work creatively alongside them to achieve these. We help them to build skills and social connections so that they can become more independent.

ACCOMMODATION-BASED SUPPORT

Having a suitable place to live is a hugely important factor in working towards leading a fulfilling and independent life whilst experiencing mental distress. We provide a range of services that support people to live in the accommodation that is right for them.

CRIMINAL JUSTICE SERVICES

Too many people who experience mental distress end up stuck in a cycle of offending because their needs aren't identified and they aren't supported to access the help they need. We aim to help people at every point of the criminal justice pathway – from when they are first at risk of coming into contact with the justice system, to when they are on probation.

ADVOCACY

Advocacy plays a crucial role in giving people choice and control, by ensuring their voice is heard. By making sure that people understand their rights and can express their views and wishes, our advocates promote equality of opportunity and create a safe and comfortable environment for people to make sense of their circumstances and options.

For more information about our work, visit:
www.together-uk.org or follow @TogetherMW.

NOCTURIA

Nicholas Royle

Nocturia is a country you visit only at night. It is a land of dark reflections in mirrors you had forgotten were there, so that you meet yourself coming back. A land of grainy images, writhing and swarming in and out of focus. A land of fear and confrontation.

In Macclesfield, there's two of everything.

There are two trains to London every hour, and two trains *from* London, if you assume that one in every two scheduled services will be late. There are two platforms in the station, one for trains going to London and one for trains going to Manchester, or, more to the point, one for trains coming *from* Manchester and one for trains coming *from* London.

There are two pharmacies in the immediate vicinity of the so-called Health Hub, known to locals, older locals at least, as the doctors'.

There are two Thai restaurants, if you count Chilli Banana.

There are two women with pink hair on the High Peak bus idling at the stop and two men who walk past you, one after the other, at the south end of Sunderland Street giving you looks straight out of the middle of the night, each pushing a bicycle. Even the two bicycles contrive to look aggressive, with their thick rubber tyres and spiky lettering.

Around the corner on Park Green, there are two yellow lines outside the row of shops and two Range Rovers or Land Rovers parked on them. In Spearing's there are two beautiful butchers serving customers and the sight of them in their white coats and aprons – one blue, one red – as they dance around each other cutting and chopping and passing cuts and chops across the counter to customers who come and go stops you in your tracks and you remember that there are two ways to start this story. One sees you walking down Sunderland Street and turning into Park Green and the other has you heading out of the station to Waters Green in search of the steps up to Sparrow Park, but of course there are two sets of steps up to Sparrow Park, one by the Nag's Head and the other, known as Step Hill, just past the Travelodge. Whichever set of steps you take (the Nag's Head steps are easier to go up, Step Hill easier to come down), when you get to the top and pause to catch your breath in Sparrow Park, you will find in the text on the interpretation panel that describes the view down over the railway, the Macclesfield Canal and towards Tegg's Nose Country Park and Macclesfield Forest two hyphens that should be en-dashes.

There are two possible reasons for getting off the train from Manchester to London at Macclesfield. The first is you either live in Macclesfield or you are visiting. The second is you are hoping to get all the way to London without having your train ticket checked and the train manager has just announced he is going to be doing a full ticket check once the train has departed from Macclesfield.

Among the ex-rental DVDs for sale in Macclesfield Library are two good films – *Enemy* and *It Follows*. In Denis Villeneuve's *Enemy*, Adam, played by Jake Gyllenhaal, rents a film and sees in it an actor who closely resembles himself. This is Anthony, Adam's double. It follows that he is, of course, also played by Jake Gyllenhaal. Adam, who clearly has not read Edgar Allan Poe's story 'William Wilson', or any other story involving doppelgängers, decides to track down Anthony. The title of *It Follows* reminds you of *They Live*, but its lingering images of slowly pursuing figures in American suburban streets is more reminiscent of an earlier John Carpenter film, *Halloween*. 'It' could be the fear of a sexual predator, like in the film, or it could simply be fear, and its shadow, anxiety.

In the same collection of ex-rental DVDs for sale there are two copies of *Unsane* and two copies of *Godzilla*.

Visitors to Macclesfield have two possible motivations: need or desire. Equally, there are two reasons why you might not have any qualms about ripping off Virgin Trains. One: nine years ago the cheapest advance ticket between Manchester and London was £11 and within a year that had risen to £22. Two: Sir Richard Branson.

There are two Turkish traditional barber shops offering haircuts and shaves. There are two green Viridor waste bins outside the Pizza Joint and Grill. There are two closed-down businesses at this end of Mill Street. A charity has quit its premises at nos. 71 to 73 – temporarily taken over by Incubation Arts – leaving a ghost sign that still reads 'British Heart Foundation' in crimson on something closer to scarlet, while the window of the Alternative Tanning Shop across the street at no. 76 has been whitewashed in an unusual fish-scale pattern, the inhabitants of Macclesfield having presumably found an alternative to tanning.

It is possible to form a strong bond with – or reliance upon – your general practitioner, so strong that when you move out of the catchment area for the practice, you are reluctant to unregister. In this scenario, assuming you are determined to carry on seeing your doctor, there are two ways you can go. Either you fail to inform the surgery of your change of address or you attempt to appeal either to the doctor or to the practice itself, informing them that you are moving but explaining that you really, really want to be able to carry on seeing your doctor because you feel they understand you very well and have a positive effect on your anxiety levels even before we get to the matter of how good a doctor they are, how patient they are with you, the patient, and your anxieties.

There are two men wrestling with a washing machine at the bottom of the alleyway beside the Pizza Joint and Grill. One tries to tip up the washing machine while the other struggles to slip the lip of a trolley under it. Across the road, there are two sleeping bags in the entrance to the closed-down Vibe Clothing Factory Clearance Shop with a poster in the window announcing 'Opening Offer Everything £5 or Under'.

If you get off the London train at Macclesfield to avoid the full ticket check that has been announced and walk around the town for an hour before returning to the station to catch the next London train – let's say you are going to London either to visit your girlfriend or for a work thing that will barely pay for your travel even in the long term – either you could face a ticket check anyway, on the train an hour later than the one you had originally been on, or you could get lucky.

On Chestergate there are two businesses that each have two separate premises each on the same street. The East Cheshire Hospice has shops on both sides of the street, diagonally opposite each other, and Norburys Garden Machinery Specialists have two outlets on the same side of Chestergate but separated by Bridge Street.

Assuming you appeal to the doctor rather than the practice, which is less likely to be flexible, the doctor's response could go one of two ways: either they refuse, or they agree, perhaps adding the proviso that you try to avoid requesting a home visit.

Since Bridgfords closed its doors, there are two estate agents at the top end of Church Street. One of them, Whittaker & Briggs, has two doors; on one of them it says, 'PLEASE USE THE OTHER DOOR'. The other door doesn't have a letter box. The only door with a letter box is the one that says, 'PLEASE USE THE OTHER DOOR'.

If you get all the way to London without having your train ticket checked, it's possible that you might accidentally reuse it, assuming it's an off-peak return ticket, if you make the same journey again, to see your girlfriend or for another work thing that again will barely cover the cost of your travel, before the ticket's expiry date. If in the meantime you happen to have booked a single advance ticket from London to Manchester, perhaps avoiding Virgin Trains altogether by booking from Euston to Stoke on London Northwestern Railway and from Stoke to Manchester on Northern Rail, you can save a considerable amount of money on your journey, bringing its total cost down to around that of the cheapest advance tickets offered by Virgin Trains some nine years ago.

There are two traffic wardens walking up the narrow cobbled Churchside, where there are no vehicles to be seen, either parked or in motion.

If you go to Macclesfield to see your doctor because you want him to conduct an examination that will determine whether your waking regularly in the night to visit the bathroom – a condition known as nocturia – and resultant catastrophising and spiralling anxiety is caused by reasons sinister or benign, there are two possible outcomes. He can provide you with either reassurance or a referral. When, on this occasion, he tells you that everything feels normal, that there is nothing to worry about, that he is happy, you experience an immediate feeling of euphoria that is comparable to sensing the light and the heat of the sun as it comes out, at long last, from behind dense cloud. You shake the doctor's hand. You want to offer to buy him a drink and sit and chat and give your relationship time to grow, but you remember he's your doctor and he's got other patients to see and so you thank him and leave the surgery and because you've got time to kill before your train and you're too elated to even think about sitting on a platform you head back into town and there is only one man with a newsboy-style flat cap and funny-looking beard who smiles at you as he cycles down Waters Green. There is only one woman wearing bright-red lipstick and an aqua-green vintage coat looking slightly lost but happy in the middle of Market Place. There is only one Market Place and only one Treacle Market and only one Treacletown. There's only one life and for these precious moments you know how to live it.

THE NOTE

JENN ASHWORTH

There had been a rain shower – heavy but short-lived – between Amanda getting home from work and sending Joe out on the evening dog walk, which meant when he brought the note in to her it was sodden, the paper fragile. Joe offered it on his palm like a waiter with a calling card on a silver platter. He was laughing, the dog dancing around his ankles.

'You've got another one.'

He flourished the note, offering it and drawing his hand back as Amanda reached for it, her throat tightening.

'Joe, give it here...'

'*You park like a...*'

'Don't—'

She caught her son's wrist, gently drew it towards her, peeled the note from his palm. Joe laughed again and wriggled away.

Joe was referring to an older, celebrated note Amanda had received one afternoon, emerging from a three-hour-long meeting to the emptied car park, finding a scrape down one side of the Honda and a note on the back of a leaflet for a veg box company letting her know what the car-scraper thought of her parking. She'd found it – if not the scrape – funny at the time. They all had. Joe had stuck the note to the fridge with a Blackpool Tower magnet and Ella had delighted in pointing it out to guests – showing off her reading and comprehension – until Maria had taken it down and thrown it away.

'You *do* park like a cunt sometimes,' she'd said in bed that night.

'I know,' Amanda admitted humbly, and they laughed together.

It was difficult to imagine laughing like that now.

❯ • ❮

In the kitchen, Amanda squinted and held the wet paper up to the light. The children were at the table with Maria, their meals in front of them. This second note (the second? Or could there have been other, missed notes? Forgotten notes? Blown away notes?) had been so heavily rained upon that the ink had washed away. There was a suggestion of something – a loop of a 'g' or a 'y' and something that could have been an 'ook' – but whatever message the note-writer wanted to convey had been lost.

'Your chops are getting cold,' Maria remarked. She wasn't annoyed. Not yet.

'Start without me,' Amanda said, and Maria didn't answer.

Amanda thought she'd been able to sound cheery. She'd meant to sound cheery. But there was something in her throat – some constriction, an unseen hand gently squeezing at her windpipe. The sensation was a warning.

'Are you coming?'

'I just need to pop out for a minute.'

> • <

The pavements were wet and the bonnet of the car was beaded with water, but the rain had stopped. The car was parked nicely, tucked in at the kerb. There was a fair, if not generous, ten inches between the Honda and the car in front, and the one behind. She was not – could not, by any stretch of the imagination be said to have – parked *like a cunt*.

She stepped back, tried to see the car and her parking the way a dispassionate observer would. Or better than that, the way someone touchy and unreasonable and tired might see it. Was there anything to complain about?

That fluttering in her chest had started. Amanda could feel Maria and the children back in the house, their attention pulling at her like little wires attached to her forehead, her elbows, the backs of her knees. She should be inside. Eating with her family.

'Just one minute,' she muttered irritably, under her breath but loud enough to be overheard if someone had been walking past her. That person would have thought she was talking to herself. Would have mistaken her for a mad person, or a drunk. She'd better watch out for that. She glanced at the houses that overlooked her on both sides of the street. Some of the windows were lit, some not. Nobody stared back. That feeling, though – a prickling on the skin. A primitive instinct, perhaps. There was someone watching her standing in a darkened room, or peering from behind a curtain. Wanting to see how she'd react to the note. Why else leave it?

I've done nothing wrong.

She didn't quite speak the words out loud, but her tongue moved in her mouth, her lips twitched, and the words, half-spoken, felt like lies.

She moved around the car, conscious of being observed, trying to make her movements casual, unconcerned. She needn't assume the worst. (What was the worst? She saved the question for later – promised herself she'd consider it once safely back inside the house.)

Perhaps the note had been written by a friendly neighbour, wanting to alert her to a flattened tyre, or something else wrong with the car. She kicked the tyres. Nothing wrong there. Amanda got on her knees, wondering about oil leaks or dripping radiators or leaking brake fluid or the myriad of other things that could go wrong with cars. The wet from the pavement soaked through her trousers, and she saw nothing unusual. She leaned forwards, the chill from the pavement seeping into her hands.

People die, don't they, when their cars are badly maintained? When something blows or breaks or snaps or... She doesn't know a lot about cars, and finds the trips to the garage for repair and maintenance purposes – the way this task always falls to her, and the conversations she is expected to have across the counter at Kwik Fit – painful. But sometimes, even in a well maintained car, something just *goes* – and you're hurtling down the motorway one minute and the next the car is smashed against the central reservation, and all your children dead.

Amanda does not, however, tend to hurtle down the motorway. Or anywhere. She is an extremely careful driver. Always has been. More so, of late. She stood in the street imagining her dead children, parts of them scattered over three lanes, bleeding and – impossibly – still screaming.

It's not my fault, she wanted to say, but the note seemed to say otherwise.

> • <

She returned to the house, absent-mindedly ate her chops, and made encouraging noises as Joe and Ella gave her details about their days. But as soon as she could, she escaped from the table to stand in the kitchen under the halogen spotlight so she could scrutinise the note again.

The paper had dried but the writing was no clearer to read. It was even less clear than before, given that the wetting and drying had erased the indentations of the pen from the paper entirely.

The 'ook' (*look? Took?* Or could it be *fuck*?) had disappeared. She could just have imagined it.

Look what you've done!

Took [sic] your car to the garage ☺

Fuck you!

Maria was at her shoulder. She put an arm around her waist.

'What's wrong? Something happen at work?'

Amanda was immediately defensive. She knew she should not be, for the sake of maintaining the peace, and so she said nothing. But why would Maria assume she'd made a mistake at work? She'd say that she didn't mean it like that, but she did – Amanda knew she did. Maria always assumed if there was a problem it had been caused by Amanda making some error.

'What is it?'

'Nothing, nothing's wrong,' she said, and stepped away from her. She couldn't – didn't want to – get into it with her now.

She meant to screw up the paper and throw it away. She could honestly say that had been her intention. That was why she was in there, why she'd left the dining table and skulked into the kitchen. She'd meant to screw the note up and put it in the bin. Put it *underneath* something in the bin – something disgusting like the bloody absorbent mat the chops sat on inside their plastic tray from the supermarket – so there was no temptation of coming back later, retrieving it, and investigating the matter further. She knew herself very well.

Amanda knew, for example, standing there with the note still in her hand, that yes, partly she wanted to hide the note from a returning future self, but also – there's just a glimmer of this – there's the sense that the note itself might be proof of something or other. That *someone else* might want to investigate the matter further. She saw the car again – not her car, but someone else's – upside down on a verge, flames licking about through the underside of the chassis. Herself, speeding away safely home in an untouched Honda after a risky manoeuvre that had caused the other car to swerve. It didn't matter that this had not happened. The fact was, it could have happened. It could have.

And she could have repressed it.

The possibility of there being an unpleasant and unknown truth about her own culpability and the slimy, sneaky way she'd driven away, not looking at the mess in the rear-view mirror, bloomed into being. Anything was possible. People were full of secret rooms, after all. Why not her?

If a person repressed a memory, would they know it? Not the memory itself, but the fact of repressing? Would there be (Amanda searched inwardly, as if for a tumour) a heat? A heaviness? A tightness? Would the body know?

She resisted the urge to smell her clothes for smoke, for burning petrol, for blood. She smiled at Maria and tucked the note into her back pocket. She needed to keep it safe, and also private. Very private.

The note might be (she avoided the word, and it intruded in on her anyway) *evidence.*

In bed that night, Amanda thought about the note, still in her trouser pocket. She dug around inside herself with her fingernails, searching for the tumour, making herself bleed. Maria snored. The fact that Maria could sleep any way, anywhere, and at a moment's notice was a running joke between them. It used to be funny, the way she could catch some zeds on a bus journey, during the ten o'clock news before the late film, and in the car during swimming, Brownies or cricket. But as the whistle Maria's breath made as it came and went failed to distract Amanda from her ruminations, she realised it stopped being funny a long time ago.

'Just relax,' Maria would say, 'no need to be so tense,' as if the shared burden of their lives – the kids' dentists appointments and vaccinations and diets and discipline and times tables – could be kicked into the long grass. Maria dozed and smiled, carefree in the sunshine, because the burden she had shrugged away in favour of her relaxation, her spontaneity, her fun, had been shouldered by Amanda, and Maria had forgotten the note existed.

Part of being a couple, Amanda had learned, was not only the day-to-day management of who emptied the bins and who remembered to buy the milk; and not only the intimacy, the myriad and sensitive negotiations of how much sex and of what type; and not only the tendrils the couple sent out into the wider world towards parents, friends, family – how much, and in which direction; but also, and maybe most importantly of all, it was the story the couple told each other about the way things were between them.

Maria would not, for example, accept this story of her shrugging off adulthood in Amanda's direction, skipping off lightly into the sunshine towards the beach and leaving Amanda shouldering the windbreaker and beach towels and sun cream, the bags of juice and foil-wrapped sandwiches, the timings of low and high tide, the parking permit, the change for the meter, the spare shoes and blister plasters and antiseptic cream and – worst of all – the matter of mysterious and sinister notes implying all kinds of sins and disasters.

Maria's story – and Amanda knew this because she had heard it from Maria many times (after all, what was an argument, other than two parties arm-wrestling over whose story should prevail) – was extremely different. For Maria, Amanda was more of a ghost than a person. Someone who was there, putting money into the joint account and making the milk appear in the fridge, yes. But a body – only a body – a bag of skin with a newspaper draped over the front of it, dead eyes, no presence, no get-up-and-go, no pleasure or joy or enthusiasm for anything. Amanda might be in the room – so Maria's story went – but really, she was somewhere else entirely. It was sometimes true. That night, Amanda was not in bed with her wife. She was in her car, mowing down pedestrians, feeling the crunch of bones under the car tyres, the gentle bump as the wheels crushed skulls, femurs, little ribcages. It was dark, but Amanda screwed her eyes up tight anyway, against those little corpses strewn across the motorway, the car upside down in flames on a verge, the passengers screaming.

At three in the morning, Amanda gave up, put on her dressing gown and slippers, and went out to the car. She repeated her inspection of earlier, finding nothing new. Was the fact that there was nothing to find suspicious? She circled the car and checked again. She walked away from it, then turned suddenly, trying to catch it in the act, trying to view it as a stranger might, as a neutral observer. As a *witness*. She stayed out there for an hour.

Back in bed, Maria still sleeping and oblivious, Amanda tried to logic herself out of the spiral. If she had forced another car off the road, damaged a child, killed a person, caused a death, a fire, or some other mayhem, then a witness would have called the police immediately. The police would not be informing her of this via a handwritten note tucked under her windscreen wiper on a rainy day. It did not work like that. They had a system, and could look her up via the registration plate on the car and find her in two minutes flat. She was being ridiculous. Her imagination was running away with her. She was not stupid and so she should not act as if she was stupid – there was a wrongdoing in this. It wasn't that she was uninformed or uneducated or weak or feeble and that it couldn't be helped. Quite the opposite. So for her to succumb to this (she could hear the children screaming – hers and not hers – their little bodies on fire on the side of the motorway, their arms and legs flapping about, the stink of petrol and blood filling the air) was something more than an act of human frailty. She should know better. She did know better. And still.

Maria turned over in her sleep, her mouth full of her own hair. She snorted a little, sighed, and rubbed her hand over her face, all without waking. Her face was clear and unlined and peaceful. It wasn't fair. It was a family car. A shared car. They were jointly responsible: they had a joint account, both their names were on the mortgage and the car belonged to both of them. And yet Maria slept on, as if none of this mattered. Amanda hated her.

❯ • ❮

Eventually, morning came.

'You look terrible,' Maria said. 'Are you sick?'

Amanda could *feel* she looked terrible. Two hours' sleep, if that, listening to the rain and watching the horrific drama of her own thoughts unspool over and over again: the fire, the corpses, the various ways and means she could have been responsible for both.

'I need to check the car,' she said. Her voice sounded strange to her own ears, as if it came from someone else's mouth. As if it came from someone else's mouth some other time, and in some other place, and had been recorded badly, and was now being replayed, from a room just to the left of where she was standing right now.

'For what?' Maria said, irritably.

'I just want to make sure everything's all right,' Amanda said.

'Maybe you could help me get the kids ready first?' Maria said. Today was obviously one of the days – there had been more of them, recently – where she was 'running out of bandwidth for this'. Sometimes she was reassuring. Today she sounded brittle, sarcastic, at the end of her tether. Perhaps she was tired too.

Amanda imagined she had woken her last night, and in the early hours Maria had stood at their bedroom window watching her sitting in her dressing gown in the parked car as the rain fell, trying the engine, revving it, turning it off and on again. Checking the lights, the indicators, moving through the gears. Amanda tried to imagine what she had looked like, what kind of crazy Maria would have seen – and not for the first time – what kind of crazy she was getting tired of. The urge to explain herself had long since left her. It was not possible. Not possible to let someone else into the logic of this, the way the inner arguments unfurled, and grew more knotted and complicated the more she tried to unravel them.

An image surfaced: Amanda as Sleeping Beauty, lost and absent and tucked away inside the castle; and Maria out the outside, hacking away at the thorns and briars that curled around her, creeping into her hair and around her wrists. That was Maria's story – the one where she was the one with the burden, and Amanda was the one who was away somewhere else, dreaming her silly dreams. Maria as Prince Charming, wrapped up in someone else's mental brambles. She'd get hurt, or she'd give up and go home. Sleeping Beauty would sleep on. That would be a proper, more realistic ending to that story.

> • <

During breakfast, as Amanda was sipping her third coffee and Maria was in the kitchen making three packed lunches (*how's that for shrugging off responsibility*, she could have said, and didn't), the doorbell went. Maria came into the living room, raised her eyebrows; Amanda shrugged (*the police, the police are here*, a voice inside her said, and she gulped her coffee – her last coffee – so quickly it scalded her throat) and Maria huffed and answered the door herself.

There were voices. Laughter. Amanda gripped the hot coffee mug in her hands and waited. Tried to commit the house to memory before they took her away – the crack around the top of the fireplace they were always meaning to have filled. The way the wallpaper was peeling a little behind the radiator. The expensive mustard velvet armchair with the grease spot on the arm. She would remember these things. She would take them with her.

'This is Sam,' Maria said, bringing someone into the room. Amanda smiled, her face feeling as if it was made of plaster. 'She lives across the road.'

'I'm so sorry to disturb you at this time,' Sam said. She was dressed for work in a good trench coat, a leather bag over her arm. 'Only you didn't come over and knock and I wanted to clear the air, or it would have been on my mind all day.'

'Clear the air?' Amanda said dumbly. She heard her own heart – like water rushing through a broken pipe – throbbing in her ears. Maria took one look, and knew, and helped her out.

'She bumped the car,' Maria said, 'and left a note.'

'I'll pay,' Sam said, standing stiffly in the doorway, politely not looking at the mess, the wreckage of breakfast, the unhoovered floor. Unhelpfully, the dog leapt at her and left a smudge on her skirt. She pushed him away gently without looking at him. 'I'm ever so sorry. Only I was in a rush, and I thought there was no real damage, and you could come over and we could swap numbers or…'

'I checked the car,' Amanda said. 'I checked it and I checked it for bumps. All over. I've…'

'The light. The front light is gone,' Maria said, 'it's just a tiny thing.'

Sam stood there politely. Stricken.

'But I checked. I don't see how I could have…'

Maria waved a hand. 'Please don't worry. Sam, is it? We'll call a garage. Get a quote. It's very good of you,' she said, shooting Amanda a look. Sam sighed, relieved, and Amanda (she saw herself as she would no doubt appear to them, sitting there in her dressing gown, puffy-eyed, with mud stains on the knees of her pyjamas) became another unkempt feature in the room that the neighbour was polite enough not to stare at. 'Don't worry about it. Nobody was hurt, that's the main thing.'

The two of them were laughing as Maria guided her out towards the door, chatting away about the horrific parking, and how perhaps they should write to the council and get a residents parking scheme set up, and how there was no harm done and don't be silly, nothing to worry about.

> • <

Sam went. Back to her own house, relieved. Unburdened of her own little guilt. Amanda got up and watched her go from between the curtains in the living room, standing amidst the mess of Lego and colouring things and odd socks, and marvelling at how quickly life had been returned to her. She breathed. Breathed again. The air tasted good, as good as if she'd been drowning and had just been heaved onto dry land.

She might stand here all day, just enjoying the mess in the front room, breathing in the smell of toast and grubby carpet and coffee. It was almost post-coital, this breathing. She had never smoked but imagined herself with one now, naked against some rumpled white sheets, high thread count, the entire room spotless and herself at the centre of it, exhaling a great plume – impossibly large – of post-orgasmic smoke into the sunlit air.

'That's that, then,' she said quietly, when Maria came back.

'Oh love, were you anxious about it?' Maria laughed, and kissed her on the cheek. 'You weren't having one of your frets, were you?'

There was a lie between them now. Maria knew full well Amanda had been 'having one of her frets', as she'd taken to calling them. 'Episode' was the word she used, during an argument last month. Rather than acknowledge it, mention it, even help her out with it, Maria had decided to ignore it. She was not, she'd said, during the argument last time, willing to go on 'enabling' this business.

'No, I was fine, just wondering,' Amanda said, her knees like water, the thrill of guilt and punishment deferred collapsing now to one distinct sensation: the hot stickiness of shame. Now she'd added a lie of her own to Maria's, and they were even.

'Good,' Maria said, shortly. And they understood each other.

I must not do this to myself again, she thought, and wondered about writing a note to herself, explaining what she is like, the way her mind runs away with her sometimes, gets her into hot water, dead ends, tangles and thorn bushes and dark places. The next time (there would always be a *next time*, she had accepted this with despair a long time ago) she would read the note, and obey the advice from her previous self. Would that work?

How would she start a note like that? In pencil? A document on her computer? A text message to herself? A little scroll, kept behind glass in the kitchen like a fire blanket? Break here in case of emergency.

Dear Amanda, remember, sometimes you think you have killed people, or done all kinds of terrible things, but the truth is...

What was the truth? Exactly?

Inside, she felt the tumour start to stir. It bulged. Flexed like a dormant, hibernating monster disturbed in its sleep. It sent out its tendrils.

You would say that, wouldn't you? it whispered back. *A terrible person would come up with all kinds of excuses and methods to prove that they weren't terrible. Doesn't mean it isn't true. In fact, isn't a note like this proof that it is true? Normal people – good people – don't need to write notes to themselves like this, do they?*

Maria was still looking at her, searching her face for something. Amanda stopped mentally composing the note because the certain knowledge that arguing with this tumour, like bothering a mosquito bite, only made it worse, reminded her of how hopeless the entire enterprise was. She smiled. She made herself smile.

'You're not here. Where are you? What's wrong?' Maria said.

Amanda shrugged her away – annoyed. Maria couldn't demand the pretence then get annoyed if she wasn't acting her part well enough. It was totally unreasonable. 'Everything's fine,' she said, 'stop getting at me, will you?' and Maria frowned and now they were going to have another one of their terrible arguments. Amanda could feel it coming and it would all be her fault.

LONELY SOULS IN QUIET HOUSES

Laura Mauro

That big house in the West Virginia sticks had felt like the biggest failure of Lissa's life. The shabby grandeur of it: white-painted wood peeling like old sores, the porch overlooking a half-acre of overgrown weeds and looming trees. It was her uncle's house, and he had extended the offer for her to stay for as long as she needed with the terrible pity of one who knew exactly how badly she had fucked up the entirety of her life. He hadn't said as much, though; her uncle, ever the true Georgia gent. 'It's a shame for a house like that to sit empty,' he'd said, as he'd handed her the keys. 'You could give it a little TLC. Keep your mind occupied.' As though her mind were not continuously occupied, a veritable 24/7 house party complete with smashed windows, singed curtains and vomit on the metaphorical carpet.

Oh, but she'd known exactly what he'd meant. *Your mind*, that charred and steaming bombsite, that acrid garbage-fire which had won her – and eventually lost her – the wife her entire family had collectively agreed to regard with distant politeness. And it was a small miracle that her uncle had offered her the house at all. On those sleepless nights, with doom weighing heavy on her tight and aching chest, she had assumed that complete familial disownment was the logical next step in the steady downward trajectory of her life. So the house – all of it, its mildew and disrepair, its worn carpets and cracked bath tiles – was a precious gift, a crumbling roof over her head, a place where she might get her proverbial shit together; where she might *keep her mind occupied.*

The house came furnished. Cheap white plywood; worn-smooth sofa, sun-bleached and patchy. Dark oak dining table built to seat an entire family, huge and imposing, disapproving of her aloneness. When Lissa first walked into the master bedroom – sad, sagging box spring, shambling wardrobe stuffed full of someone else's musty clothes – she had placed her suitcase on the floor, and sat down beside it, and sobbed silently into her hands.

Four days later and she was still living out of that suitcase. She did not want to touch the clothes in the wardrobe, with their mothball stink and strange, faded colours; there was something tainted about them, as though to touch them would be to inherit ill luck. On that first night, she'd slept in the car, unwilling to submit her exhausted body to the stained mattress, redolent of the bodies of strangers. She'd driven into the next town the following day, forked over an exorbitant amount for a mattress she could have got for $60 cheaper on the internet, except that 'three to five working days for delivery' translated to the better part of a week camping in her car, shivering in the back seat, the cries of unseen animals echoing in the dark. And still, that would be better than the old mattress, jaundiced with other people's sweat, their shed skin.

On the second night in that fading, white-painted house she had crawled into her new bed, her sickeningly expensive new mattress, too exhausted to contemplate her catalogue of failures, though they still chittered away in the dark recesses of her brain, desperate for acknowledgement. The air tasted different here. The night-time sounds were alien; the laborious creaking of the house as it settled, arthritic, a symphony of stiff bones. The faraway sounds of wild creatures high in the mountains, echoing across the empty distance. She had slept alone since Claudia left, and the absence beside her in the too-big bed still felt as large and empty as a wound. And in spite of it all – the mattress, the isolation, the clothes in the wardrobe, accoutrements of a life – the ominous noise inside her head had blessedly subsided until it was only a whisper, the distant ocean heard through the pink mouth of a seashell.

They'd met on the internet, because as her friend Ying had always said, it was easier to be queer in digital than in the flesh. Dating websites felt gauche to Lissa, who resented the requirement to present oneself as something to be bought, to be appraised: *lightly used, one careful lady owner, in fair condition but requires some renovation.* Claudia Rose had been the friend of a friend, a spontaneous connection over a shared love of obscure sci-fi films. Casual at first, the coy exchanging of 'likes' like confetti scattered sparingly; late-night conversations conducted via Messenger, the blessed anonymity of text bolstering Lissa with a confidence she did not have, had never had. On the internet she was breezy, dryly humorous; she could carve off all her neuroses, keep those in a box and shove them into the back of the cupboard to fester in the dark. She would not visit her madnesses upon Claudia, so sane, so *normal*; Claudia sold handcrafts online, went walking on the beach on the weekends, baked cupcakes for fun. She posted chirpy status updates about positive thinking (*#blessed*, though there was not a whiff of the church about her). She was fit and tall and bronzed, broad-shouldered, a sun-goddess with brine-stiff hair, and Lissa imagined she must taste like the sea.

Lissa hadn't told Claudia about her swirling maelstrom of mental illnesses. Claudia hadn't told Lissa she was three months pregnant. It seemed a fair trade.

She woke with a start. That noise again, always, from deep inside her head: a distant siren, the whispers from *somewhere else*, all-knowing, warning that something was wrong, that something bad was going to happen, forcing her anxious hands and feet and maladroit, panic-sweaty self into action: *take off that necklace or someone will die. Don't touch anything red or you'll get fired.* The non sequiturs of a misfiring brain. The illogic of it all had never been lost on Lissa, and yet there was no way she *could not*, no way to circumvent the bizarre rituals, because the consequences were too great, too much.

Lissa sat up, pulling blankets around her like a heavy robe. The house was always cold. Thin mountain air, the sharp breath of first snow like a threat. It was an old house;

single-glazed, the central heating temperamental. It was the kind of house that fuelled fantasies of rustic country living, infinitely Instagrammable and barely liveable, and it stung a little to think that Claudia, who'd never so much as spent a night camping before she'd met Lissa, would love this house, or at least the idea of it. Claudia collected dream lives the way other people collected trinkets – the eco-friendly 'tiny house' in the Oregon woods, the lakeside cabin in deepest Maine – but she was a city girl, and her lungs were black with gasoline, her fingernails black with industrial grime. Nature, to Claudia, was a pool in which one dipped one's toes on occasion, but never for too long, nor too deep.

The hazy shapes of someone else's furniture materialised in the dark. The strange silence of rural America, oppressive in its stillness, though she had grown up with it; when she'd first moved to the city she had struggled to adjust to the swollen-river roar of constant traffic, the shrill avian cry of passing police cars. The absence of it felt like an amputation. When had it become so normal to her, the noise? When had the broken radio chatter of the street below become so familiar, the pulse of faraway music, bathing her in ambient sound; seeping into her ears and her nose and her open mouth like amniotic fluid. And she had loved it. A world full of noise to drown out the sounds in her head. She would have to buy a radio, she thought, as she clambered out of bed. Even if she could not find a working station out here, the soft hiss of static would be comforting.

The stairwell loomed like a black hole. She gripped the banister, carefully testing each step; the answering whine of old boards confirmed solid ground underfoot. Audrey had been afraid of the dark, and Lissa – who understood what it was like to be afraid of the strange and the intangible – had bought her a nightlight shaped like a canary, like in the song. Audrey had been mesmerised by the soft blue glow; 'birdie' had been among her first words, and Lissa had felt, for the first time, a connection to this small and vulnerable human.

Moonlight seared through the gaps in the blinds, bathing the kitchen in slivers of bright white. Last night's dirty dishes scattered across the countertops, a strange paradox; Lissa, terrified of other people's residue, as though bad luck could be transmitted, but not of germs. The perception of the germophobic, hand-scrubbing obsessive–compulsive had kept her from diagnosis for years: how can I have OCD, she'd asked, when I'm such a fucking slob?

She ran the cold tap, filled a glass with water. The nagging in her brain had subsided a little with motion, but was back again, clamouring with indistinct noise. Back in Boston she would have slipped into her running shoes, quietly left the apartment; she would have chased the street lights until her breath came fast and the thunder of her heart drowned out the insistent tug of anxiety. She would have slipped back into bed and Claudia would have mumbled, sleepwarm and muzzy, and she would have felt something like security. All of that was gone now.

A creak of floorboards from the guest room; a low whine, like a kicked dog. She turned, sharp, spilling water down her bathrobe. In that strange lunar light the kitchen looked perfectly still, a black-and-white snapshot. She counted down ten seconds as she walked: *nine, eight, seven*, acknowledging the pulse in her throat, the flutter of her heart. The guest room stretched out into grey, empty darkness. *Four, three, two.* Calm silence. She exhaled, slow. Had it been a whine at all? The house often spoke to itself; it creaked and groaned, timber pressing against timber. Like a living thing, a large and ancient cat purring itself to sleep. She had grown up in houses like this. They all had their own secret voices.

There, at the very back of the guest room: a flash of bright eyes, disappearing into the dark as something slid through a gap in the floorboards. Her heart lurched; she pressed a hand over her mouth to keep from crying out, realising as she did that she was alone, that she could shout all she liked and nobody would ever hear her. It's just an animal, she told herself, swallowing down her terror; you're not in the city anymore. It's just an animal, and it's more afraid of you than you are of it. She stood very still, watching, barely daring to breathe, but whatever had glanced at her across the dark room was gone.

You're afraid of everything as it is, she scolded herself, ascending the stairs with careful feet. You can't let yourself be afraid of the house too. It's not like you have anywhere else to go.

She had practised being normal for so long, and worn her disguise so well, that when she did break down – four weeks after Audrey was born, and Claudia still half-bedbound, stitched abdomen like a full-body grimace – it felt like a natural disaster, an act of God. In hindsight, it had been inevitable: carting all her belongings to a brand-new city to shack up with this goddess, this perfect woman who had revealed, when it became too obvious to hide anymore, that she was pregnant, had been the entire time. And Audrey, oh, but she'd been so small, so fragile, and Lissa had held her tiny, howling body – shock of red hair like her father – and hated herself for feeling only terror.

We'll work through it, Claudia had said, when Lissa had let it all out, the hideous truth of her flowing like corruption from a wound. A gentle kiss to the forehead, strong arms wound around her: *We'll figure it out.* Because Claudia had lied, yes, but Claudia was perfect; she was never afraid, never angry, and she forgave so freely. And so Lissa – with all her ugly anger and fear and sadness, festering under the skin like an abscess – she too would forgive Claudia. She would forgive her anything. Even now, with her life in tatters, she would think of Claudia and feel only love, remote and cold as the stars.

> • <

She noticed the scrape marks on the floorboards a few days later. Shallow, but deep enough to accumulate a thin layer of dust; she could not be sure how old they were, but she knew they had not been there when she moved in. The board held firm. Whatever had made the marks had reached up from beneath, had worked claws between the gaps in the joins. Had fought to push through and been thwarted by the weight of the boards.

'Opossum, I reckon,' her uncle said, pressing tobacco-yellow fingers to the scratches. 'Big one, too, judging by them scratches. Probably living in the crawlspace. Best let it alone, unless it dies down there.'

'How will I know if it's died?' Lissa asked.

'You'll smell it,' he said, with a wry grin. He got to his feet. Sometimes, Lissa thought that maybe her uncle only owned one set of clothes; that he'd worn those same faded khakis every day for the last twenty years. 'Opossums mind their business. So long as you mind yours, it won't bother you.'

'They don't bother me anyway.' As though she'd gone soft from her years of city living, she thought, a little sourly; as though she'd forgotten how to live alongside nature. She thought about the whine she'd heard, that low, sad sound. That creak of floorboards. 'Just didn't want mice chewing through your wires, that's all.'

'You given any thought to picking up some work round here, Melissa?' He glanced cursorily around the kitchen, the dining room: spotless, tired, the way it had been the day she moved in. Empty. Like she didn't live here at all. 'I don't know that there's much call for personal trainers and the like up here, but I'd bet you could get something in town.'

'I've not been a personal trainer for a long time, Uncle Graham.'

He shrugged. 'There's a big Walmart up past Grafton, if you don't mind driving. Be good for you to meet new people.' He paused; her hackles rose instinctively, but he smiled, soft and a little sad. 'You're still young. Can't be good for you only to have an old fart like me to talk to.'

'I'll think about it,' she said, and knew she would not. She had wilfully clothed herself in isolation, worn it like armour. The terrifying visions that had haunted her since Audrey was born had mercifully dissipated; human interaction was a small price to pay in exchange. You could not hurt people if there was nobody around to hurt. You could not lose anyone if there was never anyone there to begin with.

❯ • ❮

Intrusive thoughts, the therapist had called them, months afterwards, when the damage was already done. They can't harm you, she'd said, not really. Lissa had laughed, abrupt and bitter. It's not me I'm worried about, she'd said.

Imagine you're in a car, the therapist had continued. Imagine you're driving. You've got a passenger in the back seat. You feel in control. But the passenger keeps freaking out about all the things that could go wrong. Worse than that: they keep freaking out about all the things *you* could do wrong. *What if you drive the car into that tree over there? What if you drove right off this bridge? What if you rammed the car right into that group of pedestrians?* You would never do something like that, of course. You know you are not that kind of person; you know you would never want to harm anyone else, or harm yourself. But the passenger won't stop panicking. And after a while, it starts to get to you. You start to think that maybe you *are* that kind of person. All because your passenger won't shut up. That's what intrusive thoughts are.

How can I get him to shut up? she'd asked.

Maybe you can't, the therapist had said. Maybe he'll always be there. Maybe he's scared, and he's vulnerable, and he's shouting because the world is big and overwhelming. Maybe what he needs is for you to let him speak, to acknowledge his concern. Just for a moment. To tell him you have heard him, and you have understood him, but you're going to keep driving anyway, because you know you are a safe driver, and you know you would never hurt anyone. You *know* this. Your passenger does not. You can't control him, but you can reassure him. Does that make sense?

She had sighed. Balled her hands into fists, pressed them hard against her temples. I can see myself doing it, she had said, teeth like a vice. It happens so fast. I can't stop myself. She's so light. So small. I just. I pick her up, and she doesn't weigh anything at all, you know? And she smiles at me. That's the bit I can't stand. She smiles at me with those big blue eyes, and I know she trusts me. I know she *loves* me. And the window is wide open, and I just…

You don't have to say it out loud, the therapist had said, gently. But it won't magically happen if you do. Words don't have that kind of power.

We lived on the ninth floor, Lissa had said; the bite of her knuckles against her skull, a sharp clarity. I wouldn't let Claudia open the windows. I couldn't tell her why. For a while, that was okay. But it's never enough, is it? Because what if I open them without realising? What if I open them in my sleep? In the end, I had to keep the blinds drawn just so I couldn't see them. So I could pretend they weren't there. We lived in darkness for weeks until Claudia couldn't stand it anymore and asked me why.

The therapist had said nothing. Patient. Waiting. She'd known what came next, could piece together the timeline. And Lissa had inhaled, long and slow, and raised her head – knuckles tight and pale, the prickle of blood-rush – and the therapist had gazed at her, placid, because the words were important. The words had destroyed everything.

I told her that I was afraid I would throw Audrey out of the window. That I had seen myself do it over and over again. That I could not trust myself not to hurt her. Three years, she'd supported me. She knew I was mad and she married me anyway. Audrey called me Mama Liss. Three years, and I blew all of it apart in three minutes. She told me not to come back until I'd sorted myself out.

Okay, the therapist had said. And isn't that what you're doing?

Lissa had looked down at her hands. At her nails, bitten to the quick, the livid red of inflammation. At her pink knuckles. The dance of nervous fingers. It's not enough, she'd said, at last. It will never be enough.

> • <

When she thought about Audrey, it was with careful distance, like looking at a photograph of someone else's child. She knew she could not hurt Audrey just by thinking about her, but you could never be too careful. Memories were allowed. They could not be tampered with; even if her mind invented alternative endings, they were movies she had already watched, books she had already read. A life she had already lived.

She did not drive into town, though she did scope out the Walmart, gazing up at its high ceilings and endless aisles, the nightmarish glare of artificial light. On the way home she stopped on a quiet stretch of highway, clambered out of the car and up the slope, where the trees had already begun to blush red with autumn colour. The rich smell of leaf litter, the cackle of nearby birds. She climbed further up the bank, the shift of shale underfoot, the dove-grey silk of the sky threatening rain. She could smell it in the distance, could sense the thunderheads gathering high in the mountains. There had been parks in Boston, but it had never felt the same: feet pounding the pavements on those late and anxious nights, cars every-fucking-where, the inescapable murmur of engines no matter how fast or how far she ran. The empty highway stretched out into the distance like a ghost road. There might have been nobody but her within those ragged green margins, not a single human soul. That would be all right, she thought, as the sky opened, fat droplets of rain filtering down between the leaves. That would be just fine.

> • <

The storm passed in a surge of atmospheric anger; a short but intense tantrum of shuddering thunder, a silvery wall of rain. She stood on the back porch, smoking cigarettes beneath the awning as the weather subsided, and tentative fingers of sun pried back the heavy cloud. She had never really explored the back yard. Calling it a back yard at all seemed grandiose: it was a sprawling patch of crabgrass and chickweed, a spattering of white clover. The heavy boughs of old and tilting trees cast a permanent shadow. It was not an inviting space, but there was a pleasant wildness to it. The sense that humans did not belong here, and never had.

She stepped out onto the lawn. The spongy-soft texture of moss underfoot; fat globules of rain sparkling in the grass, reflecting pale sunlight. High in the trees a cluster of crows bickered and cawed, the infuriated flutter of black wings. A clutch of black oak trees abutted the grass, a small and isolated copse carpeted with jewel-green moss. Her uncle had told her that these trees had been here long before the house; this had all been woods, once upon a time. It would be beautiful in the spring, she thought; bright dandelions and lilac speedwell and the grass gleaming in the sun.

It was quiet beneath the trees. The thick canopy seemed to blanket the interior, forming a protective shell through which sound could not penetrate. She wound her way inside, stepping over gnarled old roots. She marvelled at the deep green ceiling, the scent of loam. As a child, she had loved places like this. Places where it seemed that the world had gone away, that there was nothing left but trees, and birds, and quiet. Perhaps she would come here when spring came and read beneath the trees. Sprawl out on the soft moss and watch the birds come and go. Perhaps if she lay there long enough, the moss would subsume her; perhaps it would swallow her skin and her bones as it had the exposed roots and rocks, and nobody would ever know she had been there at all.

Her foot bounced off something hard. At the base of the tree there was a rock, squat and weatherworn; incongruous, with its smooth plane facing outwards, as though someone had placed it there deliberately. She ran her hand across its moss-choked surface, exploring the uneven topography. Who had put it here, this odd tablet, in this secret place? Her fingers found a shallow indentation, traced it slowly; she scraped away the moss with her thumbnail and crouched beside the rock, staring at the shape. A cross, rudimentary but definite, crudely chiselled into the stone. A memorial, then, small and worn and humble. The resting place of something long forgotten.

A cluster of crows burst from the trees, barking in mutual antipathy. Lissa stood, staring down at the rock a moment longer. The trees had been here long before the house, her uncle had said. Had those who'd built the house also placed this lonesome stone, or had it come after? Had it sat here between the trees, overlooked, keeping its secrets for decades? How sad, Lissa thought, as she turned back towards the house; how lonely it must be to have been forgotten for such a long time.

> • <

That night Lissa sat sleepless by the flickering fire, wrapped in a comforter, playing out old memories of Claudia and Audrey against the aggressive quiet. Audrey in her bright yellow wellingtons, dancing through the wet leaves at Jamaica Pond, and Claudia insistent that she be allowed to wander as she liked; Lissa, choking down the anxiety of such a small child running wild beside open water, not wanting to tread on Claudia's toes.

Her own mother had been a hands-off parent. It hadn't surprised Lissa that it had been her uncle who'd reached out to her when she was in dire straits. She'd been living in Connecticut when her mother died. A Facebook message from her half-sister, curt: *mom passed away. gramps wants you home for the funeral.* She had not gone home for the funeral. Georgia was not so far away, relatively speaking; flights were cheap nowadays, and the gym would've given her the time off if she'd asked. But the thought of returning to that small, dusty town had filled her with a cold and unshakeable dread. She'd felt nauseous at the thought of their eyes following her, parading before them as she had at school, in church; there goes Melissa Jackson, half a dago, almost certainly a dyke, and destined for the fiery bowels of Hell at that.

Dozy in the firelight, warmth like sunshine. She buried her face in the comforter, inhaling the scent of clean cotton. Audrey in the autumn sun, her hair like fire. Hand-in-hand with Claudia, strolling lazily. Audrey singing the songs she'd learned at kindergarten, off-key and charming. Audrey in the black water, sinking, and Claudia screaming, Claudia so far away.

She snapped awake. Her heart thrummed painfully in the base of her throat, sick and full. The fire had burned down to ashes; a few glowing embers still burned deep in the pile, red on black. It had never happened, she told herself; it had never happened and it never would, because you could not dream someone to death. Audrey was taller now, older. She would not have those same yellow wellingtons anymore. She would not be singing the same silly songs. 'It's only a dream,' she murmured, rearranging sleep-stiff limbs. 'Dreams can't hurt people. They are not real.'

Lissa slid off the sofa. The floor was cold against her bare soles, but her skin was flushed, damp with sweat; she must have been too close to the fire. She would stand on the back porch for a bit, let the chill mountain air sweep away the lingering traces of her nightmare. That was the key, she thought: she needed to spend more time outdoors, in nature, where she felt safe and anonymous and alone.

Something ground beneath her heel. A fine scattering of grit. Her heel was coated in fine grey powder. Ash, she thought. Had an ember leapt from the fire? She looked down. Footprints like the tracks of a wild animal, leading into the kitchen; the egress of fast little feet. Something had been in here. Something had watched her while she slept.

An opossum, her uncle had said. How big did opossums grow? These footprints seemed too round, too large. A cat, perhaps? Weren't there bobcats in the mountains? She'd heard stories of coyotes grown bold, entering homes; there must be a window open somewhere, she thought, padding alongside the dark little footprints. Something must have come in while she slept. We never had this problem in Boston, she thought, grabbing the broom from behind the kitchen door.

The kitchen was silent. Whatever had found its way inside had either left the way it came, or was hiding somewhere in the dark. Step by tentative step, Lissa traced the fading footprints, the scant scattering of ash trailing towards the guest room, wielding the broom as though it might stand any chance of protecting her against a trapped and terrified coyote. No, she thought, it can't be anything so big as that. Wouldn't I have woken up? Christ, I'm sure I was only out for a few minutes. On and on until the footprints petered out, and there, at the back of the guest room, that gap in the floorboards.

She crouched, prying gently at the frayed board. The hole had definitely got bigger. There was no fur caught in the splinters, no telltale animal smell. She lay her head beside the gap, staring down into the thin black seam. It seemed unbelievable that anything bigger than a rat could fit into that space. But the footprints had led this way, and there was no other route of escape. Something was living in the crawlspace. Something was coming up into the house at night while she slept.

In the quiet, there came a sound. Low, distant. As though something were crying. She pressed her ear to the floorboards. Echoing in the crawlspace, eerie. She'd heard cougars scream in the deep mountains; she'd heard foxes cackle and shriek in the warm Boston night. And yet that soft and desolate sound reminded her of Audrey most of all. Of the way she'd cried when Lissa and Claudia had spent their first weekend away, and her dramatic sobs had subsided into an exhausted keening. Those footprints, Lissa thought, had been around the right size for a toddler.

But that was ridiculous. No child could possibly have squeezed through such a tiny gap. And in any case, a child so young would never have survived for so long in that empty crawlspace. But there *was* something down there, and it sounded like it was in a bad way. She would call her uncle in the morning, she decided. There was nothing that could be done about it now.

Her uncle sent a boy down into the crawlspace armed with traps. When he emerged, he was nonplussed. 'Ain't nothing been down there in a long time,' he said, brushing cobwebs from his hair. 'No tracks, no scat, nothing but a bunch of spiders. Sometimes you might get possums or rats nesting but there's no sign of anything like that. Your crawlspace is clean as a whistle.'

'I don't understand,' Lissa said later, watching her uncle temporarily patch up the gap in the floorboards with a sheet of ply. 'You saw the tracks, didn't you? And something had to have made that hole. I swear, Uncle Graham. I heard something crying down there last night.' *I'm not going mad,* she almost added, but bit her tongue.

He shrugged, almost nonchalant. 'Things come and go, Melissa. Maybe there was something down there awhile, and maybe it's gone now.'

'It sounded human.' She shook her head, running hands across her cheeks. 'And I know it couldn't possibly have been, but just for a moment, you know? Just for a moment, I thought maybe a child had gotten lost down there. Doesn't that sound ridiculous?'

Her uncle put down the hammer. He brushed his hands on his khakis, shedding fine splinters. 'You spoken to that kid of yours since you moved out here, Liss? It's been, what? Best part of a month now? She must be wondering where you got to.'

'She's not my kid.' Anchoring her fingers in her hair. The guest bed creaked beneath her weight.

'All right, so you never gave birth to her or nothing, but you raised her, didn't you? You're as much her mama as your wife is. Okay, so things are rough right now, but that don't stop her from being your kid. And that don't mean you can just disappear.'

I kept thinking about killing her, Lissa thought, tightening her fingers. I kept thinking about throwing her out of the window. I am a monster. I don't deserve to be Audrey's mama. I don't deserve to be anything to anyone. 'In a few years' time, Audrey will barely remember me. Claudia will meet someone new. It'll be better for everyone, Uncle. She deserves more than I can give her.'

He scoffed. 'All this big talk about *deserving*. Melissa, you see this town? All these towns hereabouts? They lost a lot of men during the Civil War. Lot of women left without husbands. Kids without fathers. Even them who'd lived in big old houses like this.' The floorboards creaked as he got to his feet. 'Back in them days, sometimes a mother'd struggle to feed her children. Sometimes they ended up in orphanages. Sometimes she'd starve herself half to death just so they could eat. And sometimes that still wasn't enough.' Pale blue eyes, faded, like an old photograph. His brow solemn. 'Some of them were lucky and got found before it was too late. But there were others. Babies left in ditches, in the woods. Babies in the river. And before you think them monstrous, just imagine. You've four mouths to feed, but only food enough for three. Do you let your older children starve, aware as they are? Do you let yourself starve and leave your babies alone to fend for themselves? Or do you give up your babe in arms and pray every night to God in Heaven to forgive you for what you've done?'

She thought of that mossy stone, small and forgotten between the trees. That hand-carved cross worn smooth with time. Heat prickled behind her eyes. 'It's an impossible choice,' she said.

'Maybe so, but they had to make it just the same.' He shook his head. 'You talk about deserving, Melissa. All kids deserve to be loved. All kids deserve food in their bellies and a roof over their heads. All kids deserve to be safe. Some kids don't have those things. But your Audrey, well. You loved her, and you kept her, and you never so much as raised your voice at her, because that's the kind of person you are. So what kind of better does she deserve, exactly?'

'You don't understand, Uncle Graham. It wasn't safe for me to stay there anymore.'

'Like hell. Your wife got scared. That's okay. People do, sometimes. We're all scared of what we don't understand. Hell, I don't understand you myself.' He gave a wry little laugh, and she smiled in spite of herself; he was trying so hard. 'But whatever it is swirling around inside that head of yours, you just have to forget about it. I know in my heart that you'd never hurt that little girl. You know it, too. And that's more than I can say about some people.'

An awkward silence. Lissa glanced up at her uncle, who was fumbling in his pockets for his cigarettes, and she had never felt so fond of him; this gruff and straightforward man, who'd lived alone since her aunt died. The only one who'd never lectured her about her sexuality, or commanded her to go to Jesus. The only one who'd reached out when everything fell apart. It did not come easy to him, this kind of emotional sincerity; men of his generation were taught to keep it all inside, to never speak freely about feelings.

'What do you think I should do,' she said, 'if the opossum comes back?'

He slipped an unlit cigarette between his lips. 'Let it stay,' he said, with a shrug. 'Ain't doing you any harm. Maybe it just needs somewhere safe to bunk down awhile. Opossums mind their business.'

She smiled. 'You told me that before.'

'I know.' Regarding her with those solemn eyes. 'Problem is, you never listen.'

> • <

In the thin autumn sunlight she crouched beside the stone and gently, slowly, began to scrub it clean of moss. A wire brush and a bucket of hot water; the scrape of bristle against stone, a rhythmic hiss. She scrubbed until the jewel-bright green gave way to mottled sky grey, the uneven surface of weather-beaten rock. The cross, amateur, but carved with great and obvious care; no half-hearted tribute was this. Whoever had placed this stone had meant for God to find it.

When she was done, she carried an armful of asters she'd plucked from the verge and laid them before the stone. It felt like a poor offering. This stone had been placed with love. It had been placed in the hope that this soul – small and secret, but still a soul – would live on in some way; bathed in dappled sunlight, gazed upon by passing birds. And perhaps it was irrational of her to feel as though this clutch of drooping flowers would keep their memory alive, but irrationality was what Lissa did best.

The sun bloomed bright through the trees then. In among the emerald foliage and deep brown earth the scrubbed-clean stone seemed so pale, so stark. And there, beneath that crudely carved cross, the sun had illuminated a set of marks which looked, to Lissa, like a name. She ran a careful thumb across this new topography, squinting in the warm light so that she might interpret the letters. Decades of wind and rain and moss had worn the edges smooth; nature had almost obliterated this final human trace, but she felt each letter with the pad of her index finger, reading with her skin: *mattie*.

She knelt in that sunlit grove, her palm pressed against those small, halting letters. Her pulse was warm and strong as she looked back towards the house, in all its faded splendour, and blurred now through hot tears. This house, which had stood through war, through famine; which had overlooked this grove since the day it was built. The quiet voice of the house at night, whispering its history. Tiny footprints cast in ash. The evergreen shadow of the grove, deep and still, the better to swallow up secrets. And that name, scraped into the stone like a message.

❯ • ❮

It was almost dawn when she heard, at last, the faint stir of something moving in the guest room. Outside, the sky had begun to lighten; the perfect tranquillity of the gloaming cast in watery shades of lilac, the blush of a slowly rising sun. The fire had burned down to embers, and the room was cold, but she sat curled and waiting on the sofa, so still that she might have been sleeping. Lissa hardly dared to breathe as the sounds coalesced into footsteps, small and distant. The sound of Audrey slipping from her bed at midnight to join her and Claudia in theirs; warm feet on cold floorboards, her sleep-muzzy face at the bedside, perturbed by some nightmare or another. But Audrey was hundreds of miles away, and Mama Liss was too far away to murmur words of comfort, to smooth that wild red hair as she drifted back to sleep.

The footsteps paused at the threshold of the living room. It sensed her, she thought; even in her stillness, it sensed her. 'It's all right,' she said, softly, so as not to startle. 'You can come in, if you want to.'

For a long time, nothing moved. She wondered if perhaps she'd imagined it all; if her brain, in its perpetual dysfunction, had spun a wild story. A replacement for Audrey, one she could never harm, for the harm had already been done a long time ago. And just as she began to feel terribly, unbearably stupid, the footsteps once again began to approach: slow, and halting, as though a skittish animal were moving towards her in the dark.

'Your name is Mattie, isn't it?' Gentle, coaxing, the way she'd speak to Audrey when she was afraid or upset. 'Maybe you don't remember. It's been a long time, hasn't it? You must have been very lonely, hiding down there all by yourself.'

Another pause. It felt as though someone were listening. The burn of curious eyes upon her, though there was nobody there. 'It's all right, Mattie. You don't have to hide anymore, if you don't want to. You can even have the guest room, if you like. It's nice and quiet, and nobody will bother you there.'

She felt a gentle pressure on the sofa beside her. Her heart quickened as the unseen guest gently clambered up; the rustle of fabric as invisible limbs settled into position. There was nothing there. There was *observably* nothing, and yet she could feel it, wary but curious, watching her from the other end of the sofa. Lissa had always been acutely aware of her own madness. Even in the throes of suffocating anxiety, some small part of her had always known that none of it was real; that this terrible, crushing sensation, this apocalyptic pressure, existed only inside her mind. But as she sat quietly on the sofa, watching the first pale threads of morning light filter through the heavy curtains, it seemed to Lissa that nothing had felt more real than that absent little being beside her. This was not obsession, or compulsion; it was not the frightened passenger in the back seat, crying catastrophe. This guest-room child. This lonely little ghost, forgotten no more. Perhaps I will call Claudia, she thought, as she closed her tired eyes. Perhaps she might even visit.

Author's note: the 'guest-room child', or Zashiki-warashi, is a type of yōkai in Japanese folklore. They are small spirits that take the form of young children and typically cause mischief – leaving sooty footprints, turning the pillows of people trying to sleep. Some theorise that they are the spirits of children lost to infanticide, a historical practice carried out during lean times to reduce the number of mouths to feed. Zashiki-warashi are considered good fortune, and those lucky enough to have a zashiki-warashi often leave food and sweets as offerings to keep the spirit in their home.

SE⏅BOUND

ALISON MOORE

May had spent her entire life in that clifftop house. She did not remember a time when she had not known Dylan, who lived next door when they were young. Dylan was older though. May tagged along when he went down to the beach, which was where he liked to be, peering into the rock pools or wading into the waves, looking for ships.

While May was still at the local secondary school, Dylan was already working, and talking about getting away from this dead-end place. He wanted – he had always wanted – to go to sea.

'I don't want you to go,' said May.

'But one of these days,' he said, 'I will go.'

May did her best to keep him with her. When she told him she loved him, he said he loved her too. When she told him she would always love him, he said, 'Come here,' and stroked her hair. When she told him she was having his baby, he said, 'You're welcome to have it, but you'll be on your own.' He was joining the navy; he had already been accepted.

May tried to persuade him not to leave, but it was like throwing coins into a wishing well: she could throw in all the coins she liked and tell him all her wishes but it would not make them come true. 'I love you,' she insisted. 'You said you loved me.'

'I *do* love you,' he said, but at the same time, he was putting on his boots. May believed he did love her in a way, but she was not the sea, which was where he really wanted to be, which was where he felt he belonged.

While Dylan was beginning his life at sea, May was giving birth to Daisy. She continued to live with her parents, raising Daisy in that clifftop house and waiting for Dylan to come home. And he did return, from time to time, for a few weeks every year, seeing his parents, seeing May, and Daisy, who was shy of him.

Daisy never called him Dad; she called him Dylan, when she called him anything at all. She was stiffly polite towards him, as if he were an especially important or unwelcome guest. Occasionally, Daisy lowered her guard and befriended him, and then he left again. He never wrote letters, never phoned. As a young adult, Daisy sometimes refused to see him, and when she moved away – when her career took her inland – she ceased to see him at all.

After giving his best years to the sea, Dylan retired. His parents were no longer living, and even their house was long gone, but May was just where he had left her, and she took him in. He had no more possessions than he could carry on his back. He often fell asleep in an armchair, with his clothes and shoes still on, as if he were ready to leave at any moment. He'd barely returned to dry land when his heart gave out.

After the funeral, Daisy asked her mum to move inland, to live with her.

'I've spent my whole life here,' said May. 'All my memories are here. All my things are here.' She felt at home, in that house on the cliff edge against which the sea beat.

> • <

Daisy phoned every few days to see how she was, and May said she was fine.

Except sometimes she was troubled in the night. All alone in the big bed that had once belonged to her parents, May dreamt she stood in the shallows at the edge of the sea, which sucked the sand from beneath her feet. She went deeper. Vast and cold, the sea climbed her bare legs. It was rough, but she stood her ground. Sometimes, when she woke from these dreams, the sea was so loud it could have been right there in her room.

Daisy phoned. She said she was redecorating the guest bedroom, and sent a picture of the wallpaper she was going to put up. May eyed her own wallpaper, which had probably been there as long as she had, along with the curtains, faded by sunlight, and the carpets, worn thin. Her window frames could do with repainting, or replacing; double glazing might help. But redecorating would mean having to move everything. The house was full of stuff, unused things, unread books. She was a hoarder.

The dreams got worse. She dreamt there was a man made of water, who came to her house in the night. She heard his wet feet in the hallway, and on the stairs as he climbed to her room. He came to her bedside. Really, he was just the *shape* of a man, an *idea* of a man, a disruption in the darkness, but she knew he was there. Sometimes she woke from these strange dreams to find her nightie and her bedding damp and smelling of salt.

She put her nightie and her bedding into the washing machine, and opened a window to get some air into the room. She looked out at the garden, which had once been extensive, but over the years so much had been lost. The sea was hurling itself at the cliff face. Its spray, carried on the wind, flung itself against the walls of her house. She closed the window again.

Daisy phoned. She told her mum she worried about her, and May said she was fine. But the erosion was getting worse, said Daisy, who saw how the sea was clawing its way towards the foundations of that clifftop house. She did not want her mother to be one of those people refusing to budge even as the house she was living in was falling into the sea.

There was damp in the walls. It was coming through the bedroom wallpaper, which was going to spoil. The walls would have to be stripped and treated. And mould, black mould, was spreading so fast she could not keep it at bay.

'It's bad for your health,' said Daisy.

'I know,' said May.

When, at night, the seaman came, moving through darkness or moonlight to her bedside, she knew he was looking for something. He did not seem to see her. She asked him, 'Is it me you want?' and then, in the silence, 'What do you want?' He did not seem to hear her. What troubled her – as he came closer, looking, wanting, not seeing her, not hearing her – was that she knew perfectly well what he had wanted all along.

> • <

May opened the little dark-wood cupboard next to her bed and removed the urn of ashes. He had wanted his remains to be scattered at sea. Even Daisy knew that, and had asked her mother from time to time if she had done it yet, and May had had to say no, not yet, until eventually she had said yes, she had done it, it was done, and hoped that would be the end of it.

May carried the urn downstairs. She put it on the kitchen table and kept it there while she made her breakfast. She ate lightly. She had never seen much point in cooking for one. She made a pot of tea, and drank the first cup at the table and the second cup at the window. She could see that the wind had dropped. When she put down her empty cup, she said to the urn of ashes, 'All right then.'

She put on her coat and her walking boots and left the house clutching the urn. She walked from the clifftop down to the promenade. People were out and about, alone and in couples and families. It was still cold though. She was almost alone on the beach.

She passed the rock pools, which filled up when the sea came in. It was coming in now. When she reached the shore, she stopped. She took the lid from the urn and, bending down to be closer to the water, poured the ashes into the shallows. She kept her walking boots out of the way. It was oddly like emptying the ash pan after a fire, or even – she did it with such care – pouring flour into the bowl of her kitchen scales to make a cake with Daisy. The sea washed in and out, carrying the ashes away.

When the urn was empty, May replaced the lid. She stood for a moment and watched the horizon, looking for ships. The clouds drifted by. She was, she realised, as she turned away and left the beach, quite hungry now.

From the promenade, she could only just see the clifftop house in which she had spent her life so far. Just in front of her was the little cafe to which she used to bring her daughter.

The bell above the door rings as she enters. Inside, it is warm. May chooses a table next to the window and puts the urn by her feet. When someone comes to ask her what she wants, May asks for coffee. It feels like a long time since she has slept well. She thinks of her mouldering bedroom, that house full of stuff she doesn't need. While she waits for her coffee to come, she watches the birds: the gulls and the sparrows. She prefers the sparrows. She thinks of the garden birds Daisy has on the wallpaper she's putting up in her guest bedroom. It sounds nice.

First, she will have her cup of coffee, and a look at the menu. Then she will call Daisy, whose number is stored in her mobile phone. She will ask about the guest bedroom. Then she will begin the journey back, knowing, now, that he will not be returning.

GOODBYE, JONATHAN TUMBLEDOWN

TIM MAJOR

The five flights of stairs really *felt* like five flights of stairs. Paul noticed his pace slowing as he ascended. It had nothing to do with tiredness.

His father was waiting in the single doorway on the uppermost floor. He looked thin, his face gaunt, his fleece jacket filled with air rather than flesh. Paul reminded himself that it had been only three months since he had last seen him.

Paul put on a smile as he reached the top of the stairs. He initiated a muddled hug, pulling away quickly, wary of assessing the size and shape of Fabrice's body beneath the bulbous fleece.

'Thanks for coming to see how I'm getting on,' Fabrice said.

In truth, it was only nagging guilt that had brought Paul here. 'It felt weird not having seen the place.'

He edged past his father and into the flat. He slipped off his boots and tucked them into low shelves beside a coatrack.

'Do you recognise that?' Fabrice said. 'The shoe rack?'

'Should I?'

'It's yours. Used to be a bookshelf. It went into the shed after you headed up to…' He trailed off.

Paul frowned. 'Edinburgh.'

'Yes. And when I left too… well, I gave it a new lease of life.' His voice shook a little. 'So now when I put on my shoes, I'm always thinking of you, and—'

Embarrassed, Paul padded along the dark corridor, peering into a narrow galley kitchen, a plain bathroom with a shower but no bath, a bedroom barely bigger than the double bed it contained. The three pictures on the walls were all photos of Warwick Castle. Hardly his father's sort of thing.

'This feels like some sort of inspection,' Fabrice said.

Paul knocked on the wall with his knuckles, then shifted along a few inches and knocked again. In response to Fabrice's puzzled expression, he said, 'You'd always do that any time you entered a new building. Checking for load-bearing walls.'

Fabrice only grunted in response.

As he entered a narrow sitting room, Paul inhaled sharply. It was strange, seeing so many familiar objects in the wrong place. The carriage clock that had belonged to his grandad, one of the pair of sofas his parents had always owned, a muddle of family photos out of chronological order. Even the curtains had been imported from his father's old study. That study – the one in the family house now occupied only by Paul's mother – was where Paul would be sleeping tonight. He had dumped his holdall there before venturing to the south end of town. It had been entirely stripped of character, a single bed in the centre of a bare space. A nothing room.

'This stuff is all yours,' Paul said. 'Doesn't Stacy have any possessions?'

'She doesn't live here.'

Fabrice tapped the frames of each of the family photos in turn. Paul watched his lips move. He was counting the photos. When he reached the end, he began again.

Paul sat on the sofa. 'She wasn't keen?'

His father turned. 'Very keen, Paul. But I need my space, and...'

'I just thought you'd take the opportunity when it was given.'

Fabrice's expression clouded. 'I haven't been given anything, Paul.'

'You're saying that something's been taken from you, then?'

His father gestured at the room, as if it constituted proof.

'You were forced to move out of your home,' Paul said, determined to retain a measured tone. 'You lost your marriage. You'll lose half of your combined savings. Is that what you mean?'

'All of those things, yes.'

'But don't you see that nobody did that to you? You gambled and lost. You took from Mum, not the other way around. And worse still, it was...' He stood and faced the tiny window. Before he had pressed the doorbell, he had stared up at this blank attic window of the Victorian building, uncertain whether his father might be looking down at him, uncertain whether it might not be better to turn around and return to the north end of town.

He studied the patterns of condensation on the glass. 'You were cheating on Mum for seven whole years, Dad. Seven years you were on borrowed time. You could have called it a day at any point, you could have shacked up with Stacy, but you didn't. You strung it out, adding lie upon lie. And you would have kept spinning those plates if you hadn't been caught out.'

'Emotions are complicated, Paul, and…'

It was a familiar trait, this tendency to finish statements with 'and'. Paul often thought it a frustrating assumption, a placeholder to prevent anybody from chipping in when he might think of more to say. Now the frustration was that Fabrice seemed to have nothing to add.

'What about morals?'

His father didn't answer. It occurred to Paul that Fabrice had never apologised for unravelling so much of Paul's own life, his own memories, through his actions.

They were silent for more than a minute, Paul staring at the grimy glass, Fabrice hovering behind him. Then Paul jolted at a sharp chiming sound from the corridor.

Fabrice plodded out of the room. Paul heard a low buzz that signalled the unlocking of the outer door. 'Stacy's on her way up.'

'She doesn't have a key?'

'I'll make a brew.' Paul detected no trace of the French accent which tended to undermine his father's almost-lifetime of British citizenship when he deployed colloquialisms.

Fabrice was still in the kitchen when there was a tapping at the door of the flat. Paul counted to ten, then opened the door, saying, 'Morning, Miss Shields,' wincing at his mistake.

Stacy dumped two carrier bags on the landing and threw her arms around his neck. She was shorter than he remembered.

'You were always so polite,' she said breathlessly. 'It's so good to *see* you, Paul. And you're doing so *well* these days.' She retrieved her bags, swung them into the flat and deposited them in the doorway of the kitchen, where Fabrice was pouring water from the kettle into a cast-iron teapot that Paul had given him on a Father's Day long ago. Then she kicked off her shoes and took Paul's arm, leading him towards the sitting room.

Stacy was wearing skin-tight jeans and a loose grey jumper that slipped off one shoulder. Back when she had taught him at secondary school, she had worn mainly dresses and tights. Paul had been hypnotised by those legs whenever Miss Shields perched on the edge of her desk.

'I know this must seem quite strange,' she said. 'Does it?'

'It does a bit.'

'Of course. But I don't want you to think of me any differently than before.'

Paul gave a hollow laugh. 'You still want me to think of you as my French teacher?'

She grasped her mass of blond curls and fixed it with a hairband. Now that her face was fully visible, Paul saw the differences the years had made, the new creases around her lips. She had always been a smoker, often spotted looking furtive in the teachers' car park or accepting cigarettes from ex-pupils in the pub.

'I mean we've always been friendly, you and I, haven't we? And maybe you should teach *me*, Mr University Lecturer.' She paused. 'How's your mum?'

Paul stiffened. As far as he knew, the only time his mother had met Stacy would have been at parents' evenings, a decade ago, with Fabrice at her side.

'She was still at work when I arrived on the train,' Paul replied. 'She's keeping busy. She's strong. I think she'll be okay when she's in her new place.'

Stacy chewed her lip. 'This house sale, huh? It's taking such a very long time.'

Paul noted her unease. His mother had told him that, when she had finally confronted Fabrice with the evidence she had gathered, his drunken admissions had hinted at more misdeeds: his affair with Stacy had lasted seven years, but it had been only one of many.

His father padded in with a tray. He deposited it on a small oval table – the only table in the flat, so this dim corner must be where he ate his breakfast, lunch and dinner – and as he did so, the anglepoise lamp illuminated his face. The skin under his eyes was dry and cracked. How much of him was similarly broken?

Fabrice filled his mug from the pot. 'How's the lecturing going?'

'It's English Lit, isn't it?' Stacy added.

'Creative Writing. I suppose it's the same thing. I fully expected the first term of teaching to be manic. This time next year it'll all be second nature, I hope.'

'It's lovely that you've followed Fab into the creative arts,' Stacy said brightly.

Paul choked. 'Fab?'

'I've always called him that. And he is, isn't he? Fab, I mean. And it always seemed so *right* that we'd hit it off together, both of us being so creative, and the French link, of course.'

'Aren't you Welsh?'

'I mean *teaching* French, silly.'

'Do you have projects on the go?' Paul said to his father. 'I've just realised I haven't seen your studio here.'

'I haven't felt the need,' Fabrice said. 'And supplies cost a lot. And...'

Paul frowned. 'But it's what you've always done.' He almost added, *in order to cope.* His father had always been anxious and melancholy, but the triumph of creating new work tended to keep him on track. 'Even on holidays you'd have us trawling the beaches for finds, then you'd squirrel yourself away, turning them into something new.'

His father's eyes were rheumy and pale, and the thought struck Paul that there was nothing beneath that sea-blue surface. When he wasn't working, part of his identity was missing.

'For me it was those craft magazines that come in lots of parts,' Stacy said. 'Sew a quilt over fifteen weeks, that sort of thing. Very creative. Do you think it was being involved in Fab's art that made you a creative person, Paul?'

'No. It was Jonathan Tumbledown,' he replied.

He watched his father rub at a mark on the table, absently at first but then faster and faster, his jaw working with concentration. This behaviour was new.

Quietly, Paul added, 'You must remember those stories, Dad?'

'Yes, of course.'

'Is he a writer, this Jonathan what's-his-name?' Stacy said.

Paul shook his head. 'Dad would tell me stories about this invented character, Jonathan Tumbledown. I don't know who came up with the name, me or him.'

His father watched him with polite interest.

'There was no real thread to the stories. Jonathan Tumbledown might be anywhere in the world, doing anything you can imagine. Sometimes he was a kid, sometimes the prime minister. He was friends with my toy rhino and He-Man and Phillip from next door. Every night a new story.'

Stacy stretched across the table to take Fabrice's hands. Paul looked away in embarrassment.

'It just goes to show,' Stacy said, 'just how caring Fab has always been, and how clever...' She turned to the window. 'Perhaps he'll get another chance in the future.'

Paul's eyes flicked to his father. Was he planning a new family, at his age? Stacy must be almost forty. She still had time, but they would have to make the decision fairly soon. But when his father met his eye, Paul read his expression as pleading, a dull panic.

Fabrice said, 'I'll wash up,' and shuffled to the kitchen.

Paul took the opportunity to abandon Stacy. The only room he hadn't ventured into was the one beside the sitting room. He pushed the door open and squinted in the bright light streaming from two skylights in the angled roof. He could see why his father might have been tempted to take this flat, five flights of stairs and all. The idea of establishing an art studio in this bright space was tantalising.

But there were no art supplies, no canvases, no projects in progress. On a desk pushed against the far wall were piles of papers, miniature chests of drawers and weighing scales. The left wall was lined with shelving that reached almost to the eaves, which held rows and rows of wooden crates of different sizes. His father's boxes.

He slid out one of the crates carefully. It was slightly larger than a shoebox. The dovetail joints at the corners were misaligned and splinters pressed into his palms without puncturing the skin. He rotated the box to look through its glass window. Inside, three wire figurines vibrated with echoes of the motion. The smallest figure had a face made from a Heineken bottle cap, and it was angled as though he or she were gazing up at the large, gnarled tree root that seemed to lunge from a pool of water made of crumpled netting. The other two figures had pebbles for heads and inked mouths, but no eyes. They sat around a campfire of wooden struts painted the colour of amber.

Until a few months ago this box had been installed at the foot of the staircase in the family home, where now there was only an incongruously light patch of plaster on the wall. In his mind's eye, Paul could climb the stairs of that house and see it as it had been before his father had been thrown out, and he could name each of the dioramas in turn. The monster from the lake. The camera house. The flood of peas. The dance of the cork ballerinas. The library of sand. The punishment of the angels. Each of the boxes must be here on these shelves, pushed together and facing one another.

As he turned to leave the room he saw another, freestanding, shelving unit. On one of the wire shelves was a cardboard box. Parcel tape was applied to only one edge – Fabrice must have run out; the spent roll lay on top of the box – and the lid had come free. A handwritten address label covered most of the upper face. The address was long and ended with *GUANGDONG PROVINCE, CHINA*.

Paul lifted the lid. On top of a mound of bubble wrap was a certificate with an embossed silver badge. He put it to one side and parted the bubble wrap. The wooden crate was face-upwards, allowing him a glimpse of the diorama within: a plastic Playmobil pirate facing a mound of brightly painted film canisters. A golden plastic medal was fixed to the back wall, ringed with colourful patterns drawn in felt-tip pen.

'Get the hell out of there!'

Paul spun around, still holding the open box.

'I helped draw these patterns, didn't I?' he said. 'Have you really sold this to someone?'

His father glanced at the diorama, then clapped a hand over his eyes. Blindly, he pushed the lid of the cardboard box down.

'I saw it,' he muttered angrily. 'I saw it, so it'll need certificating all over again.'

'What do you mean? What was that certificate?'

'Go into the other room. Let me gather myself.'

Reeling, Paul obeyed. Stacy was lying on the sofa, her knees tucked up like a kid.

'What's going on with my dad's boxes?' he said. When Stacy didn't respond, he shoved her shoulder. 'Was getting rid of them your idea? When the house sells, he'll have half the money. Surely you can both hold on that long.'

She stirred and rose to a kneeling position. Her face was pale. Perhaps she understood that a long-term future with Fabrice was just a pipe dream.

'I've no influence on him really,' she said thoughtfully. 'Fab has always had more going on than just me… Perhaps money's part of it. Who knows.'

'But those boxes contain memories,' Paul said, annoyed at his whining tone. 'They're my memories, as much as his.'

Stacy's face crumpled. 'Then you already know?'

Paul froze. 'Know what?'

As Fabrice entered the room he was already speaking in a false, bright tone. '—nothing unusual, just a temporary situation. You can appreciate that money isn't as freely available as it was.'

'Paul knows about the associations,' Stacy said.

Fabrice glanced at Paul. Paul forced himself to stay silent, for fear of derailing a confession.

'Every artist sells his work,' his father said.

'You said those ones would never be sold,' Paul snapped. 'You said they were ours as much as yours. But that's beside the point. I don't think that's what Miss Shields – I mean Stacy – is talking about.'

His father rubbed his eyes. Paul grimaced at the scratching sound as his fingertips ran over cracked skin. Slowly, Fabrice said, 'I swear to God.' It sounded like a threat, possibly aimed at Stacy.

'Tell me what's going on, Dad.'

His father exhaled. His eyes darted across the collection of family photos on the wall. Perhaps he was counting them once again, a barely conscious reassurance. 'I told you, times are hard. I'm paying for this place along with my contributions to the old place. And even when the house sale goes through, my income is… Well, it's almost nothing. So yes, I've been working through my old possessions and selling what I can online. I started with knick-knacks, but it turns out that there's nothing so lucrative as my work.'

'Dad, why didn't you just say that upfront? If your art's coming back into demand, that's something to be—'

Fabrice interrupted him. 'It's only those boxes. And the people buying them have no understanding of artistic worth. They're not art collectors.'

'Then what are they?'

His father laughed mirthlessly. 'I don't know. I'll never meet them. At least, I hope not.'

Paul paused to think. 'What was that certificate in the box?'

'Proof of authenticity. And proof that the correct procedure has been followed. It's by far the most expensive part of the arrangement.'

'You said you'd have to do it all again. Because you'd seen the diorama.'

Stacy was watching the exchange anxiously. 'Tell him, Fab. You might as well.'

Fabrice blinked very slowly, as though he might fall asleep at any moment. He rubbed his hands together compulsively. He nodded. 'Paul, I stumbled across this dealership. They facilitate art sales... but it's a little more involved than that. The artworks must come packaged with the certificate and everything that involves.'

'Which is?'

'Which is the transfer of the artist's associations with the artwork in question.'

'Like a written testimonial of some sort?'

'*Transfer*, Paul,' Stacy said. 'A total transfer, not just a written account.'

Paul stared at her. 'I'm not following.'

'There's a place out of town,' Fabrice began. 'That's where I go, once a sale has been arranged. It isn't much more than a warehouse, and it's distinct from the dealers, who I've never met. The procedure is nothing invasive. The machine looks like those big dryers in women's hairdressers. Barely a tickle. It doesn't take long – I'm in the swing of it now, so I don't even have to concentrate. I just look at the diorama in question and I let the machine do its work. And then it's done and the work can be packaged up. But the dealers say it has to be me that sends the parcel, and when the money comes through they've already taken their commission.'

Paul opened his mouth, but couldn't think of anything to say.

Fabrice continued, 'Then, when the buyer receives the package, the combination of the certificate and the artwork triggers the transfer. At which point it's all theirs, lock, stock and barrel. When they observe that artwork, they recall all the associations that are bundled in with it. And I don't have them anymore.'

'But what you're saying is insane,' Paul managed at last. 'It's not possible.'

His father shrugged. 'I'm told that my boxes are particularly prized because they have so many constituent items, each with a different association. It makes for a heady mixture.'

Paul wondered whether the pair of them were having fun at his expense, but a glance at Stacy told him otherwise.

'It's normally okay,' Stacy said thoughtfully. 'But. Well, I mean, it isn't always. Is it, Fab?'

Fabrice waved a hand dismissively. 'It's hard to tell which are the lodestones, that's all.'

Paul stifled an urge to rush at his father, to shove him so hard that he fell backwards into the hallway, sprawling beside that stupid shoe rack. But instead he said, 'What's a lodestone, in this context?'

Fabrice cleared his throat. 'It seems that some items are more imbued with associations than others. It's the dealers' job to assess which is which, but they don't always get it right. I try to avoid selling any lodestones, of course. But every so often there's a mix-up.'

'Meaning what?'

'Meaning that I give away more of my associations than I'd intended. It's only when the transfer completes that I notice the extent – or rather, Stacy notices the lack of some memory or other that was once there. But put it this way, Paul – these days I could do with a little more free space up here.'

He touched his temple twice, and Paul thought again of his tapped-knuckle search for load-bearing walls.

If it were true, the dangers seemed enormous. Losing associations meant risking the loss of foundational memories. Gambling on upsetting the lower parts of a house of cards.

Slowly, Paul said, 'Your accent has gone.'

Fabrice's eyebrows performed a complicated dance of restrained emotion. He rubbed at the webbing between the thumb and forefinger of his left hand, where the skin already appeared chapped. Stacy gripped his arm.

In a desolate tone, Fabrice said, 'Sometimes I wish more might be taken, not less, and…'

'What on earth do you mean?'

His father's head bowed. His body convulsed. But when he looked up, there were no tears. 'I don't enjoy remembering some of the things I've done, Paul. I don't enjoy dwelling on the fact of your mum being a victim. If I could only carve out and discard the right parts, I would.'

Paul found that he had no impulse to comfort him. Despite his obvious suffering, his father's sentiment seemed utterly selfish. 'You wish you couldn't remember what a shit you've been.'

Stacy actually gasped, despite having been one of the most liberal teachers, who wouldn't have balked at swearing in the classroom.

'Remember who you're talking to,' Fabrice said, without conviction.

'I remember full well,' Paul replied. 'What do you wish had happened, Dad? Do you wish you'd made different choices, or simply that you hadn't been caught?'

His father stared at him blankly.

> • <

Paul pulled into the driveway and shut off the engine. He bent to peer through the windscreen.

When he had written this address on the envelopes of Christmas and birthday cards, his mental image of the house had been very different. 'Hazel Cottage' sounded picturesque, though in his mind's eye Paul had given it cramped dimensions and significant decay. His father had mentioned in one of his short, matter-of-fact emails that Stacy no longer taught, and the £150,000 share from the family house wouldn't have gone far. But the building was far larger than his mother's new semi-detached, bigger even than their old home. It was a new-build with unweathered cornerstones and fluted columns either side of the front door. Fabrice had always sworn his hatred of new houses, claiming they had no soul.

Paul started counting to ten, but opened the car door when he reached seven, a trick he often used when he was reluctant to do something. His satchel knocked against his thigh as he approached the house.

The front door opened. Stacy wore a pastel green dress that reached her knees, and her hair was long and lacked its usual curls – it must have taken a lot of effort to straighten it.

'It's Paul!' she called over her shoulder.

She launched herself at Paul before he could defend himself. He eased her away. 'It's good to see you, Stacy.'

'Not Miss Shields anymore?'

'No. Especially now that we share a surname. How are you?'

'Really good. Really, really good.'

'And Dad?'

She grinned and took his arm, leading him into the house. 'See for yourself.'

The entrance hall was as large as the entirety of Paul's Edinburgh apartment. A large Persian rug covered most of the cream carpet. Through the doorway to his left, Paul glimpsed chrome kitchen worksurfaces, and in the sitting room to his right, a horseshoe of leather sofas. At the rear of the hall a passage led to a conservatory filled with potted plants and with dreamcatchers hanging from its roof.

'Paul, my son.'

Paul looked up to see his father – it must be him – at the top of the staircase. He wore a dazzlingly white shirt and grey woollen trousers. He had grown a goatee beard. Paul watched in silence as this stranger descended the stairs. Fabrice's face was fuller, his neck thicker. He had dyed his hair, darker than the chestnut brown Paul remembered from his childhood.

Fabrice put a hand on each of Paul's shoulders, and bent to look into his eyes. 'Son, it's good to see you. Come in, come in. Can I make you a cup of coffee?'

He had always hated coffee.

'I'm good,' Paul said. He recognised nothing in the sitting room. No family heirlooms, no inherited items of furniture. The only photos were of Fabrice and Stacy, sipping drinks, standing in front of waterfalls, wearing paper hats emblazoned with the logos of restaurants, and in formal poses at their wedding to which Paul hadn't been invited. 'This place is... well, it's huge.'

'Thank you,' his father replied, misinterpreting Paul's tone. 'Stacy's the mastermind.'

Stacy beamed. 'I guess when I was given free rein, I was able to indulge my creativity.'

Paul could hear distant wind chimes. When Paul was a kid, Fabrice had once brought the fury of the Neighbourhood Watch upon himself after firing Paul's spud gun at Mrs Aspen's wind chime, shattering it beyond repair.

'I can't understand how you were able to afford all this,' Paul said.

'Isn't that rather uncivilised?' Fabrice replied. 'Talking about money.'

Paul waited, expecting his father's customary 'and', but it didn't come. 'I suppose it is, if you *have* money.'

Fabrice cocked his head to one side, an action so unlike him that Paul actually took a step backwards in surprise. 'If you're facing hard times, son, perhaps we can help. A university lecturer can't be earning a great deal these days.'

'Neither can a retired artist and an out-of-work French teacher, I'd have thought.'

Stacy laughed. 'I know you're being funny, but you do understand I only stopped work *because* we came into money. Well… and now this.'

Even before she turned to stand in profile, Paul understood what she was showing him. She cradled her belly with both hands. Paul sat down heavily on the footstool in the centre of the horseshoe of sofas.

'Congratulations to you both,' he said in a faint voice.

Stacy sat too. Instead of joining her, Fabrice stood behind the sofa, his hands on her shoulders, as though they were posing for an old-fashioned matrimonial portrait.

'Does this mean you're working again, Dad?' Paul managed to say. 'Selling new pieces?'

A flicker of uncertainty passed over his father's face, then his complacent expression was restored. 'No.'

'Then how did all this come about?'

'The house sale, of course,' Stacy replied.

'The house sale,' Paul repeated. 'You mean the sale of the family house? The house in which I grew up?'

She nodded, seeming less sure of herself.

'But it was worth only three hundred thousand. You guys got half of it.'

Stacy gazed at him for a few seconds, then turned to her husband. 'Fab?'

'Does it matter now?' Fabrice replied quickly. 'We're happy. How is your mother, Paul? How is Harriet?'

Paul had never heard his father call his mother by her full name. She had always been Harry.

'She's fine. But her house is a lot smaller than yours.'

Stacy's hands clutched at one another in her lap. 'Fab, I don't understand. You told me that... I mean, weren't the proceeds enough to...'

Without hurrying, Fabrice walked around the sofa and sat beside his wife. He placed a hand on her stomach. 'It allowed us to start again, didn't it?'

Not only was his French accent absent, Paul could locate nothing in his father's intonation that sounded like the man who had raised him. He fought the urge to sprint out of the building. 'Dad. Where did the money come from?'

'From the sale of the house.'

'But Mum got one-fifty. You were the one who arranged the sale, and you gave her one-fifty.'

'Quite right. A half share of the accepted offer.'

'The 'accepted offer'… Not the final offer? The offer of the person who eventually bought it?'

His father smiled. 'Another buyer came forward at the last minute. Your mother didn't need to be informed, because it was a personal matter. That is, the difference in value was my own affair and the money was due only to me.'

The thought struck Paul that it wasn't just that Fabrice displayed no remorse – it was that he had no *access* to remorse.

The answer came to him. 'Those dealers. The same dealers who arranged the sale of your dioramas.'

His father bowed his head, an acknowledgement rather than sorrow.

'Fab…' Stacy said in a scratchy voice. 'I still don't fully…'

Paul felt sudden pity for her. She had clung onto Fabrice after all, but at what price? Perhaps she was so grateful that she was blind to all the changes in him. She took his apparent happiness at face value. This idea seemed more awful than if she had been aware of the theft.

'When Dad sold the house, he sold all his mental associations along with it. That is, all the memories he had accrued during…' Paul did a quick mental calculation, '…more than thirty years living in that building. All the sadness and joy of any life events linked in any way to that house.' His throat clogged, but he struggled on. 'Which would have included pretty much all the memories of my upbringing, among everything else.'

'Is that true?' Stacy said to Fabrice.

'It allowed us to start again,' Fabrice said again. 'That house was a lodestone. The number of years I spent there, combined with my work, all that creative energy, all that *life lived...*'

His manner suggested no sense of regret. He knew the bare narrative of what he had done to himself, but he had no memory of the specifics of what he had lost.

Paul shook his head vigorously. 'No. It allowed *you* to start again. It allowed you to scrape away all that guilt, the knowledge of your duplicity. You shed it all and you became... *this.*' He gestured wildly at the stranger sitting before him.

The placidity of his father's expression was more awful than anger or sadness.

'I'm happy,' Fabrice replied in his bland tone. 'I appreciate you coming to see how I am. But I'm glad to say that I'm happy. We're happy.'

Paul willed him to add an 'and' but there was nothing there.

Fabrice tapped Stacy's stomach twice. Stacy flinched each time.

Paul stood shakily. 'Firstly, I'm not here to see how you are. I felt guilty, and it was weird not having seen the place.' He rummaged in his satchel, feeling past the cereal bars, his train novel and a collection of loose pens. 'Secondly, you're *not* happy, Dad. Stacy might be – or at least, she might have believed she was – but all you've done is forgotten yourself. I understand you were suffering after you and Mum split – of course you were, of course you felt guilty and depressed. And I understand that you were never a particularly happy camper in the first place. But don't you see, that was part of who you were? You're *supposed* to be pensive and inward-looking and dissatisfied. You always were that way, even when we all knew full well you were content. But this… It's not purity, it's just blankness. That's not happiness.'

But his father really did look happy as well as healthy. He seemed unperturbed by Paul's outburst, as if it were understandable and regrettable but nothing that might affect him personally.

'I'm going to leave in a moment,' Paul said. 'But I brought you something and it seems wrong not to give it to you.'

From his satchel he retrieved what he was searching for. It was a small hardback notebook. On its cover was a cartoon elephant on a light-blue background.

'I have this box of nostalgic bits and bobs that I cart from place to place, now that Mum has no room to store anything,' he said as he riffled through the pages. 'I'd forgotten I kept this.'

He looked up. His father was frowning at the notebook. His expression wasn't one of recognition, only mistrust.

'It's doodles, mostly,' Paul said, holding up the book to display a crude picture of a pirate captain holding a trophy. 'But I wrote little stories in it, too. I suppose that's why I kept it.' He settled on a page and tapped it twice. Frowning, he struggled to read the childish scrawl. 'One day Jonathan Tumbledown was walking along the path and he saw a… squirrel – I think it says squirrel – and he said do you want to go to Malta on a… quest, maybe?… to find a magic hat.' Abruptly, Paul's eyes filled with tears. 'You won't remember this, Dad, but when we holidayed in Malta, we hired a pedalo and went too far out from the shore. It was windy, and my baseball cap blew off my head. You told me it would keep on blowing further and further out, and it would go all the way around the world. You said that one day we'd visit

Malta again and we'd find my cap, and it would be better than ever before, because it would be the first hat to travel around the world. And I didn't believe it, even at the age of six, but I liked the story. Stories became more and more important to me. I suppose all memories are stories, aren't they?'

Stacy had begun to cry quietly. She pushed Paul's father's hand away from her stomach and lowered her head until her chin rested on her chest.

'Son—' his father began.

Paul held up the book, and Fabrice stopped speaking.

'That's not why I brought this,' he said. He flicked through the pages and stopped near to the end of the book. The handwriting on these two pages was far smaller, spiky and untidy. 'You must have noted down the story titles each day. I don't know whether you would have done that before or after you told the stories, and I guess now you can't tell me.' The phrase *aide-memoire* came to his mind, and he swallowed a sob. He rubbed his eyes and began to read. 'Jonathan Tumbledown and the Mysterious Switch. Jonathan Tumbledown and the Monkey Windmill. JT and the Dogalog's Birthday. The Bow and Sausages. The Disappearing Castle. The Enormous Piece of Paper. The Invisible Canoe.'

In a halting voice, he continued, 'I brought it because I've just heard that my novel's been accepted for publication. It's a mystery story, for kids. And, I don't know, despite everything that's happened, I wanted to thank you. I wanted to show you this notebook and I wanted to thank you for kicking it all off, for doing one thing that worked out all right.' He folded the pages of the book around the ring binding so that the list of Jonathan Tumbledown's adventures became the front and back covers. 'I mean, this is a real artefact, isn't it? Talk about a lodestone.'

He tossed the book to his father. It was a good throw; it landed directly in his lap.

Paul turned to leave, but immediately spun around in response to a scuffling sound. Fabrice was scrambling backwards on the sofa, his socks skidding on the slick leather surface in his attempts to escape. His eyes bulged as he stared at the notebook.

Stacy was watching Fabrice but she didn't attempt to help him.

Then his father's body slackened. He lifted the book gingerly and raised it, cradling it in both hands like a Bible. His eyes darted from side to side as he read the list.

He began to weep. His head nodded again and again.

'I remember,' he breathed. He raised his head to look up at Paul. His wide face had become sallow, his eye sockets dark, signifiers of the same melancholy that had once been a vital part of him.

His voice cracked as he said again, 'I remember. I remember what I did. What I was. The shame. And...'

THE CHORUS

ALIYA WHITELEY

'Are they singing now?'

'They're always singing.'

'What's it like?'

He closed his eyes, tried to hold the moment. 'Later,' he said, but Sal would persist; she liked to know, afterwards. The way she wanted that from him, her hunger for his chorus, was easy to love.

'Is it sleepy?' she asked.

'Yeah.' Soft, high sounds of pleasure that he felt at the base of his stomach. 'Like a lullaby. It's good.'

She snuggled into him, pulling up the duvet. Her head was on his shoulder, her hair across his chest. She liked to be so close. *She wants to be inside me*, he thought, and then he concentrated on the ebbing away of the feeling of being inside her, and slept.

> • <

On the Jubilee Line he saw at least three heads moving in time, and wondered if the chorus was singing them all the same song. He'd found that out at school, years ago: sometimes people who were gathered together, from close friends to strangers, clicked into a kind of rhythm and shared a melody for a moment. There was a sense of togetherness to living, sometimes, that gave him comfort.

The chorus was singing low, repetitive words. The usual commute sounds. *On on on.* A reassurance.

Since meeting her, Mike had begun to pay attention to the chorus in a way he hadn't since his teenage years. It had been little more than background noise since leaving university, barely worth paying attention to. But he'd been at a party held by an old school friend, dressed as a pirate of all things, drunk and suddenly aware that his fake parrot was no longer on his shoulder, and he'd got down on his hands and knees and crawled under the table to look for it. *Your parrot*, she'd said, holding it out to him. Her legs were in glittery pink tights. He'd got up, found himself face to face with a ballerina. She loved to dance. She drank vodka and tonic. She worked with a friend of a friend of his friend; it took him ages to understand that connection, and she laughed at him throughout the explanation, so he played the fool because he liked that laugh.

She first told him that she didn't have a chorus months after that party, when he was already sure he was in love. He couldn't blame her for that.

Some days he could see how, in the future, he might.

〉 • 〈

'Not such a good day?' he asked her, walking in through the door, seeing her face. He listened to her, ordered a takeaway, put on an episode of her favourite sitcom. By the end of the night she was smiling again. He dimmed the lights and put on some slow music, and they danced, in time, in the moment. His chorus sang along, softly, harmonising.

It went on singing after the music ended, for him. Only for him.

> • <

You can't be without any chorus at all, he'd said, a few years in, when he first began to understand that it did matter, and every time he'd told her otherwise he had been wrong. *Did you see a doctor?*

Of course, she said.

Is it worth going back again? Things change all the time.

Some things don't, she said.

He felt he was waiting, and he knew he was strong. He could wait. He didn't know what he was waiting for.

> • <

'Listen to this,' he said, and read out a section:

> *Nihilcantism has been documented since the first written records, and treatments have included the bizarre and torturous. From trepanning and eardrum perforating to mutilation of the face and body, bleeding, exposure to deafening or constant sounds, then high-dosage drug programmes in modern-era science, there have been many—*

Sal turned over, away from him. Her voice was muffled by the pillow. 'Please don't,' she said.

'Sorry,' he said, 'sorry, I just want to help.' He put down the book, turned off the light and rolled against her.

'You don't need to help. I mean, you do help. But it's not your job. Stop making it your job.'

'Sorry,' he said again. He sat back up and read on, not speaking the text aloud. The chorus hummed along with the cadence of the words.

> *Commonly practised contemporary aids include meditation, mindfulness, and different forms of therapy, along with drug therapies that have reported varying degrees of success amongst patients. The question of whether a fully working chorus can ever be re-established among those who have lost their own (through trauma, etc.) or even created for those who claim to have never heard the chorus, is far from answered. The subjectivity of the—*

'Turn off the light when you're finished,' she said. She sounded so wearied. By him? He was suddenly certain he was making it worse.

He put down the book and switched off the light. He was careful not to touch her.

> • ❮

It had simply always been there, that collection of voices, that sense of agreement and inner reassurance: how could she not have it? What, then, did she have? *Silence*, he thought, while they watched television. Silence scared him. But then he thought: *maybe it's different, maybe she can't miss what she's never had.*

On the lead up to their big summer holiday that year, counting down the weeks on his diary planner, Mike began waking very early in the morning, certain his chorus had ceased. That first moment, in grey half-light, he found he could not breathe, and there was nothing, no sound, until – there. His chorus. A whisper of soothing, indistinguishable words. Then he would time his breaths in and out to its tempo until he slept once more.

Sal never woke in these moments. She lay, inert and heavy, beside him. A stone.

> • <

They decided to unpack later, and headed straight for the beach. It was one of those perfect sunsets: red sun sinking, a languid sea, the waves tame and sedate. They walked hand in hand along the shore to a small bar, the tables and chairs beside the water. The laminated menu listed cocktails at half price; they'd hit happy hour. They chose at random, for the names alone. A zombie. A fog cutter.

'Good choice,' said the waiter, and they smiled at his back as he disappeared inside.

Sal looked around the empty tables. 'It's so quiet.'

'Maybe everyone's in town already.'

'I reckon they don't even come out until midnight. Then they'll party all night. Fancy going to a club?'

'Sure,' he said. 'Let's pretend we're young again.'

'Yeah, early thirties is ancient.' She rolled her eyes at him.

'I feel old, though,' he said, plaintively.

'You're really not.'

The drinks arrived, and they drank quickly, swapping glasses halfway through to taste the other. 'What are they singing?' she said.

Mike tuned in to them for a moment, and told her, 'Just a few voices, in in in with the water, out out out. Shush. Shush. That kind of thing.'

'In in in out out out?' She laughed. 'Tells me what you're thinking about.'

'Always,' he said, and laughed with her.

'I would give anything to hear them,' she said. 'To not feel different, all the time. Empty.' Her eyes were direct, challenging him. To do what, say what? Carefully, tenderly, he did his best to tell no lies, leaving *it really doesn't matter* and *we'll get some help, we'll find a way* unsaid.

'I'm here,' he said. 'You're here. I'm not sure if there's more. I want there to be.'

> • <

He got the feeling she was still thinking about his words as they walked into town. People were beginning to emerge from their apartments and villas, and bars were filling up, turning the music higher. A man on the main strip held out flyers for a club, free entry before eleven, and inside everything was electrified, neon, smoke machines and bubble wands.

'Drink?' he said, but she shook her head and pulled him to the dance floor.

She was the ballerina again, in her smile, in the movement of her long legs. He watched her sway to the rhythm, and joined in, not caring what songs played; they all rolled together, into an endless beat, and he felt no exhaustion, no need to stop moving. More and more people joined in, coming to the floor, sliding through the lights and smoke, and he closed his eyes and let his chorus, their chorus, take hold, as everyone lifted up their arms and it moved through them.

When he opened his eyes again she was not there.

His chorus shrieked in fear, drowning out the music. He could imagine it: her running from the club, down to the water, wading out, far out, to the silence. He hadn't done enough, said enough. He pushed through the crowd and nearly missed her small voice, calling his name.

'I'm here,' she said, from the bar. She was in the push of bodies queuing for service. He came and stood next to her, and felt the chorus sigh out relief. 'Want a drink?'

'Yeah, a beer,' he said.

Once she'd finally been served they took their drinks out onto a balcony overlooking the sea, jostling elbows with a loud group dressed up for a hen night. The bride-to-be was in sparkling pink, with a spiky veil obscuring her face. Even so, Mike could tell she was enjoying herself. It was in the way her shoulders moved; she was laughing along with all the others.

Sal said something he didn't catch.

'What?' he said.

She put her lips to his ear, and said something about guilt.

'Who's guilty?' he asked her, and then realised she was right – he did feel guilt, for the chorus in him and in the world, for the way the voices sang so freely for those who did not always listen. For the deep silence in her he couldn't understand and was afraid of. For sometimes wanting to be free of it, and even for loving it for making her who she was.

She put her hand on his chest. 'I can hear you,' she said.

The hen party shrieked as one, and then rushed from the balcony to the dance floor, desperate to be part of the song.

Mike put his hand over hers. He wanted his chorus to rush into her, to fill her, and if it didn't, if that never happened—

'Okay,' he said. 'Okay. You can be quite hard to love, is all.'

Was that too honest? But she nodded, and said, 'You too. I'm so tired.'

'Come on.' He put an arm around her and they started the long walk back, along the beach, both grateful for being there, in the night, beside each other.

MEET ON THE EDGE

GARETH E. REES

The morning air felt curiously thin, as if Melissa had ascended a mountain instead of clambering into the driver's seat of her SUV. She felt a little dizzy. Maybe it was nerves or something. Silly really. She wasn't doing anything wrong. Melissa breathed deeply. Once. Twice. *Good.* Then she fired up the engine and drove out of town, occasionally checking herself out in the sun-visor mirror, humming a half-remembered Nine Inch Nails tune.

A congested single lane took her to the interchange beneath a criss-cross of flyovers. After a crawl through traffic lights she hit the dual carriageway, whizzing past car showrooms and high-rise office blocks until she spotted the rectangle obelisk of the retail park sign silhouetted against the blue sky.

B&Q was already busy. Bald-headed men emerged through the sliding doors, pushing platform trolleys stacked with merchandise. Melissa circled the mass of stationary vehicles until she reached the car park's perimeter, where a verge of bark chippings met a box hedge. Here the white lines of the parking bays were faded and scorched with rubber from nocturnal wheelspins, the kerb littered with crushed cans, cigarette butts and sun-bleached crisp packets.

In this B&Q hinterland, there were relatively few cars. Not only was it the area farthest away from the store, but it was on the other side of a strip of pine trees, bordered by a wooden fence, which jutted into the car park, rendering the store as a patchwork of orange fragments among the foliage. It was the parking zone of last resort. But even if it filled up, Melissa supposed that nobody would pay much attention to her. People were here to buy power tools and lawnmowers, tiles and flooring, paint and wallpaper paste. The car park was nothing more than a tarmac sea, to be crossed as quickly as possible. She watched them hurry from their vehicles as she bit her nails, hoping that Letitia would appear, as promised.

Melissa had first bumped into Letitia the previous Saturday morning. Sick of being stuck in the house, she'd volunteered to buy paint for her eldest's bedroom. Axel wanted black walls, inspired by his discovery of her old Placebo CDs. She was pleased that he was crate-digging her teenage music collection – but black? No, no, no. Her in-laws stayed in his bedroom at Christmas. Black wasn't conducive to a harmonious visit. 'It's very gloomy in here, Melissa.' 'Is Axel on drugs, Melissa?' That kind of thing. Neither would black fit with the sophisticated neutrals from Farrow and Ball throughout the rest of her house. Besides, Axel was one of those kids who went through phases faster than pints of milk. No doubt he'd be a hippy in a month's time when he discovered her Kula Shaker CDs and they'd have to paint his room again. So Melissa encouraged him to choose grey, to match his bed frame. To get the hues right, she opted for B&Q's colour matching service. The paint needed mixing by the lad with the buzz cut who manned the counter. Once he'd blended the colours, he slid the pot into a Valspar Paint machine and pressed a button. The mixer juddered so hard that the counter shook. Melissa heard guffawing and turned to see a plump woman in a tie-dye top and blue jeans, sporting an astonishing number of bangles on one wrist and rings on every finger.

'I love this bit!' Letitia cried. 'Gotta get me one of these for home, wink wink.' She nudged Melissa so roughly that she almost fell over.

The more the machine juddered, the more Letitia laughed, setting off the lad behind the desk, who also began to laugh. Suddenly Melissa was at it too, HA HA HA HA HA, she couldn't help herself. HA HA HA HA HA HA. She laughed her guts out, folded over, holding onto the counter. HA HA HA HA HA. It felt like an exorcism. All the months of stress over work, the arguments with Matty about the kids and who wasn't pulling their weight with the cleaning and shopping and childcare. It all came roaring out of her.

'You alright?' said Letitia.

'Christ no,' said Melissa.

'Come here often?'

It was what a bloke might have asked Melissa at a pub, back when she could freely go to that kind of place. It sounded so funny here with the sawdust smell and pot-bellied men bumbling around with trollies full of U-bends, brushes and beading.

'I come here as little as possible,' said Melissa. 'And you?'

'Can't keep me away. I've got a thing about paint machines.'

They talked for a while about the weather and how the

disruptive roadworks in town were taking far too long to complete. Neither of them cared about the roadworks, nor the weather. But it distracted them from the raucous drum'n'bass of the paint mixer. And ten minutes later, when they bumped into each other again at the checkout, they laughed once more, this time for no obvious reason at all.

As Melissa returned to her car, Letitia followed, both of them swinging their tins of paint by their sides, chatting breezily. It turned out they were parked near each other. Letitia said that her van was on the other side of the dented shipping container which had been dumped on the perimeter. Melissa laughed at the idea of her driving a white van, like some kind of cat-calling builder.

'Don't be so prejudiced!' cackled Letitia. 'I'm doing good work busting clichés here. Not like you with your people carrier. Just how many people do you *have*, girl?'

'I'll happily swap. Then you can go home and feed my kids tonight!'

Their banter felt so comfortable, Melissa didn't want it to stop. She was overcome by a compulsion to ask Letitia inside the car to chat for a while. Anything to delay the drive home. She hadn't talked in confidence to another soul outside of her family for so long it felt thrilling to sit with a stranger, especially this one. Letitia had an infectious warmth and piercing eyes – stark black rings around green irises that seemed to whirl as she smiled. Those eyes remained fixed on Melissa, with barely a blink, which was disconcerting at first but soon became comforting, as if they were somehow pulling her closer. Melissa was unable to resist. As she started to speak, feelings tumbled out which she had never consciously formulated into words. She told Letitia that she was sick of the life in which she'd ended up, surrounded by flatpack furniture, pasta machines and Nigella Lawson cookbooks, enslaved by sulky children and ignored by a husband whose only remaining passions were football and Rachel Riley from *Countdown*.

It hadn't always been like this. Before she met Matty she'd enjoyed a misspent youth of mascara, speed and ear-bleedingly loud rock music. Now she had found herself parked somewhere she had never meant to stop. Marriage and two kids had scrubbed out any expectation that anything genuinely new could happen. Nothing of significance, anyway. Nothing that would redefine her. It was as if time had stalled and the future had vanished. Every day was another circling of the same airspace.

Letitia listened eagerly. She nodded at the right times and made the right noises – like 'ummm' and 'ahhh,' and 'oh yes' – consuming Melissa's troubles like a fine wine. At the end of the confession she said, 'This can happen in life. But we all have the power to change.'

She told Melissa about how she used to be a junior building surveyor but tired of valuing properties she could not afford herself. When the pandemic struck, she was furloughed. With extra time on her hands, she started decorating the house she shared and discovered a real knack for it. After restrictions eased, she would do up her friends' and neighbours' homes at the weekends for cash. Soon she was getting enough work through word-of-mouth to cover her rent. That was when she abandoned her career.

'None of it seemed important anymore, what with the world going to hell. People dying. Racists on the streets. Bigots in my office. Fuck that. I'd rather fix things up.

Hammers and nails, glues and paints. In all the madness, they're things I can control. I use them to make something beautiful. For me, each day is a fresh canvas.'

'I'm so envious. Do you know that before I came into the store today, I parked up and sat for a while? Just because I was out of the house. Just because I could. How sad is that?'

'Oh, I saw you,' said Letitia. 'As I came out of the van this morning, I saw you well enough. I see lots of you out here, sitting alone.'

'Is that why you talked to me – back at the paint counter? You felt sorry for me?'

'Nah, course not. I like to listen, that's all. It feeds my soul.' Her eyes narrowed. 'You know what I mean?'

Letitia wanted a cigarette, so they stood on the verge behind the SUV, like girls on a school trip. Melissa cadged the occasional puff, enjoying the headrush. Must have been fifteen years since she last smoked a fag. The feel of a cigarette on her lips, it was like hurtling through a time portal. She had a sudden craving for a can of lager. That metallic tinge you only get from drinking a tinny outdoors. The taste of youth.

'I miss this,' she told Letitia. 'Not the nicotine. Just the not-giving-a-shit.'

Ever since she settled down to marriage, career and kids, Melissa ditched the drugs, pubs and gigging and tried to do the right thing. Being a good team leader at work, even when most days she didn't care because she knew, deep down, that the company didn't care about her. Chatting with mums at the school gates, pretending to enjoy their gossip. Making costumes for World Book Day, even though she could barely sew on a button. Hosting dinner parties, replete with scallop entrées and chocolate fondants, at which she never allowed herself to tell the wicked jokes that popped into her brain or dared challenge the anodyne generalisations of the braying men who dominated conversations. She kept her unruly edges hidden, so that she could be the kind of person everyone got on with. Yet she doubted anybody really knew anything about her beyond the generic working mum schtick she'd been so desperate to uphold.

During the coronavirus pandemic, few bothered to get in touch, or invite her to their Zoom chats. After the restrictions began to lift, what little social life she had was nothing more than a series of 'likes' and comments on other people's Facebook posts. She told Letitia that she doubted anyone outside her family would bother much if she vanished suddenly. They'd make some consoling noises to Matty, but it wouldn't make much difference to them. It wouldn't leave a hole.

'You are not a hole, girl,' said Letitia. 'You're a whole girl, do you get me?'

Melissa laughed. 'Thanks.'

'I'm serious. I'm getting something from you, and it isn't nothing.'

Afterwards, Melissa and Letitia both agreed that it had been good to talk. To get things off their chests. That they should meet the next weekend and do it again. Same time, same spot. Letitia would need to return to B&Q for more supplies, while Melissa could make up any old excuse, as Matty wouldn't listen anyway. They said goodbye and Letitia sashayed between rows of cars that glistered like disco balls in the sunshine.

It only occurred to Melissa later that evening, staring at the bedroom ceiling while Matty snored, that she had gone in a completely different direction to where she said that her van was parked.

> • <

The following Saturday morning, Melissa made her excuses and left Matty with the kids in front of Netflix while she drove out of town, bristling with an excitement she couldn't place. As she entered the B&Q car park she thrilled at how the centrifugal force from the curve of the access road tightened the seat belt against her chest. She enjoyed the way the speed bumps rattled her buttocks as she made her way alongside a grey gabion wall, passing a parked Vauxhall Corsa with its door wide open. A man in tracksuit bottoms sat with his legs outside the car, head hung down. He glanced up and momentarily caught her eye with a desperate look as she continued around the corner to the space she had occupied the week before, near the dented shipping container.

After all that anticipation, the wait was interminable. Melissa switched on the radio to pass some time. A news reporter talked about the latest moor fires. People were fleeing towns and villages in the Peak District. They said it was the worst year for it yet, right across the northern hemisphere. California. Siberia. Greenland. All that permafrost melting and those long summer droughts. Global warming had gone past the tipping point, the reporter said. Melissa kept hearing this over and over, that the catastrophe was already under way. But at B&Q, everything looked the same as it always had. It was the end of the world and she was totally bored.

The next news item was about eight deaths during riots at the migrant detention camps in Kent. Three of them children. With a sigh, she switched the radio off. There was too much bad news these days. It had become unbearable to listen to current affairs shows the way she used to. But whatever passed for popular music on the radio wasn't for her either. So she sat in silence with her phone, grimacing at her friends' Facebook updates, hoping to find one from someone leading a duller existence than her own. Rachel Hagerty, recently remarried, was off to Borneo and looking really fucking happy about it, obviously. Melissa's cousin had just got an Open University degree in Forensic Psychology. There was a photo of Alan and Fee Granger doing star jumps at the top of Ben Nevis. A colleague from her company had announced that she was leaving to focus on her inexplicably successful Etsy business, selling earrings made from bottle tops. Worst of all, Julie Thompson had posted a picture of a sunrise with the words: 'Start by doing what's necessary; then do what's possible; and suddenly you are doing the impossible.'

Melissa craved a post where someone admitted that they'd made a bad choice. That they'd wasted their time. Fallen off the rails. Like when the little-miss-perfect head girl from her schooldays admitted that she was battling alcoholism. Or when that QAnon prick Alan Smedley posted an incoherent rant about how a paedophile network at the bank had stolen money from his account. These posts made her feel better about herself. It was awful, she knew it. Like she was a pitiless Facebook predator, hunting her newsfeed for weaklings to feast upon.

A sudden commotion disturbed her. A few feet away, a couple of crows fighting over some discarded fries were interrupted by a gaunt, bald man in a dirty anorak who looked a bit like Nosferatu. As the birds flapped away, he stopped to observe Melissa for a few moments, rocking slightly from side to side, chewing his lip. He stepped forward as if to approach, then changed his mind and sidled behind the shipping container.

Bloody weirdo.

She hit the internal door lock, glancing around her for the nearest security camera. Mind, even if there was a camera, who would be watching? Who would put a stop to anything terrible happening? She'd read all kinds of stories about people in superstore car parks getting stabbed or robbed. Cameras never seemed to make a difference. She doubted they were ever actually recording.

Melissa was grateful when Letitia emerged from between a Nisan Micra and a Ford Mondeo. She leapt down from the SUV, beaming and waving. Almost as soon as they'd hugged and said 'hi', Melissa felt the overwhelming urge to release all that pressure which had built up inside of her. She told Letitia about how glad she was to find someone she could talk to, truthfully, about how she really felt. And what she felt was tired. Tired of Matty. Tired of being a parent. Tired of customer service management. It had only been meant to give her some income after university while she sought a career in publishing. But by the time she realised that seven years had passed, Matty was on the scene and they were buying a house, so it seemed foolish to switch career and jeopardise their mortgage. Now she was forty-one, running her team online because the office had closed during the pandemic, never to reopen. Endless days of working at home. Endless evenings watching television with Matty while Axel sulked upstairs and her eleven-year-old daughter Macy stared at her phone like a zombie.

Was this how modern life was supposed to be? Or had she done something wrong? It felt like they were in prison, awaiting some heinous sentence for a crime they did not know they had committed.

Melissa became shamefully aware that she was the only one talking, but Letitia was an eager listener. She gripped her arm tightly, as if to take her pulse, the numerous rings on her fingers digging into her flesh, throat pulsing with tiny swallowing motions, murmuring with enraptured empathy.

When it was over, Letitia breathed deeply. But instead of responding with words of wisdom, she pulled out a cigarette and lit it. The ensuing silence wasn't exactly awkward. Just strange. Melissa had thrown Letitia a ball, expecting her to play the game, but Letitia had simply pocketed it. She seemed distracted. Her nose twitched and she sniffed the air, as if she had caught a scent. She tossed the cigarette butt into the woodchip mulch and grabbed Melissa's shoulder.

'That's it, girl.' she said, without her usual smile, those green eyes drilling into her. 'Until we meet again.'

Melissa desperately wanted to say something to make her stay, but she felt glued shut. Fixed to the spot, she watched in dismay as Letitia ambled towards the pine trees without looking back. Once she was out of sight, Melissa slumped against the car, feeling drained. Light-headed. A little bit sick.

There was a rustling behind her. A rat scurried towards one of the Rent-a-Kill traps poking from beneath the fronds of the box hedge. It stopped near the entrance hole, as if to consider its options.

'Don't,' said Melissa. 'Just don't.'

> • <

After the kids were in bed, Melissa stood at the back door while Matty watched *Match of the Day*, looking out over their Astroturf lawn, smoking a sneaky cigarette. She thought about her last trip to the car park. Letitia's farewell was so abrupt. 'Until next time,' she had said. Did that imply they'd meet again at the same place, next Saturday? Or was that just a big brush-off?

She wished she had asked for an email address or phone number. She scoured Facebook looking for Letitias but none of the profiles matched. She googled 'Letitia decorator', but nothing.

That night, Matty asked her for sex, something they hadn't done in a long time. For the first few minutes, all she could think about was Letitia. Her kindly face, listening to her moans and groans, nodding fervently, tell me more, Melissa, tell me more about your problems. Give it to me. Give me the hard stuff. Then it wasn't Letitia at all, but the B&Q store looming over her with its massive orange face and its dirty edges, those pine trees thrusting upwards, the Valspar paint mixing machine hammering away and the sound of someone singing 'You can do it when you B&Q it'.

She begged Matty to stop. No more. No more.

But it wasn't over. Later, she had a dream that she went to B&Q with Macy but once they were inside it looked more like a supermarket, not a DIY store. When they opened one of the upright freezers, there was a creepy man inside with dark holes instead of eyes, who handed them a box of fish fingers. Macy screamed but Melissa turned to her daughter and told her that it was okay. He lived there because he had nowhere else to go.

The next morning, she was still thinking about B&Q. Days turned into nights, into days, into nights, and the yearning to go there and talk to Letitia did not go away. And when Saturday came round again, she returned to the same spot, where Letitia's cigarette butts, stained with her lippy, lay on chippings that bore the faint imprint of their feet from the last encounter. She reversed into the slot and waited, scrolling through Instagram, occasionally looking out the window, hoping to see her. It was a long shot, but not an impossible one.

After a while, a Vauxhall Astra reversed into a space about four empty bays away. The sole occupant was a man around her age, wearing a beanie hat. Once parked, he didn't get out of his vehicle or switch off the engine. For over half an hour he sat there. It was disconcerting. She just wanted him to do something. Eat a sandwich. Make a phone call. Anything. His presence was unbearable. *Go away, you sad little man,* she thought, *be gone with you.* It was usually alright, being parked out on the edge with her thoughts, but not when guys like him made it feel tawdry and desperate.

Melissa was about to give up and leave when she saw Letitia, cutting between two vans, carrying a new pot of paint. But she didn't approach Melissa's car. She didn't seem to see her at all. Instead, she walked towards the man in the stupid hat. Melissa slid down into her seat as far as she could, watching Letitia approach his passenger door. His window rolled open and she bent down so all Melissa could see was her buttocks waving from side to side. They talked for a while like that, but she couldn't hear what they were saying.

From this angle, Letitia looked disconcertingly like a sex worker propositioning a John, but she was not like that. It couldn't be that. But then, what was it? Did they know each other? Had he been waiting for her all this time? Was this a rendezvous?

Eventually, the man got out of the Astra and stood in front of Letitia. He was wearing ironed jeans and a denim shirt that was far too big. It was as if a wizard had shrunk him inside his clothes. Double denim. Never a good look. But on him it was a catastrophe. It looked like he had been crying but he was smiling now that Letitia was here. Well, she couldn't blame him for that.

The pair talked some more. This time Melissa could make out fragments. 'Ex-wife… depressed… we used to come here… bad memories… socket button screws… bedsit… wish they would come and visit… Bosch combi drill… discount sale.'

Letitia nodded as he spoke, just like she did when Melissa poured out her heart to her. She clutched the man's wrist in the same way with that same backward tilt of her head. Then she said something to him. It must have been significant because the man's Adam's apple bobbed up and down as he tried to swallow back his emotions. *What a baby.* It was hard to imagine Letitia falling for this nonsense. But at the end of this excruciating exchange, Melissa was mortified to see them walk together through the car park in the direction of the store. The man paused once to activate the remote-control lock of his Astra, and then they were gone.

The air inside the SUV was stifling. Melissa jabbed at the button for the electric window. It opened with a buzz that sickened her. All this pointless convenience. All this hopeless luxury. All this wasted energy.

Enough.

She abandoned her car and began to walk away from it. She couldn't face driving home. Not right now. She needed air. A brisk circuit of the retail park would let her gather her thoughts and calm the fuck down a bit. Perhaps on the way she might bump into Letitia. She could pretend that she was heading into the store to buy more paint and that their encounter was a happy accident. *Oh hello*, they'd say to each other in unison, *do you come here often?* Or something like that. And then they'd laugh at their little in-joke. HA HA HA HA HA HA HA. Letitia with her big laugh. Melissa slapping her own thighs, doubled over. Like the day they met. And after they recovered, Letitia would calmly explain what she was doing with that ridiculous man in their sacred spot on the edge of the car park and everything would be okay.

The clouds sat heavy and low. An occasional drop of rain bloodied the dry tarmac as she traversed the cracked lines of parking bays, tracking the box hedge as far as it would go. She passed a woman in an expensive Mercedes, slowly applying red lipstick while a mournful love ballad blared from the stereo; a Volvo with tinted windows, its solitary occupant a shadow within; a Ford Fiesta, parked at an angle, the driver with his forehead on the steering wheel, face obscured. She tarried a few moments, observing him closely, concerned that he was dead, until he reached out his left arm, clenched his fist, and began to strike the dashboard repeatedly.

Okay then.

Eventually she reached a thick mass of cotoneaster, bursting with berries. There was a crude break where people had repeatedly forced their way through, the trail littered with disintegrated McDonald's packaging. Probably those late-night car cruisers who left figure-of-eight marks on the tarmac, stomping to their makeshift racetrack with drinks and burgers.

Melissa felt compelled to step into the gap. As she did so, a whiff of cotoneaster flashed her back to a moment in time. She and her mates at the Tesco near their school, sneaking into the maze of hedgerows with a spliff during a lunch break. She remembered bursting into hysterics at the sight of discarded underpants covered in shit, and how they found women's stilettoes in a little clearing – 'right scary' they said, puffing on the joint, coming up with elaborate theories about the murderer who left them there. Funny, she hadn't thought about that incident in decades. She'd pushed it to the back of her mind as a childish misdemeanour, best forgotten. But now it felt like the happiest time ever.

At the other side of the hedge, a grassy slope led to a lower car park for the other major stores in the retail park: M&S, Currys and Halfords, as well as a Costa Coffee and a McDonald's Drive Thru, its golden arches glowing like a neon church.

This car park was smarter. Cleaner white lines, less litter and fewer people lingering. Red walkways for pedestrians were lined with shrubs in giant pots and ornate cast-iron litter bins. There was a smell of hot dogs. In contrast to the drab corrugated grey and orange of B&Q, the modern glass-and-steel edifice of Marks and Spencer reflected a shimmering vision of the car park back onto itself. It was like staring into a parallel dimension. She strained to catch herself in the reflection but she was too far away to register in the seething mass of metal machines; nothing more than a footnote in the story of cars.

As she made her way along the pavement, a besuited man gave Melissa a suspicious stare. When she looked down, her jeans were dirty. There were a couple of tiny leaves in the creases at the knee. He must have thought she was one of those saddos lurking at the edges of car parks. How embarrassing.

Melissa hurried on until she came to a little wooden bridge, surprising amidst all the concrete and tarmac. She stopped in the middle and leaned against the barrier. A few metres beneath was a narrow gully filled with shingle and lined with blocks of old, worn stone. In the lower car park, it was only a shallow trough running between the trolley bays, but once it passed under the bridge it became a deep gorge that cut through the elevated B&Q car park. Steep banks on either side were littered with dead needles from the pine trees she'd observed from her parked car these past few Saturdays.

How curious. It looked like a dried-up stream, or perhaps a trackway from a time before the retail park existed. It was remarkable that despite all her visits over the years, she had never noticed it. Then again, why would she?

There was a slope leading to the track at the side of the bridge with a muddy trail gouged into it. Perhaps formed by the same nocturnal denizens of the car park who created the gap in the cotoneaster. Melissa was tempted to follow it. She could walk up the path and see what was at the end. Maybe an interesting historical feature. Sure, it was a little foolhardy. A lone woman in a concealed alley beneath B&Q. But it was unlikely that anybody uncouth would be there in the daylight. Besides, she enjoyed the shiver of trepidation. It took her back to those Tesco truancy days. That time when life was still wide open and even smoking a poorly rolled joint in a stinking hedgerow could be an adventure. If this was teenage life, with all its restrictions, she marvelled at what thrills adult life had to offer. In the forbidden edges of the local car park, she had once dared to dream.

Nervously, Melissa entered the gorge, feet crunching on stones. She noticed that there were circular iron hatches along the sides of the channel. They looked old. Victorian perhaps. The light was already gloomy because of the amassing black clouds and the canopy of bushy pines above her, but there was a thickening of the darkness as the vale narrowed. She stopped and checked for an escape route. It would be easy to scramble up the bank in a few seconds, she figured. While she couldn't see it, the car park was still there. She could hear a man barking at his kids. An engine turning. A baby crying. These sounds drifted into the gully and settled like mist. Offered her some comfort. This was silly, a woman of her age, doing dares with herself for the hell of it, but she continued onwards, wondering how the path could feel so much longer to walk than it appeared from the outside.

Soon there was another noise. But this time it was from up ahead, around a slight bend. A voice. Quiet and whiny, almost mewing, but certainly human. Melissa slowed to a more cautious pace, readying herself to make a dash for it. A few steps more, and she could see that the route terminated in a circular area, walled with mossy stone. Yellow water seeped from the cracks and dripped a glutinous beat on the concrete floor. In the centre was a bench and a bin for cigarette ash.

There were three people there. One of them was the creepy bald man in the anorak who she had spotted earlier by the shipping container. One of them she couldn't see properly, because he was lain on his back.

The other was Letitia.

She and the bald anorak man were on their knees, on opposite sides of the prostrate figure, bowed as if in prayer, faces close to his chest. For a moment, it seemed like they might be giving him CPR. Or that they were already weeping over his demise.

With rising panic, Melissa ran forwards. 'Letitia! Is he okay? What happened?'

Letitia stood up quickly, pivoting to face her – startled – like a kid caught smoking. Melissa could now see that the man on the ground was wearing double denim and a beanie hat. It was the sad little guy from the Astra. His eyes were closed but he murmured a feverish, whimpering babble.

'They don't respect me... they don't... I never see them anymore... it's not fair... all the lies... I never... all lies... they don't come to see me... I'm building them a bunk bed...' He started to choke up. A horrible strangling noise like a distressed cat. The bald anorak man grinned, nodding his head up and down to the rhythmic undulations of the sound.

'Is he alright, Letitia?'

'My, my, aren't you the curious one?' said Letitia, frowning. 'I have to say, I didn't expect to see you here. You must be in far worse shape than I thought, girl.'

'I wasn't... looking... for – I was – I was just having a wander. But really, is he alright?'

'Does he look alright?'

'No.'

'That's your answer, then.'

Letitia sounded odd. Rather cold. A bit aggressive. Then again, what did Melisa really know about her? Aside from that opening gambit at the paint counter and her inspiring story about ditching her career, she had not revealed much more than was necessary to start a conversation. She had made a simple cut in the flesh and then waited for Melissa to bleed out. It was always Melissa talking while Letitia listened. She was a good listener. Always listening.

'Shall I call an ambulance?' Melissa reached for her phone.

'No, he's not that kind of ill,' said Letitia. 'Nothing a hospital's gonna fix, anyway. Tell you what, sit down here with me. Let's talk about it.'

'I don't think...'

'Come.' Letitia gripped her wrist and drew her to the bench as if she was a naughty child. It didn't feel right to complain about her life, what with the distressed man lying there on the ground like that, and that weirdo in the anorak hunched over him, doing nothing to help. But one look into Letitia's eyes and Melissa numbly acquiesced, feeling faint suddenly. She noticed that there were a lot of sealed tins of paint and orange B&Q bags around the bench, like discarded props.

'I missed you at the car park earlier,' said Melissa woozily. 'I thought – I hoped – we were meeting again, but then... you were with him...'

The double-denim man was muttering something about divorce settlements while the anorak man uttered little grunts and sighs of appreciation. Neither of them seemed to notice Melissa's presence at all.

'...I didn't know if you saw me or if you wanted to see me,' said Melissa. 'But then I came to look for you. Sorry. God. I don't mean to sound weird. It's not like that. You know.

Not weird. I'm not weird. It's just...' Her words began to slur. She felt a heaviness in her bones. Prickling skin and shivers. Like she was coming down with the flu. 'It was just that I needed to talk. I really needed to talk... to you.... to anyone really... anyone... I hate it at home... I hate me... and I don't know why but I...'

'Yeah, it's okay, tell me all about it,' said Letitia, cradling Melissa's scalp gently, easing her back onto the bench. 'You must be very tired.'

'I am, I am.'

'So tired.'

'Yes...'

'You say what you need to say, Melissa. Don't hold back.' Letitia leaned over her, lips parting to bare brilliant white teeth. 'Let it all out.'

> • <

It was dusk when Melissa clambered up the bank of the gorge and stood for a while by one of the pines, looking over the fence into the car park where a fine rain sparkled in the glare of the floodlights and oily puddles welled in the tarmac. Her head was thick. Mouth dry. She had no idea how long she had been down there or what had happened to her. Her left hand felt unusual. It took her a few moments to realise that her wedding ring was gone. Oh well. It didn't matter. She would find another ring. There were always more rings. More fingers. More hands. More people. So many people coming from miles around to congregate in this car park. They wanted to buy home improvement goods but what they really needed was a banishing ritual to

Gareth E. Rees

release them from their burden, like those liberated young car cruisers who scorched black rings into the tarmac at night to keep their demons at bay.

She could see them now, the weary remnants of B&Q's congregation, leaving the infernal church. A woman in a hijab pushed a pallet trolley towards a Perspex bay, while her husband loaded their purchases into the boot. A man in overalls approached his white van. A young couple ducked into a smart car, headlamps flashing as their vehicle swung out from its space.

These people were too strong and healthy for her, But at the furthest edge of the car park were those who sat alone in motionless silence, staring out the window or gazing at their smartphones, scrolling through social media feeds in an interminable hunt for consolation, desperate for help which they never believed would come, and so – unable to think of an alternative – remained in limbo. Even in the dimness of the evening, she could tell which cars they were because a greenish aura emanated from them. Domes of loneliness shimmering on the perimeter. A scent, too, like rotten meat, carried on the breeze to her lair in the trees. It made her hungry, but not in a way she recognised. A heart hunger. A hole in the chest that must be filled.

Eventually, it became too hard to resist. Melissa clambered over the fence and made her way to the perimeter, where a Skoda was parked, throbbing with phosphorescent light. Inside was the silhouette of an elderly man. Melissa was fully aware that she looked a bit of a state. Pine needles and cotoneaster leaves were stuck to her clothes. Hair damp from the mizzle. But she knew that the old man would wind down his window when she knocked upon it three times.

He would find it surprising when she said, 'I'm sorry for bothering you, but are you okay?' A little odd, perhaps. Yet at the same time, he would feel relief that somebody had asked him and an overwhelming desire to reply.

He would speak. She would listen. And when heavier raindrops began to drum on his roof, he would invite her inside the car to talk some more.

THE FORLORN HOPE

VERITY HOLLOWAY

Vultures wheeled above the walled city of Perdu, their shrieks carried off by another surge of harried bells. In the fossilised desert below, an army tended to its rations and other essential business.

'On this day, the 12th of June 1813, I, Captain Matilda Cross, being sound in mind, make these directions to be carried out in the event of my death. I make this final Will in the presence of two witnesses, Sergeant Garrick and Private Welby of the 45th Infantry. In this, my thirty-sixth year—'

At the camp's heart, the girls were boiling beef and singing.

Billywitch, Billywitch,
Fly away home,
Your house is on fire,
Your children will burn.

'—and so many miles from my place of birth, I trust unto my executors – is that what you call them, kid? – to carry out my wishes to the letter.'

Welby was a nice little thing, if a touch bovine. A failed scholar, she had a fair hand and didn't pull any faces. Garrick, as expected, had done nothing but gripe since Cross had called her to the tent.

'Ma'am—'

Captain Cross scraped back her hair and treated the Irishwoman to one of her stares. 'To my sergeant, Rose Garrick, I leave my rifle, on account of it being better than hers at almost everything, chiefly hitting Frenchies. My boots... I don't know. Whoever they fit. My sword I leave to Lady Amelia Fitzmichael of Whitewater House, Surrey, in gratitude for her teaching me letters back in ninety-five. She always did like a trophy above the fireplace.'

Garrick made the throaty sound that usually meant the latrines were ripe in the midday sun. To her, Lady Fitzmichael was *That Woman*. But the sergeant had at least made tea. She was as good at brewing tea as she was at killing, which was slapdash but fast, and precisely when Cross needed it. 'Beg pardon, Ma'am,' she said, passing Cross a tin mug. 'But I expect the good lady will prefer you alive.'

'The good lady has forty acres and a strapping husband worth five hundred a year. She can't have everything she wants.'

> • <

My own dear Mathilde,

What is this I hear of you burning my letters? Have you forgotten my million eyes? Or is this silence your crude method of wounding me? Alley cat. Only ever come running when I turn my back...

〉•〈

''S just as I see it, Ma'am.' The sergeant slapped a mosquito on her swarthy forearm.

A fresh clamour of bells rang out over Perdu. Welby jolted, sending a fine spray of ink across the document. That morning, artillery had made a mountain of the city wall. They were all still chewing on the dust. With a telescope, Cross saw the mess the Billywitches had made of the golden city since they took it in the spring. Like the vermin they resembled, the creatures left nothing unspoiled. Bright pennants hung in ribbons. Temple domes reduced to eggshells. Of the citizens she saw no sign, but she knew the 'Witches were in there, the way she knew a scorpion was in her boot without needing to tip it up first. Every city, it was always the same. How they got in, no one was sure. Pagan excess, the army chaplains said; tainted meat, said the surgeons. A half-dead priest they found in Shallamar said there had always been such things, things of carapace and claw, things that chase, but he was mad with fever and would have said anything for a drop of water.

When Cross used the handful of local words she knew to question the nomad shepherd boys, they clicked their tongues and rode away. Welby was the linguist, but when Cross sent her out to speak to them, she came back pink with embarrassment and apologies.

'Come on, then,' Cross demanded. 'What did the little buggers say?'

Only that they were wary of the woman with the yellow hair and the black look.

〉•〈

My own dear Mathilde,

Silence still? Sleepless, I unlocked the chest in the attic and spent the night barefoot among your dazzling old letters.

Despite this and all the rest, I still show my face at church on Sundays. Picture me beneath my widest bonnet with the veil of lace – what did you used to call it? My mosquito helmet. I sit there in the family pew and listen to the neighbours trotting out the usual topics. Births, marriages, and you, my dear. Everyone reads of your daring deeds. Mister Dalrymple boasts it was he who first gave you the notion of taking the king's shilling. Wasn't he the one you oh-so-carelessly pricked with a toasting fork when he made that snide remark about dirty petticoats? He says he saw potential in you, the way one sees it in a man. I think about that fork daily.

Missus Dixon is just as bad. She and her hideous coterie all claim they remember you here, that they shared some special little interaction with you when you were nothing but my maid, though we both know that's a lie and a poor one at that. The motherless waif, Matilda Cross. That particular untruth was your own, was it not?

I miss your barefaced lies, Mathilde. I miss your promises, sweet as your threats. You will come home to me this instant. You will.

> • <

The volunteers of the Forlorn Hope would go up at daybreak. The first over the rubble. The first to see the whites, the yellows, the reds of their eyes. Captain Cross's name was dry on the roster before anyone else had the chance to sign.

'The girls are welcome to raise a glass in my name if they see fit,' she said. 'Sergeant Garrick can have any last pennies to my name, what good they'll do her. As for my body...'

'Ma'am?' Welby looked up from the page. Brown eyes, unplucked brows. She was a decent soldier, but looking at Welby, Cross found her brain crowded with cannonballs and agues and festering wounds, and she resented the private for flaunting her fragility, for passing on that burden.

'My body is not to be repatriated.'

Garrick flashed her teeth. 'What about Sophia?'

'She took a vow of poverty. She has no need of any baubles from me.'

'She'll want to bury her mother, Ma'am.'

The bells rang out. Rose Garrick's broad handsome face was the same grim mask Cross first laid eyes on in the column that scorching summer in Spain, when the enemy was merely Napoleon. Cross missed Boney. That was soldiering, not this grinding routine of ruins and rumours. When the word came down from Horse Guards that the Billywitches were Boney's secret weapon, Cross slung her sword over her shoulder and strolled down the line. Any day now, she promised the girls, they would capture one of the bastards, cut it open and make sense of it, just like any other bit of kit. When it became apparent Boney was fighting the 'Witches too, Cross found she had no words of reassurance.

It was around then that the letters started again.

That flawless arcane script, waiting for her on the camp bed. At once she was undone, staring down at the brown ink Amelia favoured, bloody and costly, like all her favourite things. Cross had taken those memories and killed them, or so she believed; but now they were crowding the tent with her, threatening to whip away the canvas and expose her to the whole battalion.

Sophia's name brought that unsteady feeling back. She recalled her grown daughter in the rough-spun habit of a nun, that dust cloud of hair, so like her own, pinned and covered until she could be anyone's daughter, or no one's. The only thing that linked them that final day as the elders sang in the bell tower was a shared love of uniform. '*When your grandmother was young...*' she almost said. But an officer never lowered her guard, especially not an officer baptised in the oily effluvia of the Birmingham Inkleys.

And what would speaking accomplish? *When your grandmother was young*, she fastened my dress to hers with a length of twine. She told me the neighbours pressed their faces to the mouseholes and took note of our comings and goings. That if she let me out of her sight for even a second, they would spring from their hiding places to snatch me away and she would die, die, die, Matilda, do you want that? They're ringing my death knell across the parish, listen...

Young Matilda cut that binding rope and fled before the worst of the poison could travel down it. And yet Captain Cross still felt the tug and chafe of it. Especially that day, when she left Sophia in the Sacred Heart where the water came clean from the mountains and the bells only marked the passing of hours.

> • <

My own dear Mathilde, alley cat, wretch...

There's no problem you cannot take a blade to, is there? Always something to prove. When I found you, you were everything they say about the tenements. The perfume of the slaughterhouse. I had to burn your clothes to kill the lice, and no matter how hard we scrubbed your filthy skin or how prettily I taught you to simper and bob in the presence of your betters, you were a corroded thing, eaten up with the need to bite and scratch and claw your way out of the Rag Castle streets, and when you saw you could not win this coward's battle, you turned tail and scurried off the way your kind are born to.

Damn you, Matilda. I've been sitting here debating whether or not to destroy this page, and now my coffee is cold. You always did delight in wasting my time.

There's a splinter in me. Always has been. Perhaps that mutual savagery is what drew us to one another. You read my letters and curse me for my cruelty and my pride? Of course you do. Each note I send to you, I send loathing myself. Do you ever recollect those long evenings together, with J at his club and the house empty? The two of us, free! To talk and to dream. With my money and your bravery, we had the means for every adventure under the sun. How privileged we were, in our secretive way. And now you are so far away, and I am split in two.

I won't let you make a fool of me, speaking to thin air like this. Be a good girl and write. I have something for you.

> • <

Garrick grimaced at the gritty film on her tea. 'It's a damn fool thing you're doing, Ma'am, and I don't mind you knowing it.'

'I've been promised certain death in a hundred places. But *this*. This is certain promotion.'

'You're in one of your moods.'

Cross could feel Welby holding her breath. The little private spent the four months at sea hugging a bucket. Cross weathered the relentless swell and plunge with gritted teeth, fighting the urge to speculate how many of her girls could swim. She steered clear of the ship's doctor and his offer of soothing tinctures, preferring to spend her restless nights questioning the Indian Sepoys about their destination. But they knew as much as she did, missionaries' tales of beastly red fruits wet on the outside, spiked toads you could lick to lose a memory, shifting sands the colour of a week-old bruise. To her relief, all wonderfully true. This disconcerting island everyone despised was migraine bright, too addictively treacherous to allow space in the mind for anything or anyone else. Cross knew people like that. You could disappear inside them if you didn't keep reminding yourself of your own dwindling solidity like some fanatical faith.

Four months of salt water between her and Birmingham. A year in the desert.

Everyone else spent their last days of home leave full of gin, scrawling their names and kill tallies on the inn walls, but not Captain Cross. She boarded the dawn coach to the Inkleys with a knife in her boot and her money sewn into the lining of her greatcoat.

'They pulled the tenements down, Miss,' the barmaid said, sopping up spilled ale with a rag as grey as the hollows under her eyes. 'A good ten years past. Well overdue, if you ask me. Forgive me, but I don't remember any Harriet, Miss. We see a lot of people come and go.'

But Cross wasn't thinking about that now.

'Welby, cover your ears,' Garrick said.

THE FORLORN HOPE

She blinked owlishly. 'Sergeant?'

'Think loud thoughts, you silly chit. Matilda, remember Dundril. You were doing well there. Sleeping. Eating. This shithole was known for its doctors. I got talking to the nomads—'

'Quacks and mountebanks, is it?" Cross snapped. "Some piss prophet who'll stick a leech on my arm and tell me all I need's a good man?'

A plume of smoke feathered out above the *battlements*. A bad colour, to Cross's eye. And those unceasing bastard bells. Welby – with her inky hands over her ears, why had Garrick made her do that? – was staring out at the ruined defences as if the Billywitches might come pouring down in an avalanche while they slept. It knocked the wind out of you, the first time. Private Welby hadn't had many first times.

Cross felt Garrick watching her. She was always watching her, it was her job, and Cross had come to rely on those following eyes, hard mirrors in which to gauge her decisions. But now there was something unfamiliar there, and it was making Cross's sword hand itch.

'I hate to ask, Ma'am,' said Garrick. 'And you can tell me to button my lip. But what has that woman—'

'Nothing.'

> • <

My own dear Mathilde,

A drizzly afternoon here in Surrey. A day for shawls and novels, and, for the lucky ones, the company of a friend. When did you last see drizzle? I'd wager you miss it on some animal level, your dismal habitat. Has your skin bronzed in all this time away? I worried about that, you know, seeing you trussed up in that red tunic for the first time. Life is cheap but good skin is a luxury few can afford.

Since my last letter the fruits in the Whitewater gardens have ripened and fulfilled their destiny as jam. Fashions, too, are changing. Missus Dixon and her friends are cavorting around in gowns embellished with gold frogging and slippers of finest faux Billywitch leather, their mode of supporting our heroic soldiers overseas. I attach a sketch for your amusement.

Time is passing, dear Mathilde, and still you have not written to me. I could take this to mean you are dead. If that were so, I could wear darkest crepe and collect my tears in a bottle like all the other decorative widows. But my million eyes know better.

Do you ever look about you at your comrades and wonder who among them is doing my work, watching over you? It could be anyone. That hulking Irish woman, the one who hates me? That would be a comic turn. You trust her. Remember when you trusted me?

My million eyes watched you all those months ago when you took the dawn coach to Birmingham. You once told me no one ventured into the Inkleys from the outside. All too easy to slip inside and dissolve into the shadows. No, no one takes that coach alone, not unless they are looking for something. Fights and flesh, you always said.

What about family?

> • <

Cross saw the sting on Garrick's face. With care, she tried again. 'Rose, I've no special inclination to die tomorrow. But if it pleases you, find the 'Witch that kills me and take its head. Boil it up and send the skull to Sophia's convent. You can do all of that before you ever march me to any poxy physician. But I mean it – you do not put my bones in a box and send them back to England.'

Garrick chewed on nothing. 'So I'm up there picking through the rubble and see you lying there and I do what?'

'You keep going.'

Garrick tossed her tea away in disgust. It sank into the sand leaving hardly a trace. 'A fine sergeant I am.'

The tent was thick with baleful silence. The night was rolling in, bringing with it that uncanny rush of cold the women had come to crave, peeling off their woollen tunics to let their aching hides breathe. Still the vultures made their grim circuit over Perdu. Little Welby saw Cross neglecting her tea to watch them.

'They kill plague,' Welby said. 'The miasma will survive the death of the host and jump to the nearest warm body, but a vulture can put an end to it by eating the infected flesh. Like a living furnace.' The private spoke with a zest for information that made her easy to tease, but now no one was laughing she looked unsure. As she trailed off, she picked bashfully at her inky nails. 'It's… quite beautiful, really.'

Garrick met Cross's notorious stare with one of her own.

'Cowbag,' the sergeant muttered.

> • <

The things I do for you, my Mathilde. The places I go. The things I discover.

Dear old Harriet. She knits beautifully, you never told me. Despite her arthritis, she stitches away like a busy little squirrel, and when you compliment her handiwork she grunts churlishly. You really are terribly alike.

My dear, your mother will live out her days in perfect comfort. I found her – for you. You needn't know where or in what circumstances, for I know they will cause you pain. No chains for her, no public viewings. I bought her a private room at Rubery Hill. Good food, country air, the companionship of a sweet, strict nurse. As far as she knows, kind-hearted benefactresses keep old widows out of the madhouse all the time. What a nice world she inhabits, up there in her head.

It doesn't all have to be degradation, Mathilde.

You will come home when your posting is over, and I will take you to her. And then, when you have dispensed with this pig-headed obstinance of yours, you will allow my physicians to examine you for traces of Harriet's splinters. Yes. You will. Modern ideas. You will be well, and we will be happy. I would hate to disturb Sophia at her convent, but you will agree it is only right a member of the family is involved in Harriet's care. Sophia hasn't met her grandmother, has she? Would you like her to?

Picture a million eyes, Mathilde, every one of them brimming with love.

> • <

'For I know my Redeemer liveth, et cetera,' said Cross. 'It's done?'

Welby blew gently on the ink. 'All but the signatures, Ma'am.'

They both looked to Garrick. She took the opportunity to pack her pipe with tobacco, licking the crumbs from her fingers where they clung to the callouses ground deep by years on the road.

'She's poison is what she is, Ma'am.'

Captain Cross turned her face away to the walled city of Perdu, little more than a noisy inkblot against the darkening sky. Here night mugged you, it sneaked up behind on silent feet and clamped a hand over your mouth. The vultures took their leave with the daylight, though where they bedded down in this barren land, she couldn't guess.

OBLI⊙

RICHARD V. HIRST

Beyond the window, I can see three balloons hanging in the air over the graveyard. I am sitting up in bed, listening to the radio alarm, a news report in Italian, and watching them glint in the sun and sway in the light breeze. Behind me, coming from the room next door, I can hear music, very faint. Beneath the window across from me is another bed which is neatly made, evidently unslept in.

I get up and stand for a moment looking out of the window at the concrete graveyard. It is in fact a mausoleum, a grand building, domed and framed by palm trees, at the rear of which is what looks like an alien village. A network of squat crypts, the size of bungalows, gives way to long rows of headstones, crooked yet serried and all uniformly white, which taper into muddy and untidy undergrowth, with the graves beneath the window looking collapsed or shattered. Some even look plundered. Beyond the wall is another world: the small concrete yard of our apartment building, a few potted plants in each corner, a clothesline criss-crossing the patio, a cat sleeping in the sun.

The balloons are foil and shaped like animals: a parrot, a giraffe and an elephant. They are tethered somewhere in the graveyard, presumably to a child's grave, their impossibly long ribbons wound together causing them to pull at one another as they move.

I turn the radio off and the music becomes clearer: the lilt of a harmonium being played.

Koo.

I pull on my jeans and go through to the apartment's kitchen, and find her hunched over the Formica table, her right hand on the harmonium's keyboard, playing a series of notes, her left on the bellow, a wedge of concertinaed fabric which she pumps gently back and forth. I stop in the doorway for a moment, watching her as she presses on the same keys over and over, shifting between different rhythms and sequences, trying to locate the melody she's after. There's something familiar about the music – something of our childhood living room, perhaps an old TV theme tune or a song our mother used to hum. Or perhaps it's to do with a dream I was having in the night. Something about stampeding animals. There's no doubt that Koo has been up all night, riddling away at this melody.

'Sounds nice,' I say. Koo stops playing and turns to me, manages a smile.

'Oh, hey,' she says. 'Sounds okay, I suppose. You think it's okay that I used their coffee? I found some stuff in the freezer and made a pot.'

'I'm sure it's fine,' I say and move over to the countertop to pour myself a cup from the cafetiere. The place we're staying at is an AirBnB, someone's home when not being rented out to travellers like us. 'You tired?

'I'll be okay.'

'Well… okay. Just remember that we don't have to do anything today. We could just have a day off. Get some rest.'

'I'll be okay, don't worry.' She spoons the hair away from her face and takes a sip of her coffee.

I take a sip of mine and find it's cold. I open the microwave, put my mug inside, and press the buttons until it hums into life.

'You need to sleep at some point,' I tell her.

She shakes her head. 'Not today.'

I sigh. 'You know, we can just say no to journalists.'

'No, it's not interviews. We got an email from Patrick while you were asleep.'

'Oh…? Holy shit. Viner?'

Koo nods.

'Has he arranged a meeting with her?'

'No. Just sent through an address. But he says it's not far from here. We could walk over.'

'Okay, let's do that. I'll have a coffee and then get dressed. Do you want to go for a shower?'

'No, I'm okay.'

'Are you sure?' The microwave beeps. I take out my coffee and make my way back to the bedroom. 'It's been a few days.'

But she's tapping away at the harmonium, her stare fixed ahead of her.

> • <

Our love of Carrie Viner comes from a holiday Dad took us on when we were children, right after Mum died. We had a week filled with preparations for her funeral followed by an awkward, silent fortnight which the three of us filled by wandering the house, trying to speak with one another, trying to avoid one another and, very infrequently, crying. Then, late one night, Dad booked a flight which we took the next day. The silence accompanied us on the plane, Dad drinking and staring out of the window while Koo read her books and I read my comics. It was only in the hire car that a change felt possible. We listened to Dad's Carrie Viner tapes on the long drive, with him telling us all about her – both the facts, such as they are, of her life as an artist and the skill with which she composed her music, but also the importance of that music for him and Mum – until we arrived at Casadolore, a cottage in the middle of nowhere.

The atmosphere on the holiday wasn't too different from that which we'd hoped to leave behind at home. Each of us retreated into ourselves. Dad drank and cried quietly. Koo discovered music in the form of a piano in the house, poorly tuned but functioning. She would sit and play at it for long periods, picking out strange, cramped melodies from the keys, concentrating.

I climbed trees. Casadolore was surrounded by a large scrubby lawn, which would have been perfect for outdoor games, but of course we hadn't brought any. Beyond was a dense and seemingly endless wood through which I would wander. I never ventured too far as getting lost seemed a possibility, but I did grow adept at climbing, at times incredibly high. I would perch where the branches and leaves were at their densest, enjoying the breeze, the sounds of birds close to me, watching other animals – hedgehogs, foxes, large lolloping hares – move about on the forest floor unaware of my presence. I would also watch Casadolore and catch Koo wandering into the kitchen to get a drink before returning to the piano, Dad sat outside, staring blindly in my direction, or occasionally exerting himself by splitting the store of logs with a rusty axe.

Then, one day, I saw a girl. She was around my age, perhaps a little older. I caught sight of her wandering through the forest in my direction and then she stood at the edge of the wood, both hands to a tree's trunk while she peered at Casadolore. She stood there for a long time, then eventually she headed back the way she'd come, disappearing among the trees.

She returned the next day and, while I was sat high above her eating a packet of nuts, she once again spent a long time watching our cottage. I had had a bad night's sleep. Dad had spent much of the night sat downstairs, watching Italian television and weeping. As a result, I found was in an odd mood. After a while I began flicking nuts down at the girl. Most of them missed her, of course, but they did catch her attention as they pinged off the trees next to her and landed among the leaves on the ground. She looked around and then up at me.

'Hello,' I called down.

She went on staring.

'We're on holiday.' I nodded at the cottage. 'If you were wondering.'

Still she didn't reply.

'That's my sister in there, and my dad.'

She looked back at Casadolore, then back to me.

There was a long silence between us, then I said, 'Do you speak English?'

She tilted her head to one side, neither a nod nor a shake.

'My name is Fiona.'

'Maria,' she said.

〉•〈

The harmonium had cost a fortune. Koo had disappeared from our hotel room when we were in Zagreb a couple of weeks ago and returned with it a few hours later. We were in Croatia for one of the first dates on our European tour and we hadn't yet earned enough money to justify the purchase – I hadn't been at all sure at that point that we ever would – but it had been the first thing Koo seemed interested in for as long as I could remember, so when I heard the beep of her keycard and she slipped into the hotel room and settled the instrument onto the bed and began to play, I just told her I thought it was a beautiful object that made a beautiful sound, which is true.

Things have changed since then. While we've been touring, our album has been released – *Debris* – and the response so far has been positive enough for us to recoup the cost of the harmonium tenfold. In truth, I've been intimidated by the reviews. Five stars in *The Guardian*, a glowing review on *Pitchfork*, an essay-length piece of praise on *The Quietus*. Patrick, our manager, was delighted. I am delighted. But it all seems to have made Koo worse. At the start of the tour we'd begun with small yet respectable audiences, but the past few nights have been sold out. Patrick is now thinking of venue changes. When we play, I jump about the stage, thrashing my guitar from side to side. But the audiences are always focused on Koo as she stands, almost motionless at her keyboard, her expression unreadable, a lone foot tapping almost imperceptibly to the electronic beats. They must think this is all part of the performance.

Each evening since its arrival in Zagreb, Koo has played the harmonium. She comes offstage quickly and picks it up as soon as she's in the dressing room. She carries it with her wherever she goes, as though it's her handbag, her familiar. Whenever we return to our hotel room or the apartment where we're staying, she sits on her bed or in a chair in a corner and stays there until it's late, in the thrall of the instrument's drone – an endless C-note – over which she plays notes, these little tunes slipping in and out of discordance, her head nodding to the imaginary accompanying rhythm. This is the first night I've known her play the whole night through.

Maria would arrive every day at the same time. I would wait for her high up in a particular tree which she would climb and we would then sit alongside one another, close enough for the breezes to carry her odour over to me, a curious mixture of floral and fish, and at times close enough for contact, the warmth of her leg pressing against mine. We would pass the time largely in silence but punctuated by brief exchanges. I was growing close to the age where playing was rarer, exuberance subsumed into an interest in sports and imagination into social anxiety. But occasionally we did play, swinging upside down, using our legs to try to hold onto the branch without dropping to the ground.

And we would watch Casadolore, Koo and Dad moving around through the windows or coming out into the garden.

'Do you live with your family?' I asked her one day. We had been watching my dad sitting by the kitchen door, drinking and biting at his fingernails.

'There is me and my father only,' Maria said.

We went on watching Dad. He finished his drink and then returned inside.

'Do you live nearby? On the other side of the wood?'

She looked at me blankly.

'The wood, the forest, the trees.' I gestured.

'Ah, *foresta*,' she said. 'Yes, we live here. Not so far.'

Another one of our long silences grew. We looked at one another, occasionally at the house. Then Maria swung her legs over her branch so she was facing away from me and slumped in my direction, dangling from the branch, her arms and her hair trailing beneath. I did the same and we faced one another awkwardly, our faces flushed and distorted.

'*Pipistrello!*' she cried out in a high voice, swinging herself back and forth. '*Vampiro!*'

She swung at me with her arms out, hissing, her fingers crooked. I laughed and made a show of being frightened. In doing so I lost my purchase on the bark. We were very high and the fall took a couple of seconds. I felt certain the impact on the ground would kill me, but instead I landed on my back with a simple earthy thud which left me aching but conscious and intact. I began to pick myself when Maria dropped onto my chest, knocking the air out of my lungs and pinning me down. She remained there, astride my shoulders, looking down at me for a few moments, her hair hanging down around my face, her breath in my mouth.

'*Oblio*,' she said. 'You should like to see Oblio?'

'See what?'

'Oblio.'

'What's Oblio?'

She angled her head in the direction of the wood, away from the house.

'There is a *buca*— what is your word? In the floor, a space... digging...'

'A hole?'

'*Sì*. There is a hole. This is where he is living.'

'What? Who?'

'Oblio.' She stood up. 'You come see. Come. *Avanti*. Up.'

> • <

'The next right should take us out at a park, I think,' I say, checking my map app. Koo nods. We keep walking. I clutch my phone to my chest, looking down at it constantly. There's no signal here and the app hasn't fully loaded – it shows a blue dot twisting at the centre of a blank grid, a patch of green in the corner the only other detail. We look like tourists, something I tend to try to avoid, especially in places like this, a rough neighbourhood where the AirBnBs are cheap and the buildings run down. From time to time we pass a doorway piled high with refuse, binbags piled onto a torn mattress, bottles spilling out. The street we're on is long, dusty and seemingly endless. Three times we have arrived at what I think will be its end, instead for it, on each occasion, to be a bend which leads on to another long stretch of apartment buildings, silent and shuttered, laundry on lines stretching from window to window high above us.

Koo, dressed in black with her harmonium slung over her shoulder, seems as immune to the sun as to the panic at getting lost. The heat makes me sweat and I can feel myself growing irritable at our not knowing where we are. I would decide it was time to turn back if it wasn't for Viner, and I'm not sure I could retrace the route which has brought us so far.

The 1980s had plenty of famous musicians who had a run of success before drifting out of favour and producing sporadic, unsuccessful albums, but there's something unique about Viner's music that draws people in. I've never been sure what it is – her songs have slick production, catchy hooks and cryptic lyrics, but then so do plenty of her peers. But, unlike them, there's something inherently doomy about her songs, underneath all that brassy synthpop make-up you can hear genuine conflict, a combination of desperation to escape from misery and a wallowing in it – a glorying in it. The album which first led Koo and me to develop our obsession with her was *Candles,* an unconvincing grunge-inspired record she'd released in 1995 and which had been in Dad's car when we went to Casadolore. For much of our childhood the album was best known as the release which preceded her disappearing from view, with no releases or performances and crotchety interviews taking place infrequently until 2006, when she surprised everyone by releasing two records in quick succession: *Kloya*, an album of dark jazzy synth songs, and *Klik*, a handful of pared-back songs, mostly with Viner singing accompanied only by herself on the piano. These had come out at the perfect time for Koo and me. We were in our early twenties and were still impressionable when it came to music, keen to learn how to create it ourselves. While *Kloya* had been something of a success, commercially, *Klik* had been the more acclaimed of the two in the music press. Like most people, I'd preferred *Kloya*, with its catchy hooks and squelchy synths, all calibrated to remind the listener of her big eighties hits that people like Mum and Dad loved, but also lost more than ever to that distinct proud darkness. Naturally, Koo preferred *Klik*, with its slow and quiet ten-minute songs. Since then, Viner had once again sunk from public sight, earning a reputation as a recluse, having moved from London to Palermo and not granting an interview since.

'What about down here?' says Koo. She has stopped a few feet behind me and is peering into a doorway. I walk over to her and see that the doorway is in fact a narrow alleyway, through which can be seen the city beyond a set of stone steps that twist away down a steep incline.

'Let's go,' I say.

As we descend the steps they grow wider and straighter, until we reach a small piazza with a few shops and a cafe around a fountain.

'Shall we stop here?' I say. 'I could do with a drink while I see if I can get this bloody phone to work.'

We sit down at a table in the shade. Koo places her harmonium between us. Its casing is etched with a floral pattern around the rim, along which she traces a fingertip.

'Aren't you happy with the reviews?' I say. 'Have you read them? They all praise the stuff you brought to the record.'

'Well, I don't know about that.'

'They do. All the stuff like the atonal breaks and the flutes at the end of "Speak For Me" – they're the bits which were your ideas. They're the things that are, you know, pushing it over the line.'

'It was a joint effort.'

'Come on, Koo. I'm not a journalist.'

'Fine, yeah – it's great that people like all that stuff, that they see what I wanted to add to the songs. But I don't know...' She gestures airily around us. 'All this... I don't know...'

'Touring is hard work.'

'All of it is hard work. Touring, recording, performing.' She places another hand onto the harmonium, another finger pressing along its loops and curls.

'I think the deal must be that we go inside to order,' I say.

'Let's just get going – I want to see Viner. If she's going to go out for lunch we'll miss her.'

> • <

I followed Maria through the wood for a long time. I wondered if this were perhaps a tryst. Was this talk of an animal living in a hole simply a ruse? *Oblio.* Was that a local term for whatever activity I would be expected to engage in? Was I being led to some secluded area where I would be seduced, or perhaps a seduction would be expected of me?

From time to time I looked back to try to get a sense of what the route we were taking looked like, but of course all I could see was trees.

Although I was matching her pace Maria managed to keep moving ahead, leaving me lagging behind. I took the opportunity to assess her, to look her up and down. I knew men often looked at women this way and found it satisfying and, while I wasn't a man, I knew I wasn't really quite the same as the other girls at school. Still, I wasn't sure what I was looking for. Her skirt and her hair swayed as she moved and I noticed the collar of her denim jacket was sticking up slightly at the back.

Then I saw her shift her gait, turning sideways slightly and leaning back as the floor of the forest took a downward slope. I came to the top of the slope and saw that I was looking down at a clearing and amid the undergrowth, not too far away, there was what appeared to be a hole in the earth, obvious only from what looked like a threadbare campsite organised around it: a large stone with a coat draped across it and a bag alongside, a few other items littering the area too indistinct to be made out from our vantage point.

'Is that the hole?' I said, somewhat uselessly, because of course it was.

But Maria was already getting away from me, traipsing down over rocks and ivy, clapping her hands and emitting loud hoots.

'Oblio! Hi! Hi! Hi! *Sveglia!*'

> • <

The street is lined on both sides by market stalls which seem to run on forever.

Koo and I struggle through the crush of shoppers and tourists, alongside tables piled with crates of fruit and vegetables, flies hovering over them, the traders hollering out their offers from the shade.

Although I'm the one whose pace is brisker, Koo edges ahead of me. There's something about her slow saunter which causes people to part and let her through while I walk in stutters, twisting to fit past people, squeezing through gaps in the crowd, stopping to let them pass.

'Koo,' I call, and then louder, 'Koo!' She turns to look at me but I see that she's put on her sunglasses and I can't tell if she spots me or not, although I raise a hand. She continues walking. I elbow my way through to where the run of stalls turns a corner and there's more space, and stop, turning in circles to find Koo, expecting to see her slow amble among the swarm of people or perhaps spot her standing in a doorway.

'You are losing someone?' a man behind a stall asks me. He's young, younger than me, more of a child.

'Yes... yes. My sister. Dark hair. Dark clothes. Sunglasses. Carrying an instrument?'

The man shrugs, lifting both hands. 'There are so many people.'

'Shit.'

'Oh, hey. She will have gone to, I do not know how you say, *chiesa*? It is at the end down here.' He points down the crowded walkway at the end of which looms a large church, its facade lined with statues and ornate corbel stones.

'How can you know?'

'Dark hair. Dark clothes. Music. These people, they are... *costretto...*' He searches for the English word. 'They feel they must go inside.'

'That place there?'

'*Si.*' He waves a dismissive hand and begins bagging up tomatoes. 'I am sure of it.'

I move back into the throngs of people and head down the street. Along with the people, the buildings on either seem to crowd around me and I lose sight of the church. I move to the side of the street and try to get a glimpse of the church again, but it's no good, the gazebos and their awnings make it impossible.

One thing I do see is a balloon drifting above the street, unseen by those below. It is in the shape of a giraffe with a long trail of ribbon hanging from its feet. 'It must have come undone,' I find myself saying aloud.

〉 • 〈

The form at the bottom of the hole was impossible to fully make out. Although the day was bright – indeed, *because of* how suddenly bright it was out here in the clearing, along with a fringe of tall dusty grass around its rim – the bottom was in darkness. Initially, I perceived the figure to be human – a torso, limbs, perhaps a head – but then I perceived the tail, long and thin. As I saw it, it began to move. This movement too had something undeniably animal to it – brief bursts of motion touched with panic, followed by moments of alert motionlessness.

'What is it?' I asked.

'It is Oblio,' Maria said.

'But what is it?'

Maria didn't speak. She simply looked down at the hole, smiling.

I spotted a thin patch of sunlight cast close to the base of the hole, through which fragments of this Oblio creature became visible as he moved: a brief flash of what I took to be his face, pink and smooth, like a baby rodent's, and tiny black eyes. He completed another scurried journey around the edge of his space and I fancied I caught sight of a clutch of protruding teeth, thin and needle-like, or perhaps they were whiskers.

'Where did it come from?'

'From here.'

'How do you mean?'

She sat on one of the large stones that surrounded the hole – the one that had her bag and coat beside it – and took from the bag a packet of marshmallows.

'I found him on a road, not so long before you are arriving. This is old *trappola* – hole for to keep animal.'

'And you… dragged it in here?'

'*Si*. Yes. I with my *papà*.'

'But why did you put this thing in here?'

'Because he asked.'

'But what does your *papà* want to do with it?'

'No, not *mio papà*. He did not ask. Oblio asked. He wanted to be in a place *buio*… dark.'

'Where is your dad?'

Maria plucked a marshmallow from the bag and seemed to consider it for a moment, looking it over. Then she flicked it into the hole. A rustle of movement could be heard as Oblio scampered and pounced.

I follow the music. It's quiet when I first hear it, but the sound is distinct enough, as is the melody: Koo's harmonium. As I move through the crowd, listening, it's almost as if the music transmits its creator's uncanny power: for the first time today people seem to step out of my path, and the towering facade of the church I'd seen at the top of the street slips into view. I find her sat in a portico, squeezed into the space beside a statue's feet.

'Oh hey,' she says as I approach, and stops playing.

'Christ, Koo, I thought I'd lost you.'

'The apartment is just down there.' She points at a side street alongside the church.

'Yeah, I just saw one of those balloons from that graveyard behind our place. I figured we must have walked in one big circle.'

'A balloon?'

'Yeah, the animal balloons, you know? You might not have seen them. They were outside our bedroom window.'

'No, I don't mean our apartment. Down there is where Viner lives.'

> • <

'You can't just leave it down there.'

'He likes down there. *Ama il buio.*'

'But it's cruel.'

'*Cruel*? What is *cruel*?'

'It means not fair, not nice.'

Maria tutted at this, throwing her head back. '*Culattone.* Why I bring you here? I tell you he likes down there. *Ama il buio.* You want to speak to him? You stand here for a long time and you shall hear.' She grabbed me by the arms and pulled me to the edge of the hole. 'I do this sometimes. It is lonely out here, just me and my *papà*. But now I come and listen to Oblio.'

I shook my head but I didn't move. Maria returned to her stone, sat down, and continued eating marshmallows. I peered into the hole again. I still couldn't see Oblio, although I could hear his staccato movements continuing. Nothing more, though: no speaking, no voice. After a few minutes it stopped moving, falling completely silent. I expected it to emit some noises – shrieking, barking, grunting – after which Maria would laugh at me for being so gullible.

But this didn't happen. Instead, the silence just went on. I found my mind wandering. I thought about my mum, dead. I thought about my dad, drinking, splitting wood, crying, and I thought about Koo, playing the piano.

Then there was a voice, a sudden voice, not outwardly audible but like something that had been imposed into my head like a finger into a wound.

Come down here. Come down here. Come down here.

> • ‹

I'm just about to ring the buzzer again when the door cracks open and a face glowers out at us, wrinkled and rheumy but undeniably Carrie Viner.

'*Ciao*?' she says.

'Miss Viner?' I say. 'I hope you don't mind us calling in on you like this. We're musicians who were touring in the area and we just thought, well, that we couldn't miss out on paying you a visit.'

Viner shifts her gaze between myself and Koo. She's dressed in a cardigan and is clutching a packet of cigarettes in one hand, a grimy thumbnail circling its edge, the other hand still holding the door in place.

'Our first album came out just last week. It's called *Debris* – it's been getting some really good reviews in *The Guardian* and in some other places. We're called Taurig. Anyway, we're really big admirers of your music. You've been such a big influence on us. I don't know if…' I stop myself speaking. I can hear my voice growing more urgent. Instead, I smile and await a response from her. But she continues staring at us. The silence stretches out. I wonder if we are indeed not actually talking to Carrie Viner, but in fact an elderly Italian woman who just happens to resemble her. But then Viner says, 'I got used to your kind tracking me down in London. Not so much here.' She steps out into the street, letting the door fall shut behind her. 'I need to pop out. Walk with me.'

> • <

Koo found me. I have no memory of her rescue, nor of my escape, if escape is what I did. I have a dim recollection of the feel of soil compacting under my fingernails, presumably as I scrabbled back up the incline, but nothing more, and even that memory is one I do not trust entirely. Koo had taken a break from playing the piano, she told me, and had come outside to enjoy the sun for a moment. And there I was, visible as I weaved uneasily through the trees, half walking, half clambering through the dirt and the ivy, red-faced and panting, wide-eyed and tearful and, seeing me coming, she ran to me.

> • <

Viner is quick, taking long, stalking strides, both hands in her pockets, a burning cigarette lodged in her mouth. She leaves Koo and me trailing behind her in a long twist of smoke, occasionally jogging to keep up. We're on a busy high street, and to any onlookers I imagine it would look as though we're harassing her were it not for our shared silence. Koo is naturally quiet, and so it seems is Viner. Ordinarily this would lead me to direct the conversation but here the stakes are too high, even for small talk – Viner, although hard to read, already seems dismissive – and I already know the answers she would give to the most banal questions – How long have you lived here? Where did you live before? – in a way that would create an awkward dynamic. And asking the questions I actually want answers to would feel like overstepping: What are you working on at the moment? What do the lyrics on 'Buffalo in the City' mean? How did you achieve the guitar sound at the end of 'Wolf Summer'?

I'm grateful when she finishes her cigarette and speaks, tossing the butt into the road. 'So, tell me about this record of yours – what was it called? *Detritus*?'

'*Debris*,' I say. 'It only really came out a few days ago but the reviews have been really positive.'

She raises a hand. 'I know. Review in *The Guardian* and so on. You said. Why did you record it?'

Koo and I exchange a blank, panicked glance. 'Well, we were signed by Galleon Records and had three weeks to—'

'Not how. Any idiot can release music these days. *Why* did you choose to join them?' She turns and looks at us, I realise, for the first time since we set out together, an eyebrow raised. 'I assume you aren't idiots?'

'Well, we love music…' I begin, but find I sputter out. Any response I could offer seems insipid.

'We're siblings,' Koo says. 'When we were children our mum died and our dad took us on a long trip. We listened to one of your albums for about two weeks. So music – your music – is more than just music. It's important to us in a way that most people find, I don't know, conversations important.'

While Koo has been speaking, Viner has taken her packet of cigarettes out of her pocket and removed one. She stops while placing it between her lips and fumbling in her pocket for a lighter. Koo and I stop too.

Viner puts her lighter away and lets out a long puff of smoke. 'Could you play me something?'

'Yes,' I say. 'We've brought you a CD of the album.' I begin pulling my rucksack off my back.

'No, no,' she says. 'I don't have anything I can play that on. I meant could you play. Could you let me hear one of the songs?'

'What… right now?'

She shrugs.

I begin to speak but again have no idea what to say. I notice that Viner is gazing at me with an odd look on her face, perhaps a sly grin. I smile back at her but then realise she's actually looking past me. I turn and see Koo, who has moved away from us and is now perching on the ledge outside a cafe window and unfastening the harmonium case. Already I can hear it wheezing into life as she squeezes steadily at its bellows and begins to run her fingers over the keys.

It takes me a moment to recognise what she's playing. 'You Let This Happen', the single which first began to get us attention. Koo wrote it on her keyboard and we rerecorded it as the opening track for *Debris*. Here, on the harmonium, out in public, it sounds different, the tempo altered, the accentuated notes on which the melody lies now in the background while a second melody, one that was there all along but which even I had not noticed, takes prominence. Music fills a small patch of the busy street, some people stopping to watch, others continuing on their way, all of them giving Koo space.

One of the reviews of *Debris* described Koo as having a voice that sounds like light. It's true – our easy ability to harmonise is one of our strengths – our signature. As she begins to sing, I think about that review. There's always been something effortless and pure about her voice but suddenly, accompanying this new version of 'You Let This Happen', it seems almost painful in its perfection, the lyrics stretched out into long beams, clean and piercing: 'A miracle dissolved. A herd of stone. A saviour slept, swept smooth with dark: backlit and burnt but afraid in the rain.' I want to look over to Viner but I can't. Even though I know the words to be nonsense, written by Koo one night after smoking weed – and even though I've been singing them myself for almost a year – I find myself pinioned by the imagery, transfixed like an animal. I'm unable to look away from my sister, singing, glancing down at her harmonium and framed by the oblivious, chattering diners in the cafe window behind her.

It ends abruptly, both the song and its spell. Koo's singing cuts out and the harmonium's engine wheeze quickly slips into silence. She stares at us, eyes widening, posture straightening.

'What's wrong with her?' Viner says, turning to me, half-whispering as though this is part of an act.

'Oh god,' Koo mutters. She stands, staring in our direction but, it's now apparent, beyond us, behind us. She lets out a gasp. 'Oh my god!'

Viner and I turn around. Behind us, on the other side of the road, is a small square with a large fountain, tiered animals of white marble spouting water from one to another. Surrounding it are high iron railings, serrated at the top.

'What has she seen?' Viner mutters.

'What is it?' I ask.

'Look! Don't you see?' She is pointing at the fountain. She untethers herself from the harmonium, settles it on the ledge beside her, stands between me and Viner. 'There! It's on its side!'

I look to where she's pointing. There is only a fountain, a handful of tourists milling about in its surrounding shade.

'The baby!' She splutters. 'Look! Do you see? It's just there on the floor!'

We have all three of us edged closer towards the road, Viner and I following Koo's lead.

She looks at my blank face. 'Can't you hear it, for Christ's sake!' She gives a growl of exasperation and vaults through the traffic, reaching the other side and running into the fountain's enclosure. I jog across the road and watch her moving through the railings, running around to the other side of the fountain, becoming obscured by tourists and running water.

Viner arrives at my side. 'Can you see a baby?'

'No. Can you?'

'Nothing.' She lifts a shielding hand over her eyes. 'I can't see your sister.'

I can't see her either. I run into the enclosure, around to where, logically, Koo should be. Then I run back around to the other side. I run back out into the square and search around. There's no chance that she could have slipped through the gaps between the rails or climbed over the top.

But she couldn't have left the entrance without my seeing her. It's just not possible. I feel myself beginning to cry but press the urge away.

Viner watches me, her expressionless face strobed by the railings as I sprint in circles, my eyes searching the sculptures, water pouring from their faces.

STILL SHE VISITS

EUGEN BACON

You remember when you were eleven or twelve, hands fumbling with a folded cloth. The tingle of a sore nipple, the claws of muscle cramp. Each pang in your pelvis was a sword that hacked away your childhood.

Your mother waltzed into your grave-sized room. It was tiny enough to hold two coffins and a row of ghost feet. It always felt haunted. Mamm brought in her rage and suspicion in a growl that said, 'What mischief are you plotting?' even though the words were different: 'Tidy your room yet?' Furrows on her forehead, her no-nonsense gait... all now just a memory in fragments.

It was your little sister Mokgosi – her name means a call for help – who used her body to shield your secret from your mamm. Why it had to be a secret, you don't know, maybe it was to stop your mother from fraying your ears with threats about boys. How they took everything you gave, then broke you even though you were empty. How they sauntered whistling to a forever place, leaving you with mouths to feed, tiny mouths that couldn't tolerate hunger.

'Loosen, Mamm. Just ease.' Mokgosi's calming words stood in front of your stained pad and your mother, ever grouchy like a buffalo.

Mamm looked harder at your sister and your blocked self, still with rage and suspicion, but she left the room without a word, and that didn't happen all that often. You looked at Mokgosi. She looked at you. She gave you a clean pad and soaked your blood in salted cold water, washed the nasty cloth with her bare hands, because money, money, money. There was no money to take to a shop and buy tampons.

It was then that you understood your sibling bond, even though before that you were street dogs – the way you fought. This new love moved you through bad things, like when your mother left, not just your room, but this time for good.

It's an undying love that makes you see through the hollow in Mokgosi's eyes full of dusk, so you can unsee the guts like strings falling out of her mouth, her ears. Her silent aura telling you like a movie that she's dead, please be honest.

'Sorry, I...' You clang pots, bang doors in your apartment in East Melbourne. *Thump-thwack-clang-bang.* How can you be honest to such loss?

But still Mokgosi visits.

> • <

Segomotsi – your name means a comfort in Setswana. Few people here know you by that name; they call you Seggie Slacken – the Aussie you married.

It's years since you travelled home. Botswana will be a stranger, the village of Lejwana even more. But with your parents gone, and without your sister Mokgosi, what's left to call home?

A girl waits opposite you at the shrink's office. She flicks through pages of a brand-new issue of *Women's Interest*. She's chewing gum. Flick, chew. The receptionist ignores you both.

You consider the receptionist, her face sharp as a pin, her nose and ponytail equally harsh. Back home, you would chat to strangers like old friends; ask about their cows, their goats, their children. Here, folk don't do that.

The psychiatrist who retrieves you has dimples. Her pensive face is complete with lines: forehead lines, crow's feet at the sidelines, marionette lines run straight upwards from the corners of her mouth. Her room is pristine, bland colours unable to touch your moods. Her leather couch is familiar, wears an easy look like the coin-slotted massage sofa at the Jam Factory in South Yarra.

You ignore Mokgosi, her hollow eyes, oozing entrails, sitting in the corner of the room. The settee in which you recline, face up to the bland ceiling, smells synthetic. Nothing like the dusky cowhide on Uncle Kopano's chairs in Lejwana, unbleached skin and hair that smells of wet mud. This leather is coffee coloured, café latte.

'How are you?' Dr Bland. Her voice matches the insipid room.

'How is she in this room?' you say.

'How is who in the room?'

'There. Can't you see?'

'What would you like me to see?'

'She looks like death but smells fresh and sweet like gazania.'

Silence.

'She was like that in life, you know. Bright yellow, hot orange, cheery purple, her temperament, sometimes the clothes she got from *mtumba* – second hand. Face of the sun, unfussy, everything she wore just fit right.'

Silence.

'Dainty, but she was the stronger of us two. With a mother like ours who had to fight for everything she got, so much that she mistook her children for combat, you needed a Mokgosi standing with a water bottle and a towel in your corner. So here she is, fully here, to fight my demons – only now she's one too. All wretched to look at, but there's strength in her scent. Sweet mango. Sometimes durian.'

> • <

You leap into the swimming pool at the aquatic centre. Mokgosi dangles her feet in the water, makes you touch them each turn at the wall before you somersault. It feels like a call for help, but whose – yours or Mokgosi's?

> • <

A week.

'Is Mokgosi in the room with us today?' asks Dr Bland.

'Right there. Same corner.'

Mokgosi who always stood by your side, but you're the one who got away. It was curiosity for the world and a scholarship that put you on a plane, and away, away you flew.

'What's she looking at?' asks Dr Bland.

'You.'

'What's she thinking, do you know?'

'I guess – why you? She was always there for me.'

'And how do you feel right now?' asks Dr Bland.

'Cross,' you say.

'Cross – because your sister is looking at me?'

'Because work sucks. Been thinking to leave.'

Silence.

'Employee assistance programme, bereavement leave on tap, cards, flowers...' you say.

'I'm glad you took EAP – that's why you're here,' says Dr Bland.

'How can a plant so rugged be so beautiful? It grows in extreme heat, tolerates any drought, climbs out of the hardest earth to splay in vibrant colours...' You choke.

Dr Bland hands you a tissue.

> • <

A week.

'Surprised?' Dr Bland. Sometimes she's like this, prods you with a question. 'Why so? You say Mokgosi surprised you?'

'When Mamm left... her leaving was not the kind of walkaway our father did: *Grabbing cigarettes, be right back.* A beast in the wind swallowed him whole, no one saw him again. No, Mamm's leaving was the kind that happens where shadows reach into sleep and take away a loved one.' All that fighting the world finally it took its toll. 'She ate dinner one night, rested her head on a pillow, closed her eyes and never woke up.'

'So how has your sister surprised you?'

'Mokgosi doesn't hurt like when Mamm died.'

Mokgosi slips from her corner, her gazania bloom smell tightly closed – today she's odourless. She shuffles to the settee in which you recline. Traces with her gnarled finger a tear that brooks its way round your nose to the edge of your lips.

'If Mokgosi doesn't hurt,' says Dr Bland, 'then why are you crying?'

> • <

A week.

'Do you know that the gazania flower doesn't bloom on a dark or stormy night?'

'Is that how you feel today?' Dr Bland. 'Dark and stormy?'

'I feel far.'

'What do you mean?'

'Too far to mourn.'

'Why didn't you go to Botswana when she was sick?'

'Work, stuff.'

'How are you dealing with being far now?'

'I sent money. World Remit. To help with the funeral.'

Silence.

'But they didn't need it. Took them a week, a whole week for Uncle Kopano to collect it. The chief is a friend of my family. He paid for everything: hospital bill, ivory-finish coffin. They didn't need my money.'

'How does that make you feel?'

Mokgosi's hollow eyes full of dusk pouring into your soul. 'What do you expect?'

Silence.

'No Tobin Brothers Funeral services in Lejwana, you know. Nobody to wash her. Nobody saying to you: *How would you like to make your coffin look?* Or: *We'll send out the funeral notice to your friends.* It's the women who washed her, dressed her. Put lipstick on her face. Put on eye shadow, angel face. Put her in a white dress with a shiny coat. No curls in her hair; they put on a headdress.'

Silence.

'There were drums, huge drums, Uncle said. *Doomba-doo! Doomba-doo! Doodoomba-doo! Doo! Doo! Doodoodoo!* The whole village was together, they farewelled her like a queen.'

Mokgosi in her corner, smiles at the memory.

'All of Lejwana at her doorstep. They sang, they danced, they drank. They feasted: platters of meat and rice. Chief Dikeledi paid for it. People ate fit to burst.'

Silence.

'I feel rubbish.'

Mokgosi is on the settee – how did she get there so quick? She's cradled to your breast. Her aura is red with splashes of hot pink. Her scent, dear gods, her scent. An overwhelming sweetness that reminds you of a wedding.

'What do you regret the most?' says Dr Bland.

'Being seven thousand miles from Mokgosi's grave. Far, far from home…'

Mokgosi strokes your cheeks through the sadness. 'I didn't even keep the Aussie.' Your smile is cynical. 'Slacken. The divorce was a slap in the face for him, fourth year of our marriage. No wonder he went mean after that, the slap still ringing.'

> • <

A week.

Today Mokgosi looks like your mother, the rage, the suspicion, black fog swirling from her empty eyes. Furrows on her head, a no-nonsense gait.

'How are you today?' Dr Bland. She sits in a comfortable silence, palms flat, parallel on her thighs. Sometimes she sprawls her arms casually on each armrest.

'Angry. ANGRY.'

'Talk to it,' says Dr Bland. 'Talk to your anger.'

Acha! Stop! Mokgosi is shaking her head, making a gargling noise. She's rocking in a corner, back against the wall like Mamm did in the kitchenette when your father evaporated.

'Why don't they call it what it is? What it is IT IS!'

'Why don't they call what?' asks Dr Bland.

'What it is IT IS she died of.'

'What do you want to call it?'

Mokgosi leaps. Her scream is full of echoes, her arms outstretched to muffle or strangle you. Entrails like tongues rush from the yawn of her gobbling mouth.

'Break the circle of silence. It's not malaria. It's not pneumonia. It's not tuberculosis.' Hands on your throat, you can't breathe, breathe. But the words fall out of your mouth: 'It's AIDS. AIDS. AIDS!'

Mokgozi's fading cry, *Arrggggh...* Then she puffs out, leaves behind a sickly-sweet smell of formaldehyde.

Your wet face against Dr Bland's breast.

> • <

A week.

'No more Mokgosi in the room?' asks Dr Bland.

You shake your head. 'No more.'

You're surprised that something is changed in Dr Bland, in how she speaks now. She talks different. A slant in her vowels, a trail as if they're cursive with consonants. There's colour in Dr Bland. Texture.

'What do you want to talk about today?' asks Dr Bland.

'Like what?'

'Tell me anything.' Each vowel has its sound, like a sixth sense.

'I made hard decisions, the ones that made me stay. It wasn't the lightness of bills – he was more expensive to keep than me alone. I married an Aussie, but it wasn't for the fondness in his touch. Kissing him was like smooching carrion, the sex as impersonal as a bus driver's glance at dismounting passengers. I don't know why I stayed. All night as he snored, I heard sirens. *Do you have a moment?* they sang. *Tell us your name.*'

'And what's your name?' Cursive words, the tongue lingers.

You're not sure whether it's you or Dr Bland who has changed.

'My name is Segomotsi – it means a comfort in Setswana.'

You lie in bed, unable to sleep. You remember the hurt you forgot. The day Mokgosi died, your sense of loss was so keen, it pierced holes into your gut, and cannon balls entered those holes. You flick on the lights, look at the white of the ceiling speckled with the cream of the apartment sprinkler, a fire safety gadget with circular ridges, indents and protrusions. Three silver hooks fasten the clear of the translucent plate covering the bulb.

Had to happen in March?

Death is easier in November – New Year around the corner. Come January, you set your mind to new thinking. You leave death with the year gone. Sucks in March; you have to live with death the whole year.

> • <

You look at your phone: 6 a.m.

It's Saturday.

Aquatic centre, you prefer the outdoor pool. You swim like the physio instructed: 'When you turn to breathe, level your cheek with the water surface, not nose up.' You agree with the physio: this way is less strain on your neck.

Every day is winning and losing. Sometimes more win than loss, a little more now. She still visits, Mokgosi. Unfolding in bright colours of the gazania. She's an African daisy and, like all daisies, she's complete in herself. Gazanias, like tall grasses, just more radiant, appear anywhere. There she is luminescent in the water, shimmering with the waves as you swim. Hers is a big kiss, florets and golds spreading with each stroke. Now I'm a bigger bloom, she says. Her voice buzzes rich with low notes. You should see, she says in her resonant bassoon. It's a starburst here.

You swim, swim. Sweet mango and durian: her scent in the waves.

Water enters your nose, your mouth, just enough not to unsettle. Breathing cheek level with the water, you like it. It is almost like a water hug. The sun is playful. She patterns the base of the pool with her rays. A white ray bounces off a window to reflect on your tinted goggles as you breathe. Your face is in the water. The sun's rays are a comfort, like your name. The sun feels intimate.

Like Mokgosi's gaze.

> • <

A week.
   Silence.
   Silence.
   'Tell me anything.' Dr Bland.
   'Anything.'
   She smiles.
   Silence.
   Silence.
   'I know to see when I'm drowning,' you say.
   'Good. Make sure you keep swimming.'
   You smile.
   Silence.
   Silence.

BLOODYBONES JONES

SAM THOMPSON

I had not seen Rufus for three years, but when he appeared on the doorstep wanting shelter for the night, I was not surprised. He's my brother.

Up in the flat, he dropped his whole weight into the sofa. He surveyed the fitted bookshelves, the framed posters from Latitude and Electric Picnic, the screen prints Gwen's sister had made for us, the coffee table we had found one Saturday in the antique shop on the corner. His skewed canine tooth caught on his lower lip in the way it did. He let his grin widen.

'You would not believe,' he said, 'how hungry I am.'

I did not reply. Every move at this stage was crucial, and a false one could be a disaster. I walked into the kitchen, but when I came back with some cold pasta bake he was asleep, snoring, with his head rolled back and one boot resting on the coffee table. The leather was peeling away from the steel toecap.

I sat down opposite. He had changed his look. His hair was long now, hanging loose and greasy around his face. He had a cut on his cheek and his army surplus greatcoat stank of cigarette smoke. I wanted to remove the boots and the coat, clean the wound and cover him with a blanket, then grab him by the ears and shake him until he confessed why he had come.

Instead, I turned out the light and went to bed, treading carefully so as not to disturb Gwen. She had been having trouble sleeping since the start of the third trimester, and was liable to wake at small disturbances, but as I eased into bed she did not stir. If he was still here in the morning, we'd deal with it, I thought. I lay awake for a long time, but at last I dreamed I was in the back garden of our childhood home with someone who was both Gwen and Rufus. The garden was evil and would only let us go if I could perform a certain magic trick with a coin, but Rufus or Gwen kept laughing and pointing out how I was getting it wrong. I woke to find I had slept through the alarm for the first time in years.

Gwen was leaning on the kitchen counter with her crutches beside her. Rufus, bare-chested under the smelly coat, pushed the plunger of the cafetière. Adhesive sutures had been applied to the cut on his face. Usually I would have gone to Gwen and pressed a hand on her stomach to feel the strong movements of limbs under the surface, but instead I gestured lamely towards my brother.

'He's going to stay as long as he needs to,' Gwen said. 'You promise, don't you, Rufus?'

Rufus pressed his palms together, prayer-wise, and bowed.

Leaving them was against my better judgement, but I was running late. As I kissed Gwen's cheek in the hall I restrained myself from telling her not to listen to him. I only told her to take it easy. The pelvic girdle pain she had been suffering since the middle of the pregnancy had eventually forced her to begin her leave early, and she was under orders to rest up. I reminded her daily not to try and walk. Joining the queue at the bus stop, I shook my head in admiration at the instinct that had made Rufus choose now, of all times, to make an appearance.

Our most recent encounter with him had been the day before we got married. He had arrived without warning, having ignored my previous attempts to contact him about the wedding. At that time his persona was based loosely on jazz-age hedonism: he was wearing two-tone shoes, hair oil and a charity shop pinstripe suit, complete with a fedora, and he insisted on taking us for whiskey cocktails and talking in brittle aphorisms. He kept on calling Gwen 'kid' and toasting us in an exaggerated way, as if he thought approving our union was his business. We changed the programme so that he could give one of the readings, but at the ceremony he was nowhere to be found.

And now she was meant to be avoiding strain. I spent the day not phoning her, knowing that I could not afford to show concern. When I got home it was to the smell of cooking and the sight of Rufus wearing my blue-and-white apron, lifting the big enamelled casserole pot out of the oven. Gwen poured two glasses of Malbec and a blackcurrant juice for herself. Rufus had spent the day going from market to market, it turned out, gathering his ingredients. He was picky.

'You didn't have to,' I said.

He paused, letting that statement hang, cocking his head as if to catch all its echoes. He chuckled to himself. Earlier, Gwen told me, she had taken a long hot bath at Rufus's suggestion, and had spent the rest of the afternoon in a completely pain-free nap. The baby was kicking.

As Rufus stirred the pot, making spiced steam rise, he explained that it was a simple dish, the trick being in how he used the tomatoes, lemon and garlic, but that you had to find good meat as well, which was less easy than you'd think. He had picked up the recipe in Spain. He had worked for three months as a security guard in a Bilbao shopping centre last year, chasing shoplifting kids down the hidden access corridors behind the arcades. You could collar them but you had no legal right to detain them, so it was a question of what you could get away with. Usually he'd end up sitting on some angry boy's chest for forty-five minutes until the cops turned up, or else they didn't and the kid went back out to pilfer some more.

He had shaved since the morning, leaving himself a long moustache and a pointed piratical chin-beard. His towel-dried hair was caught back with a rubber band. He wore one of my T-shirts, stretched tight under his armpits, and a pair of my old jeans, showing inches of hairy shin below the cuff. As we ate he continued on the theme of his recent employments. You never need to worry about money, he said. If you want some, you find yourself a job and you work until you have enough. Then you leave. Before Bilbao he had picked apples in Belgium. Further back, he'd been a runner for a reality television production company in Mexico City; he'd driven cars coast to coast in the USA three times over; he'd worked his passage from Nova Scotia to Oslo on a container ship; he'd been a waiter in a gourmet hamburger bar in Dublin. I gave as little encouragement as I could, but he needed none. When he got bored with somewhere, he told us, he was out. Next train. Why wait? Let yourself get tied down, you might have a comfortable existence but you weren't truly alive. Of course, a lot of people would have trouble with his philosophy. But Rufus didn't need a label to tell him who he was.

I was watching for any flicker of mockery, but his eyes were fixed on Gwen. He poured himself more wine and pointed at her with the bottle.

'Live in the moment,' he said. 'Travel light.'

He raised an eyebrow.

I chewed a mouthful of the stew. The meat was so overcooked that it might have been anything. I pictured Rufus catching pigeons, wringing their necks and stuffing them into his greatcoat's pockets.

'I've got work tomorrow,' I said, as soon as I credibly could, but when I made to rise from the table he caught my forearm and gripped it with long yellow fingernails. He took Gwen's forearm in his other hand. He looked into her face, then into mine, slow and steady.

'You two,' he said. 'You guys.'

Before letting us go, I realised, he was going to give us his blessing.

'I want to say one thing, you guys, and I hope you'll remember it down all the happy, happy years ahead.'

He shook his head, smiling sentimentally. I waited, but instead of fading the smile stayed and grew broader, splitting to display teeth. His eyes showed white all the way around. He held his face in its rictus until I pulled my arm free and walked out of the kitchen.

'Night then, mate,' he called.

❯ • ❮

Gwen was breathing steadily beside me when I heard a noise: a tapping, soft but rhythmic. I slipped out of bed, crossed to the window, and opened the curtain. A big white mask of a face grinned at me through the glass. Then the grin was replaced by a look of cartoon surprise, and the face disappeared. The bedside clock said 1:38 a.m. The flat was on the first floor, and when we went down we found Rufus lying among smashed herb pots on the paving stones of the back garden. He had climbed out of the kitchen and somehow edged around the corner of the building to our bedroom window.

'I'm so broken,' he mumbled, but in fact he did not seem to have done himself serious damage. He giggled. Gwen knelt down beside him and tried to make him keep still, but he was already rolling around and getting to his feet. Half an hour later she was sitting in front of him in the kitchen, cleaning his grazes, watching for signs of concussion and carefully not asking what he had been trying to do. I went back to bed.

In the morning he was sprawled across the sofa, sound asleep under his coat. His face was peaceful.

'He's having a hard time,' she said, breathing into her tea so that her glasses misted. 'I got him talking.'

I opened my mouth. Then I closed it again, marvelling at his knack of blocking my every move. Gwen was explaining the kind of hard time that Rufus was supposed to be having. She thought he needed clinical help. He kept checking the doors and windows.

'In the end he told me he was scared of someone he called Bloodybones. Any idea?'

I shook my head. I pressed a palm to my temple, which was throbbing with the lost sleep, and went to work.

I knew I should not be leaving her with a man who was demonstrably a danger to himself, if not to others. But there was no choice, because if I stayed at home it would mean that he was calling the tune. I must give no credit to his impersonation of someone who was not responsible for his own actions. I could not blame Gwen for being sympathetic, or for imagining he did not know what he was doing when he pressed his face against our window. It was only decent of her, but I could not afford to be so indulgent.

At work I ignored the urge to phone, and the day passed slowly. I thought about Bloodybones. I saw what he was up to, of course. It had not been an important or lasting presence in our childhood, but just important enough, perhaps, for a tiny doubt. Could it be that a forgotten children's game, trivial then and meaningless now, could have affected Rufus so deeply that it was returning as a personality disorder? I knew the answer, but I had to admit he had chosen well, because the doubt was possible, or it would have been for someone not on his guard.

There were three years between us. As a child Rufus had been small and credulous, unable to resist being hauled and shoved where I wanted him, and always ready to believe what he was told. He had spent his childhood beset by fears he could not explain, and hemmed in by all the places he would not go because of the menace that lived there: the compost heap, the turn in the stairs, the boiler cupboard, the wardrobe in the spare room, the attic. If I encouraged him, it was not out of malice. There was a kind of tenderness in the way I taught my brother that something would reach a hand out of the cupboard and grab him as he scurried through the hall, and that it was sending him messages in the knocking of the central heating pipes at half past five in the morning. I do not know which of us gave the thing a name, but I know it added to the fun.

Rufus plucked at his hair, chewed his fingertips and broke things. He stamped on the toys he loved best. I understood why. He did it when Bloodybones got too close, because a sacrifice could keep it off a little longer. Of course, I know now that a twinge of guilt might be in order, but it was nothing unusual, as things go between brothers, and didn't Rufus get his own back in time? The summer when he was fifteen, he grew into his adult height and breadth. We no longer went in much for physical tussling by then, but he found an occasion for it, and I was held face down in the scrubby ground behind the house until I was gasping to breathe and there was no missing the fact that I could not get free. He never laid a finger on me again.

> • <

On the bus home I thought again of sending Gwen a message, but I left my phone alone. I had made it this far without letting him score that particular point. Send him on his way without putting yourself in the wrong, I told myself. He had come back to get something, as he always did, but what he wanted he did not deserve and could not have. And actually it was that simple, I saw. I got off the bus. I would tell him to leave. I started walking.

The flat's outer door had been left wide open to the street. Puzzled, I stepped in and eased it shut. The door gave into a cramped vestibule from which a flight of stairs ran up to the flat proper. I listened, straining into the still air of the five rooms. As I began to climb the stairs, treading like an intruder, a picture formed in my mind, and by the time I reached the landing it seemed really possible that I had made an error of judgement. Past events fell into a pattern of signs that had been plain for me to read. I saw the meat Rufus had served us, the grinning face at the window, the broken toys and Bloodybones tapping its codes on the pipes. The living room was tidy and deserted. I moved into the kitchen, weighing the odds as I opened the door that Rufus would be waiting here in the blue-and-white apron, as two-dimensional as a nightmare, standing over the remains, ready to explain that everything was all right now. But the kitchen was empty. I was alone in the flat.

Locking the street door behind me, I walked, remembering that in last night's dream Rufus had been in a kitchen preparing a meal with the assistance of some unidentified person. I had craned and jostled to see what they were making, but Rufus and the other had kept their backs to me and I could not push between. I turned onto the high street and hurried along, scanning faces. I had little hope. The evening was cold and dull, losing light. A breeze lifted river-smell from a hidden source. I hesitated in the glow of the Metro supermarket and saw them.

They were walking towards me, Gwen using her crutches and Rufus escorting her tactfully, hands ready to give support. Their pace was unhurried. Seeing them, you would have taken them for a happy pregnant couple returning from a stroll around the block. When they noticed me they smiled.

FLOTSAM AND JETSAM

MALCOLM DEVLIN

Ruth was the only passenger to alight at Benedict Lane. She stood back from the bus on the far side of the pavement, and let the driver depart. The tyres sluiced through the lagoon of rainwater that had collected along the fringe of the road, sending eddies of grey wash across the pavement to meet the scuffed toes of her shoes.

The worst of the afternoon's storm had given way to a lull, leaving only a thin skein of rain as a stern reminder that it wasn't yet done. Ruth pulled her hood up and hurried through the short alleyway connecting to Beatrice Street. It felt as though weather of one type or another had been buffeting her since she left for work that morning. The day had been busy with people and the hierarchy of them – *strangers, clients, colleagues* – had started to blur around the edges in a way that made her feel under siege. All she wanted now was to get home and close the door on the world.

Across the road, an ambulance was parked, its doors gaping. There was a fire engine beside it, similarly dormant. Both were silent, but their blue lights chased broad circles around the street.

As she neared, she saw the vehicles were parked outside Mr Carter's house, one of the old red-brick Edwardian semis that lined the north side of the road. She passed it every day, but now the house looked unrecognisable. It was usually a little tatty, because Mr Carter so rarely showed an interest in maintaining it, but this evening there was a large, dark hole where the bay window should have been, and emerging from it lay the remains of the stout silver birch tree that had once stood proud in the front driveway.

A tall fireman appeared from the open front door. Striding towards the fire engine, he saw Ruth standing there and nodded at her. She flustered. The man looked as though he was going to talk to her.

'Is he okay?' She hadn't meant to say anything, but for some reason it felt important to be the one to say something first. 'Mr Carter. Is Mr Carter okay?'

'You family?' the fireman said.

Ruth shook her head. She was going to say she was a friend but that didn't seem quite as true as it should have been. *Friend* was a title that felt like it should have been earned and bestowed, rather than simply claimed.

'I don't think he has any family,' she said. 'I knew him, but—'

The fireman looked as though he was about to say something, but his phone interrupted them with a chirrup. He hooked it from his belt and regarded it with a frown.

'Look,' he said. 'It's not my place to say. I should…' He indicated the phone, then hurried past her, disappearing around the other side of the fire engine.

Ruth took a breath, collecting herself. There was a faint smell of drains, as though a pipe had fractured somewhere.

She looked back at the house, and for some reason the hole felt darker to her than it should have done. The cracks from it snaked up the wall and along the window frame. It looked like a blot of ink on a page, its dark lines creeping between the cracks in the brickwork like spidery tendrils.

Poor Mr Carter. He had always struck her as a rather curmudgeonly sort. A retired divorce lawyer, living by himself in the house.

When she had first moved to the area, Ruth had briefly volunteered with the local meals-on-wheels service. It had been her mother's idea. A way of becoming part of the community. A way of 'fitting in'. Ruth had only got involved under forbearance, still half-believing her mother's conviction that her anxieties might be resolved with the stubborn application of brute force. She barely lasted a week. There was a certain sort of horror involved in approaching a stranger's home. A nauseating tension waiting for the door to be answered and an unforgivable *ostentation* about expecting to be seen and spoken to. Some of the elderly people on her list were desperate for her to come in, to stay, to *talk*. They wanted company that she was in no place to give.

She remembered how Mr Carter had never let her past his front door.

'I just want to be alone,' he would say as he took the plates from her. There was no please, no thank you, but Ruth didn't really mind.

'I understand,' she said, and even then, she really did.

'Tell her,' Mr Carter would sometimes add, 'I just want to be alone.' He never specified who he was talking about, so Ruth would only nod and promise to do her best.

The storm must have taken out the tree. Ruth had seen traces of damage on the bus journey home – bins felled like skittles, broken branches littering the pavements – but in the sealed shelter of the office, the scale of it had felt muted.

In the kitchen that afternoon, she'd heard Mabel and Jeffery from finance talking about how strong the winds had been. Mabel, round and gingham with pink-rimmed spectacles; Jeffery, greyer and slighter in every respect.

'Took the tiles clean off my mother's roof,' Mabel had been saying.

'I do hope she was insured,' Jeffery had replied. And then they'd both fallen silent, waiting expectantly for Ruth to finish. The kitchen was too small for the three of them. Normally, Ruth retreated there as a respite from the noise and agoraphobia of the open plan office – a necessary evil, she had been told – but that afternoon, she'd mistimed her moment and found it occupied. She felt their eyes on her as she struggled with the kettle; she'd sensed the way they were exchanging glances as she was clumsy with the tea caddy; she heard their amusement when her panic made her drop her mug in the sink, forcing her to start all over again.

Across the road from Mr Carter's house, another birch tree stood unscathed, sheltered by the high wall which ran the length of Beatrice Street. When she crossed, Ruth saw there was something trapped in its branches. A large tarpaulin. A dark, reinforced plastic sheet, its edges flapping and flickering in the remaining wind.

It was difficult to make out the exact size and shape of it. It was tangled securely in the lower branches in such a way that it looked tented and stretched. The light drizzle blurred its edges, giving it the appearance of something solid, bunched together and hanging wetly in folds through the boughs. It shifted and rippled as though – without enthusiasm – it was struggling to free itself.

Flotsam and jetsam, Ruth thought. It had likely blown free from a skip. Maybe the one outside Mrs Owen's place, the cover of which had looked as though it had been threatening to take off for the past week. Ruth had every faith that someone would deal with it, tidy it away and make the tree right again, but as with so many other things, it struck her as being a job that would have to wait until the storm had safely passed.

As she walked beneath it, the gathered rainwater tucked in its folds dripping down her hood and her cheeks, she could hear the material shifting in the breeze, making a wet and crinkling sound. It was a distinctive sort of noise, and not a wholly pleasant one. It made her think of hospital bedsheets, of cellophane wrappers, of plastic crisp packets being loosely balled before being thrown away.

She hurried onwards, searching her bag for her house keys as she went. When she reached the end of the road, she spared a glance at Mrs Owen's house and saw not only that the skip was still there, but that its cover had been securely fastened down. The bright blue plastic was trussed and still against the turbulence of the day.

She heard the sound again. The crackling, shifting, unfolding sound of something thin and plastic in almost organic motion. It was loud enough and long enough; uncoupled from the movement of the wind. She looked back the way she had come and saw that the sheet was gone from the tree, whose branches now stood stark, picked out cleanly by the blue lights of the ambulance.

Beneath it, Ruth could see that someone was standing. They were a little too close to the wall to make out clearly, but there was the clear *impression* of a someone; a stooped and silent figure in dark robes whom Ruth was certain had not been there before. It wasn't the figure's appearance that made her feel disquiet, it was its attention. The mortifying awareness of being seen.

She squinted into the shadows beneath the tree, and when the figure did move – a single confident step in her direction – there was that sound again; something plastic, shifting, moving.

She turned away and hurried home.

> • <

Ruth's ground-floor flat was warm and cosy and – with the door firmly closed and the curtains drawn – it was easy enough for her to imagine that the outside world no longer existed at all.

There was something about the familiarity of the space that made her relax immediately. She teased off her shoes and socks; she traced her hands across the closed door, then she set the radio on.

It wasn't a big flat, but it was as much as she needed, perhaps even more. The lounge and bedroom were separate, she had a reasonably appointed kitchen, and there was a full-length bath in the bathroom. There was enough wall space for three large, full bookshelves and the television, while modest in size, served her perfectly well as a window onto a brighter, noisier world that could be silenced or extinguished at the touch of a button.

Her evening routine was a simple one. She showered and changed out of her work clothes, then set some of the weekend's bolognese on the stove to reheat. The calendar on the fridge reminded her it was her mother's birthday, so she steeled herself before calling home and patiently listened to her parents' usual advice that she should 'find herself a nice man'. Experience had taught her to be diplomatic on such a point. Her quiet agreement was no more than a means to shift the conversation's gears and steer the subject to something less contentious. They talked of politics and the climate and other miserable things before the subject of Ruth Being Single returned for a second round before they all hung up.

'I just worry about you all on your own,' her mother said.

'I'm fine,' Ruth said. 'Really, I am.'

'Nobody should be alone in a big city,' her father said, as though the thought of her living by herself in the middle of a forest or on the summit of a mountain might set his mind to rest.

'I like it this way,' Ruth said, but when they said their goodbyes, she had the familiar sense that this compromise wasn't settled. The subject would come up again the next time she called.

She spent the evening paging through the television channels, but everything seemed to be showing romantic comedies or relationship dramas, which her phone call had evaporated any interest in. Even the adverts all seemed to be about happy couples frolicking on beaches, so she turned the television off and read a book instead.

Outside, the storm had returned, and was building steadily. The rain skittered on the glass of the window, the wind creaked like the timber in a ship, and the barrage had the effect of making the flat feel cosier and more secure. When the lights flickered once or twice, Ruth retired to her bed and imagined the deep rumble of the distant thunder outside might serve her as a lullaby.

>•<

It was still dark when she woke, but her dreams – so startling and vivid only moments earlier – receded from her newly sharpened wakefulness, leaving her with a restless impatience to begin the day. She remembered only that her dream had been one of suffocation, of claustrophobia, of a tight and unwelcome embrace. To find herself awake and alone in the cool of her own room was a blessed relief.

She pushed her covers away easily, but when she reached for the bedside light, the switch flicked on and off with no effect. It was only when she saw how her phone was also dark that she realised the power must have failed, and she was struck by a disorienting sense that she did not know what time it was.

The bedroom window overlooked the back wall of the building only inches behind her flat. It had never let much light in at the best of times, so she picked her way through her small familiar knot of rooms to the kitchen and parted the curtains.

Outside, the darkness was absolute. Her first thought was that the street lights – which usually filled the kitchen with a warm, honeylike glow – must also be victims of the outage. But it was a darkness her eyes refused to acclimatise to. The boxy shape of the houses across the street. The tangled branches of the sycamore trees, the wrought-iron fence that bordered the parkland? These were shapes she expected to cut themselves from the gloom and make themselves known. Was it still so early that there was no trace at all of light in the sky?

Again, she felt unmoored. Her sense of time had abandoned her, now her sense of space had too. For all she understood, the flat could have been moved while she slept. Plucked from its foundations and cast, spinning into space.

Blindly, she searched the cupboard under the sink for candles and matches. When she returned to the window, armed like a gothic heroine, her reflection greeted her like an unwanted twin. She tried to peer past herself, but the night had thickened into tar.

She took a breath and closed her eyes. Ever since she was a child, it was a trick she had used to centre herself. A personal, private darkness with no one in it but herself. She could be rational even without the horizon or the time to anchor her. It was still night, there had been a storm, a power cut. There was no reason at all to be afraid.

Although now fully awake, she resigned herself to returning to bed and waiting for the dawn light to creep in and right the world, which it occurred to her she had so carelessly shut outside. This was another fix for a better time, for someone better suited to the job than her. But as she turned her back on the window, a familiar sound arrested her. The low but sharp-edged crinkle and crackle of something plastic, something wet and unfurling.

Flushed with fresh adrenaline, she swept the candle around the kitchen and the living room. The shadows lurched and danced but there was nothing she wasn't expecting; there was nothing wrong or out of place.

She returned to the window and held the candle close. As she watched, the darkness buckled, then shifted. It wasn't the night sky outside at all, it was something large and dark and flat that inched its way across the glass, rucking into creases and crackling as it went. Bunching itself up to move onwards with the patient slowness of a slug, the lithe inexplicability of a snake.

And if *she* could see *it*, then it stood to reason that *it* could see *her*.

She ripped the curtains closed again. She took a breath and held it. The sound sparkled like dying static. From the window. The door. The outside wall. She understood she was surrounded, but that was nothing new. The flat had always been surrounded, by the outside, by the city, by everyone, everything else.

I like it this way, she had said.

It wasn't bravery that took her to her front door and set her hand upon the handle. It wasn't quite anger, either. It was something else. A familiar exhaustion, perhaps. A weariness, an impatience.

She gripped the handle and opened the door wide.

Outside was black. The same measure of thick, unsparing blackness as the window. There was nothing else, no light, no breeze, barely a sense she had opened the *inside* to the *outside* at all. Ruth took another breath to steady herself, then she reached out her hand.

It was hard to tell where the darkness was. The further she pushed her hand outwards, the more she was certain her fingers would come against *something*, but it wasn't until her hand was fully outstretched that she felt something cool, dampened by rain; something solid but supple beneath her fingertips. She brushed the surface gently and the sound it made was plastic, a tarpaulin sheet, a light and brittle skin.

She thought of her dream of suffocation. She thought of the figure she had seen beneath the tree. She thought of Mr Carter when she had seen him last.

'Tell her,' he had said. 'Tell her I want to be alone.'

Ruth withdrew her hand as though it had been stung.

'No,' she said. Her voice was soft, but there was an authority to it that surprised and strengthened her. 'No, thank you.'

A trace of wind rippled the tarpaulin, it snapped lightly against the door frame.

'I'm sorry,' Ruth said. 'I don't want you.'

And she closed her eyes.

Did she hear anything? Only the thudding of her heart, only the roar of blood in her ears. She closed her eyes so tight her whole body shrieked inside. And when she opened them again, the street was there as it should be. House and trees and fence-line all present and correct. Everything was grey and dusty blue in the early morning half-light, the yellow fringes of the dawn bruising the edges of the sky. Somewhere in the park she could hear birdsong: a bright call, a brighter response.

As she closed the door, she felt unaccountably tired. She extinguished the candle and returned to her bedroom. From somewhere there was the faint smell of drains, but she resolved to investigate when the morning had matured and she was more fully awake. Until then, she climbed into bed and pulled the covers up and over her.

They crackled like plastic and held her close.

THE LIGHTNESS OF THEIR HEARTS

GEORGINA BRUCE

They arrive by car in the middle of the long night. They are one of each kind: a man, and a woman with an infant clinging to her breast. Although it is night, and will be so for the next several hundred hours, the house is lit by a silver luminescence, a pool of light that does not extend to the dusty plains beyond: a pale shining bubble of light in a black field sprinkled with thousands of icy stars.

The man pushes open the gate in the white picket fence around the house, and carries their suitcases up the path. The woman follows the man through the front door, which has stained-glass roses in the windows. They enter the wee sitting room, where a fire burns, and a sofa is piled with cushions and blankets. It is designed to be cosy. But the woman stands at the window, holding the rose-patterned curtains to one side, looking out into the vast tenebrous night.

'Don't look,' says the man, whose name is N35i-Pickering. The woman calls him Bob. Her name is N35a-Pickering, but among other humans she is known as Alice. They are ordinary names for their time and milieu. They are ordinary humans: she, dark-skinned and taller than average. He, light-skinned, tall, and slightly paunchy. Both of them have lived four decades and a year.

The baby squalls and wrestles in Alice's arms, and she passes it to Bob while she arranges herself on the couch, unbuttoning her dress.

'I hope the journey, the conditions, didn't affect my milk,' she says.

Bob passes her the baby. She feeds it from her breast, as humans do. The fire keeps them warm. Bob draws the curtains together and it is as though the sky outside does not exist.

'Everything is roses,' says Alice, looking around the room.

'You see?' Bob beams at her. 'Everything is copacetic.'

'I wish you wouldn't use that ridiculous word,' says Alice. And the baby gives a little hiccup.

> • <

In the eight-hour, Bob goes to work. He leaves the house and drives away in the car. Alice and the baby watch him leave. The darkness swallows him, gulps him down.

Alice turns on the television but it doesn't work. It is only for show. Every channel is inky black, churning with the echoes of space. The baby cries.

In the kitchen, which we have stocked with edible gels and shakes, Alice sits the baby on the table and counts its fingers and toes, saying a little rhyme as she does so, raising her voice over the sounds of the baby's screams.

She walks the baby around the house, up and down the stairs. She jiggles the baby on her hip and names all the things they can see. *This is the table, this is the bed, this is the intralunar transceiver – I don't think it's working – and this is a mirror! Look at you! Who's that? Who's that little baby?*

The baby cries. Alice changes its nappy, feeds it, strokes its back, puts it in the cot, picks it up again. She does these things in rotation, filling the eight-hour with nappy changes, feeds, attempts at sleep. The baby screams, howls, whimpers and wails.

Alice cries.

When Bob comes home, Alice is waiting for him at the front door. The moment he steps inside, she plonks the baby into his arms. The baby stops crying.

'Oh hey, sweetie,' says Bob. 'I'm done in. This is some project! I just need ten minutes then I'll mind the baby.'

'No,' says Alice. 'If you don't take the baby right now, it's over between us. I'm serious. I'll go back to Earth and you can do this stupid experiment by yourself.'

> • <

The darkness is total, a complete engulfing obscurity. Alice drives fast, foot pressing hard on the gas pedal. The headlights illuminate nothing but blackness ahead. The radio crackles with static. There's no station to tune in to. We can only imagine what Alice is thinking.

After some time, during which she cries and then stops crying, she makes out a pale bubble of light in the darkness ahead of her. It's a house, like her house, sitting in its puddle of luminescence. It is like her house, but larger; softer, somehow. There are hazy balloons of light drifting around it, like lanterns swaying in the darkness.

She drives towards the light, but the ground beneath her wheels seems to swerve away, and although she points the car directly towards where she wants to go, it never gets any closer, and in fact, the more determinedly she drives towards the house, the further it recedes away from her. A trick of the moon.

She says, 'I wonder if it's like Alice trying to get into the garden,' an utterance we don't understand, and she turns the steering wheel and drives away from the house, into the darkness. Soon, the house appears in front of her, large and bright. The fence is strung with glowing baubles, but they're not baubles, they're babies, big fat naked babies, floating like lanterns, waving their arms and legs, leaving trails of light. They're secured to the fence by ribbons tied to their ankles. Pink for the girls and blue for the boys.

Alice stops the car. She gets out and walks past the babies, and up the path to the house. The front door has stained-glass daisies in the windows. She doesn't knock at the door, but instead peers in through the sitting-room window. The curtains are patterned with daisies. It is just like Alice's own sitting room, except it's all daisies instead of roses, and it seems empty. It seems as though no one is there. Then Alice looks up and sees a man lying on the ceiling, smiling down into the wee cosy room. The man, whose name is PQ12i-Kimble, is naked. His genitals dangle softly down. He bobs around the lightshade. He holds his hands down to the fire. When he turns his head towards the window, Alice ducks and runs away, past the gurgling babies, back to the safety of the car.

> • <

Back home, Alice asks Bob how the baby is.

'Any problems?'

'A few tears,' says Bob. 'Nothing major.'

He hands Alice her sweet, sleepy baby. Alice looks from Bob to the baby, and back again.

'Is it just me,' says Alice, 'or does the baby seem a little bigger?'

Bob grins. He walks ahead of Alice up the stairs, his feet lightly grazing the carpet.

'And lighter,' says Alice. 'It definitely feels less weighty than before.'

'I hope you feel better now,' Bob says. 'I hope you don't want to leave me anymore. I want to have more babies with you. Don't you think it would be lovely?'

They go into the bedroom, where the bed is covered with a rose-patterned quilt. The baby's cot is next to the bed, on Alice's side. Bob lies down and his body sinks into the soft bedcovers, making Alice roll slightly towards him. She smiles and rests her head on his shoulder.

'I won't leave you,' Alice says. 'I don't think so, anyway.' She strokes her tummy, which is already swelling, making room for the nub of life.

Alice drives to the daisy house as often as she can, even when it becomes difficult to wedge her growing body behind the steering wheel, even when her walk up the path becomes a waddle.

The babies tied to the fence grow bigger, but not older. They grow swollen, like fat luminous balloons. Alice hums a popular Christmas song to herself, although it is not Christmas, never Christmas. She gently pokes one of the babies as she walks past, and it giggles and sends light swaying back and forth in the darkness. Inside the house, PQ12i-Kimble floats past the window. His laughter creeps out underneath the curtains, seeps into the night.

When Alice returns home, Bob drifts down the stairs towards her. He kisses her cheek. He pats her enormous stomach. He is holding the baby, but when he leans towards Alice he lets go of it, and the baby floats between them.

'It will soon be time to tie the baby to the fence,' says Bob. 'Pink or blue? I'll get the ribbon.'

When he goes upstairs, he has to hold the banister to stop himself from falling up towards the ceiling.

> • <

The new baby cries and cries. It feeds from Alice's breasts and her nipples crack. Alice cries. She changes the baby's nappy and strokes its back and tries to make it sleep in the cot or resting on her shoulder. She jiggles it on her hip and walks it around the house and names everything they see. *Here's the mirror, look see? And here's roses on the curtains. Here's the intralunar transceiver – useless fucking thing – and here's the cupboard where we keep the tablets and gels and here's a box of pink and blue ribbons and here's the packed suitcase I keep behind the front door but it doesn't matter because we're not going anywhere anyway, and please stop crying, please stop, please.*

The baby doesn't stop crying.

When Bob comes home after the eight-hour and settles in the sitting room, Alice follows after him. She hurls the baby up towards the ceiling and Bob reaches down to catch it.

'Alice!' he reprimands her.

'I don't care,' says Alice. 'I hate it here.'

'Don't be like that,' says Bob. 'I love you. You're doing so well.'

The next eight-hour, he doesn't go to work. He floats about the house. He lies on the ceiling, chortling to himself. He holds the baby and the baby doesn't cry. The baby laughs.

'See?' Bob says. 'You'll get used to it. You'll feel better when the night is over. Only a couple hundred more hours and everything will be... copacetic.' He laughs, and dandles the baby. 'Copacetic,' he says, and the baby giggles.

'I can't,' says Alice. We wait for the rest of her sentence, her explanation. But she doesn't give it. She takes the suitcase from behind the front door and she leaves the house. She staggers down the path, past the bright sweet baby floating above the fence, bobbing and kicking against its pink ribbon. Alice gets into the car and drives away.

> • <

There are more babies tied to the fence of the daisy house now, smaller babies. The original ones are big bulbous babies, almost ready to harvest. Their arms and legs are sunk into their round moonlike bodies. Their faces are wide with toothless smiles. They strain and bob against their ribbon ties, as if telling us they are ready to ascend and take their places in the sky.

Alice sidles between two big babies tied either side of the gate, and tiptoes up the path towards the house. Through the sitting-room window, the man can be seen, pirouetting in the updraft of the blazing fire, his genitals weakly flapping in the warmth of the air.

Alice startles at the sound of the front door opening. A woman's voice calls out, 'Who's there?'

The woman, who is called PQ12a-Kimble, or Diane for short, says, 'I know someone is there. Someone must be there. Who's there?'

'It's just me,' says Alice, and she steps into the light of the open doorway, so Diane can see her.

Diane says, 'Oh, it's just you, is that right?'

And with a sudden gust of exhaled breath, the two women laugh. They seem to erupt into laughter, and then it seems they are unable to stop. Their laughter echoes in the big sky. They laugh for a long time, choking back tears as they cling to each other's arms, collapse against each other's bodies. It is strange; we don't understand their laughter.

When they finally stop laughing, Diane slips back inside the daisy house, and steps out again a moment later with her suitcase. Alice takes it from her, and the women walk to the car together and get in, and drive away. We don't know where they're going.

The babies floating above the fence gurgle and giggle. The man on the ceiling chortles to himself. We understand *their* laughter: it is normal to laugh on the moon.

THE RESIDENTIAL

GARY BUDDEN

That evening, everything collapsed.

Crackling speakers began intoning wearily. A points failure at Colindale. We should be moving shortly when we hear further information. Thank you for your patience.

When I thought of Colindale it summoned images of an eternal desert, suburban housing and grey streets punctuated by the sad dribble of Silk Stream and dirtied by the endless fumes from the M1. I'd worked there, years back.

Okay. These things happen, I reasoned. It shouldn't be long. Hold tight, don't stress out.

How many times has this happened now?

Twenty minutes were spent at Golders Green huddled with fellow travellers on the train, like wartime refugees but without the thrill of any conflict. I often dreamed of bombs ripping open the city, of something happening, but of course nothing ever did. I enjoyed reading the literature of London from the Blitz years – fear, but a sense of liberation too, a place and time where different rules applied.

The doors to the carriage were open, a freezing wind flinging droplets of water inside. Optimistic arrivals squeezed into the packed and silent carriage.

Did you know more of the underground is actually overground?

Minutes ticked by, the carriage and platform both thickening like a clogged, fatty artery. People coughed, fiddled intently with their phones, began huffing and rolling their eyes. But they were unwilling to leave the carriage, to cede space to any of the incomers. We all knew things could change at any moment, the train lurching and shuddering suddenly into life to perform its solitary purpose. There was a damp smell, like wet dog and old sweat and crushed cigarette butts.

Nothing. Whatever the problem at Colindale was, it was not going to sort itself. Failure.

That crackly voice again, dull and with a tinge of despair. That was it, it said. Off you get, line down. Make your own way home. Fuck you.

I stepped off the carriage. Out on the platform, I pushed past two baffled-looking Charedi dragging giant suitcases. You're going nowhere, I thought, with a cruel joy. A Chinese tourist in a facemask stood mutely in front of the Tube map in the blind hope it would reveal its secrets. No one assisted her.

I could have told those entering the station, as I exited, what the situation was. Turn back, don't bother, it isn't working. But they could find out themselves, like we all have to. You're alone, always. Sort it out yourself. And anyway, they'd think me a madman if I tried to help them.

Up the stairs and through the barriers and out into the open. It was pissing down with fat cold rain, the sky above north-west London grey like the skin of a persistent smoker blooming with dark bruises from a deserved beating. As a National Express coach hissed through the torrent, I allowed myself to be soaked by the polluted water. The faces of long-distance travellers were pressed up against the coach's windows, features twisted sickly by the condensation. Malformed eyes regarded the commotion around the station.

As the coach pulled away, the nagging voice started up. Always with the fucking questions.

Is this all for nothing?

This is all there is. We keep going, don't we?

Even when the lines are down?

Even when the lines are down.

Unfurled umbrellas brushed my face, the metal tips threating to dig into or lacerate an eyeball. A vivid red umbrella grazed my face, showering droplets into my beard; a ferrule scraped my ear. No one said sorry, if they even noticed. I did not begrudge them that. I would not apologise. People who did were weak and not made for this city.

Do you really mean that?

Sometimes, yeah, I do.

Chin up, son.

The bus station adjacent to the station was a desperate scrum. I thought I could smell burning plastic. My instincts were welling up, to run and run and keep running from this awful place, this city. Out of the rain, finally, to find somewhere safe and dry.

Nowhere is safe, not really.

That's true. But there are moments, happy times. Times when we are secure. If we feel it, it's kind of true, right?

If you say so.

The banality of the situation made all this so much worse. No one was fleeing anything or escaping persecution; there were no stories of heroism to be gained from everyday nightmares. We just wanted to get home so we could go to work again tomorrow. So we could keep going. In the dead light of a November early evening, my face raw from the ferule and rivulets of cold rain sliding down my back, it was hard to imagine anything better from life.

No buses appeared. The rain fell.

It made a person realise how quickly all of this, the city, the country, would fall apart if something truly went wrong. How long would we wait at the bus stop after we knew the game was up? The people of London would queue until eternity took us, standing in line even as they saw the mushroom clouds rise above the tower blocks and glass skyscrapers.

I debated summoning a taxi via my app, and checked my phone. Surge pricing. Then a surge of anger, you fucking bastards, charging the best part of forty quid to get the few miles home.

This is what you get in your neoliberal hell that you choose to live in.

I agree. Look at these commuter plebs, they just suck it up. Standing in line like pigs for slaughter.

Yet you stand with them.

I could see the anger inside of them, like rusted and twisted metal. Would they ever do anything to try and change all this? Maybe they'd cheat hard on a partner or get into the coke and booze.

Perhaps they would find veganism and hit the gym and read pacifying books about the inherent worth of the individual. We're all worth it.

A bit harsh?

Of course it is, I go to the gym myself.

They could blog successfully about their anxiety and Instagram as many pictures as they liked of them living a full and fulfilling life, but we would all still be trapped here at Golders Green in the rain waiting for a red bus that would never come.

Reality is waiting for a bus.

Ha, good one.

This is the kind of shit that gives you an ulcer. This is cancerous.

You're joking, but it's true.

I pictured tumours blooming like coral under my skin.

I looked in all directions. A collage of angry blaring horns, red lights flecked with rainwater, gridlock. People huddled like shivering sheep under the bus shelter trying to avoid the pelting rain. To think of the crowd as one bleak homogenous mass was unfair. What predators lurked there? A common question that preoccupied me was the degree of proximity I had come to, unknowingly, serial killers, paedophiles, rapists, wife beaters, trafficked girls, and so on. Did one lurk in the animal crowd right now? The chances were high, right?

That guy there with the cheap Primark shoes and the Tesco bag. He looks like a sex offender. Probably a nonce.

No more. Enough of this. Start walking and get away from here.

It was about three miles home from where I was. More than doable, I'd do three or four times that if I'd selected walking as the day's leisure activity. But it was hard for it not to be depressing after a long day at the office, after the wasted and impotent moments at the station, waiting for something to happen. It's the wasted time that wears you down. You cannot seize the day when you are stuck due to points failure. I had tried mindfulness, and only became more aware of the reality of my surroundings.

But walking – walking was good for the emotions, good for the body, good for the mind. Take a walk to clear your head, don't they say, and London was a city that could reveal its mysteries if you went on foot. The city could offer antidotes to all the abuses it heaped on its populace, if you knew how to find them.

I crossed at the traffic lights, vehicles snarled and shrieking either side, and hit the main road before quickly diving into the back streets. I had finally quit cigarettes six months back, summoned periodically by a nurse to blow into a contraption that measured the level of carbon monoxide in my blood. On one occasion, the reading had gone up when it should have gone down; I hadn't had a cigarette in over eight weeks by that point. Noticing my surprise, the nurse had asked did I walk here along the main road?

Yes.

It's the fumes from the traffic. That's why we should all be driving electric cars, or walking.

I liked that nurse. For weeks after I would watch cyclists in the city at busy intersections, getting fit and cutting down on pollution and contracting nasty lung diseases for their effort.

It was liberating, to be away from the station and the wet faces of stranded commuters. I didn't know the back streets here well, but I knew which direction I was going, and I could easily summon a map up on my phone if it was required.

Dark had fallen. Away from the main artery the streets were nearly deserted and lit weakly by sporadic streetlamps.

I walked for an hour or so, headphones in, listening to forgotten songs from the nineties.

Where are you?

I am only ever here.

Seriously, mate, I think you're lost.

I thought I was somewhere near the RAF Museum, Hendon way. But as I removed my headphones and looked around me, the streets were dark and unfamiliar, unknowable and stripped of meaning. I fished my phone out of my pocket and summoned up the digital map, but as I did so, the battery died on me.

You idiot.

I walked for another hour at least through residential streets, some of the houses pebble-dashed and others more modern. All had cars parked on their drives and neat, small front gardens. Many had UPVC windows and they all looked safe, secure and able to resist the slights of the outside world. I imagined how warm they would be inside, the central heating acting as a welcome soporific. Inside, I would lock and bolt the doors and enable the alarm system. Then I would turn up the central heating to its maximum and luxuriate in my suburban palace.

These were houses you could be proud of, as quiet as you can get in London. They were a measure of some sort of success. Yet none of them appeared occupied. No lights in the houses were on, no telltale flickers of television. The streets had been emptied of life, too; I walked them alone.

I wondered what happened to the people at Golders Green. Did their bus arrive? I hoped they all made it home, somehow.

Finally, I reached a street which had the slightest hint of familiarity, from my days working in Colindale. I felt as if I was getting closer to something.

At the end of this street, a single windowpane was illuminated by a bright light within, and I headed towards it. There was little else I could think to do, and anyway, the walk had cheered me up a little.

REPLACEMENT BUS SERVICE

ASHLEY STOKES

The cab driver still stares: itchy and twitchy, extremely annoyed. Georgia is her calmest since the text. Purse open on lap, she continues to hold out her hand. She knows she must look red-eyed and shattered as she waits for her change. She does want her change, though. Insists.

The central locking clunks. The driver shoulders the door. He pours out, looms beside her, mutters a cuss, tugs open her door.

The fare was ten pounds.

It comes back to her: she has already paid him. Ten pounds. Exactly.

She shuffles out, drags her rucksack across the seat, says nothing.

The day is white. A nothing day. A white nothing.

The station lobby: sprawling scrum at the self-service ticket machines. Two of the four don't seem to be working but people queue for them anyway, then barge into the other lines. A riot atmosphere. Georgia doesn't want to be in the middle of it. She joins a long queue in the ticket office. On the departures board above the desk, orange words next to her destination flash the most depressing phrase in the English language: Replacement Bus Service.

Now she will be late. Usually a three-hour train journey, it could end up being four, even five. She'd left as quickly as she could. The text appeared at 4:46. She'd showered and stuffed a change of clothes into a rucksack. Not for her. For Inge.

Inge is back in the dunes, hiding. The dunes are quite a walk from the station at the other end. And now: delays, detours, replacement bus service.

The queue for tickets edges forward at a caterpillar's pace. Right in front of her are two tall men in black parkas, both bald. Identical black duffel bags hang from their shoulders. One of them grumbles to the ticket seller: '…do you know what urgent means? What do you mean, you can't? You can… Of course you can… You can't? You can.'

Meanwhile, the other one oinks like a pig. The ticket seller flinches at each grunt. In the end, they buy their tickets without doing her any of the mischief they promised.

After Georgia buys her ticket and has her own gripe about the replacement bus service, she finds herself bang-smack behind them. She follows their duffel bags out of the station. As they approach the hulking black bus, she notices a red triangular logo on both bags. It reminds her of the red triangle she never wants to see or hear about again. She will hear about it again, in the dunes or thereabouts. Until then, she'll blank it out.

The big bald men look like brothers. They refuse to hand over their duffel bags so the driver can load them into the luggage hold. They climb onto the bus. Georgia follows them. To put as much distance as possible between them and her, she lets the duffel bags ooze up the aisle. She takes a place three up from the driver and stands her rucksack on the seat next to her, hoping to deter anyone from sitting there. A replacement bus service is only bearable when faced alone.

The bus is nearly full. Those bald guys – she's starting to think of them as The Siblings – have managed to occupy the back of the bus. A good two thirds of the other passengers are old: white men and grey women. Standing out are a young guy in blue, mirrored visor-like sunglasses; a girl in her late teens who pulls back the tresses of her hair as she takes a selfie with a pink phone; a thickly moustachioed hipster type with one of those hole-in-the-lobe disc earrings that make Georgia feel sick, already sunk into a book the title of which she can't see; a woman with a very round face; a kid with a strapping, US-marine-like vibe asleep against the window; and a dark-haired young woman who looks a little too much like Inge.

The driver clambers aboard and takes the wheel. The bus revs. The anxiety Georgia has felt that someone wants to sit next to her eases. The driver announces that his name is Ronnie. He spiels some safety instructions and promises anyone who lights up a cigarette or vapes on an e-cigarette will be dumped on the kerbside and abandoned to the sort of people who pick up hitchhikers around here. The bus pulls out of the station. The radio comes on. Local radio. The worst kind of radio. Something FM. Nowhere FM. A DJ called Kelly Kenyatta, who sounds like she's about to explode from all her pent-up pep and enthusiasm, announces that we're going on a long, long, beautiful joyride through the hits of 1989 – the year Georgia was born – starting with

'Americanos' by Holly Johnson, yee-haw, praise the Lord and pass the ammunition.

> • <

By the time 'Buffalo Stance' by Neneh Cherry plays, the bus is rattling along the dual carriageway and Georgia is trying to zone out the oinks from the back of the bus. If it isn't one of The Siblings pigging it up, it's the other. She wants to shout at them to stop. The others on the bus must want them to stop, too, and resent Ronnie for letting them get away with it. He should speak to them. One of the others should speak to them. She can't speak to them. They wouldn't listen to her. No one listens to her, apart from, sometimes, Inge.

The bus passes a diner, its forecourt empty of cars, its sign swinging in the wind, its logo… She can't swear it… she'll never go back to check, but that sign: red triangle. Not any old red triangle. *That* red triangle. The red triangle with the red aligned slant hovering at its left side. Inge's triangle.

She must now overwhelmingly associate Inge with the red triangle and its aligned slant on its left side. It is sad. The triangle intrudes on her memories of their time together. Inge first told her about it after she found the red triangle secretly stamped on all the boxes and bottles in the stockroom, sewed into the linings of their uniforms, and daubed on the back of the painting of the shipwreck in their chalet. At first it was a hushed joke between them. Later, a threat. By then, who it represented had been named: Arpeggio.

It surprised Georgia that Inge hadn't quit first, or packed in the job when Georgia left, that she'd stuck it out working the bar of the Silver Rose.

Maybe she hadn't. Maybe she resigned soon after Georgia, or more likely the management let her go. Yesterday she went back, though, returned to the Silver Rose to have it out with them, a final confrontation with Arpeggio.

The Silver Rose: a casino at the end of a titty bar and chip shop seafront, the only attraction in a semi-derelict North Sea resort abandoned to the washed-up and burnt-out and loved only by the dead.

The Silver Rose. She tells herself now it was a temporary job, she was only going to stay for a summer, though at the time she'd fully expected her placement there to lead to a career. It was not enough to work in the bar. She wanted to manage the bar, then maybe own the bar and somehow grow a franchise of bars elsewhere, maybe called Georgia's or GT Georgia. Or maybe she could try for something more stylish and become a croupier. She could wear a bow tie and waistcoat and spin a wheel. Maybe if she made it as a croupier, a counting, smiling, hip-sidling croupier, she could end up running a casino one day. Or she could end up running a casino after hopping streams to work in security, in-house detective Georgia Robinson, the eyes and ears of the Silver Rose, watching the hustlers and grifters, the scam artists, the drunken degenerates and degenerate gamblers.

She'd worked the bar of the Silver Rose. She fixed shorts and cocktails for the men who came in from the tables with their silent women. She poured beer for the men who came in from the machines on their own. She wore a pale blue outfit with matching gloves and cap that was an imitation of a French airhostess uniform from the 1960s. She worked nights. During the daytime, she slept in a chalet at the edge of the dunes. She would return to the chalet at daybreak. In the summer, she would sit on the step, bare feet buried in the sand, cup of tea, cigarette, the sun rising over the dunes, the rustle and rush of the sea. It was over. Some of it was over, at least.

She must have been working there close to a year when Inge arrived.

Ingeborg Erin Soo.

Such a striking and beautiful name, the first thing Georgia thought when they introduced the new bartender, the one they'd promised so Georgia would not be alone behind the bar and outnumbered by the punters. It was certainly more fun working with Inge. She had a way of beguiling and baffling the clientele.

Inge told the man in the sharkskin suit she was from Denmark, the island of Lindholm, a special, holy place where the sky and sea kiss and melt into one another. The man they called Scary Hamsters Super Creeps she convinced she was an Innuit from Nunavut in the far north of Canada. He didn't know the difference between an Innuit and an Armpit (as was explained to him after he'd bought each of them a Brandy Alexander for after they knocked off). She let the King of Drift know that her old man was inside for a twenty-two stretch but had a geezer with a Glock in every port from Southend to Scarborough (so keep your tentacles on that side of the bar, Mr Octopiss-Take). She explained to the singer from the house band, Cat Jericho and the Mucky Chickens, that his songs took her back to a sad place that was hot and dusty, where in the summer the locals performed the rite with the flails and the streets slicked with their blood. If she'd wanted to scare him away, she scared him away.

She made those long nights pouring drinks for the out of luck and out of control more bearable, almost an adventure. Until the one they called The Anaesthetist followed Inge back to the dunes wearing a surgical facemask. After that, she and Georgia shared a chalet.

Before shifts, or if the casino was empty, if it was midweek and no one had come in from the refinery or the tankers, they would wander together the long corridors of the Silver Rose, its gaping chambers, its upstairs bedrooms where no one slept, its unused offices. They would always end up outside the nerve centre on the top floor where they kept the safe and the surveillance screens, where the management and the tough guys cracked their jokes about the low rollers and those they called the spindrifters. Here, Inge would whisper what she had discovered about the Silver Rose on that particular sweep: the story of the 1922 St Crispin's Day Massacre; the man who bet his bride at roulette and lost; what happened to the Smuts Gang and their hirelings soon after; the reign of Miss Deck, Queen of the Upper Rooms during what came to be known as the Rose Period; the Mods and the Rockers they let in but wouldn't let out in '64, and the continuing story of The Room No One Has Ever Seen.

When she started to talk incessantly about the red Arpeggio triangle with the aligned slant on its left side, that's when Georgia should have known something was wrong, that she should have encouraged Inge to leave and/ or get some help, someone proper to talk to, someone who wasn't Georgia, someone Inge wasn't keeping awake all day who needed to sleep because she worked long nights in a strip-lit and airless cockpit of a bar that crawled with sleazers and bankrupts.

> • <

Oink. Oink. 'Batdance' by Prince is playing. Georgia blinks. Her mouth is dry like she's been asleep but she's not been asleep. She's just been... worried. The replacement bus has stopped. It's sitting in traffic. Stuck. Snarled. Jammed. Not even sure how long it has been like this.

Oink. Oink.

Georgia props herself up and peers over the seat in front of her. Beyond Ronnie the Driver, from the windscreen to the horizon the traffic is at a standstill. The sky is slate grey. The broken end of a rainbow sinks into distant hills. For a moment, it feels like everyone is stalled here waiting for their legendary gold. She swings around and tries not to make eye-contact with Sibling Oink and Sibling Oink on the rear seats. Out back, the traffic is solid too, the roofs of the cars like the scales of a basking metal snake. It must have been like this for a while. She didn't notice the rain when it was raining. Droplets still trickle and combine on the window glass next to her. Outside, on the verge, a family have decamped from their car. The man lights a cigarette. He looks like a friendly walrus. Mrs Friendly Walrus is taking two small boys by the hand towards a gate that bars the way to what could be a farm track. She opens the gate and ushers the children through. Georgia loses sight of them.

'We Didn't Start the Fire' by Billy Joel is playing, a song too fast for slow times.

This is bad. Very bad. They could be stuck here for ages. The replacement bus service has already added hours to the journey. It could now take all day to reach the dunes. Georgia has no idea what supplies Inge has, if she has something to eat and drink, if she is hurt, if she has slept, if she's been bothered, or if this is all for nothing because they have found her already.

They will be after her if she did what she said she did yesterday. Or the police may well be trying to find her for her own safety, just as Georgia is – in theory – dashing across the country for Inge's safety.

She should never have left Inge while she was still seeing the red triangle everywhere – in the ice cubes, on their cufflinks, behind their eyes – the triangle she insisted was the symbol of an interdimensional crime syndicate called Arpeggio that was planning world domination from the security office of the Silver Rose. The locked room, the room with the safe and the monitors, also accessed eight other portals to eight other Silver Roses in Asuncion, Reno, Pretoria, Ekaterinburg, Goa, Geneva, Izmir and Okinawa. A.R.P.E.G.G.I.O.: Arpeggio: The Compiler, The Vex Prismatic, Spider Eyes of the Multitudinous Worlds. They were making plans. They were coming for us. We know too much, Georgia. They know we know, Georgia. Georgia, they know! They know about us!

Georgia had not slept properly for a month. She left… not on a whim, but suddenly. She soon found a job working in an off-licence. A tiny shop. Out of the way. A few afternoon shifts. No uniform, but the boredom clung to her like a wet sheet. She had been there for four months at least and not contacted or been contacted by Inge until 4:46 this morning. She shouldn't have left the Silver Rose like that. Inge had no one, no one to talk her out of confronting Arpeggio.

Yesterday, Inge broke into the security office of the Silver Rose armed with pepper spray and an aerosol can of red paint. She'd held the room long enough to deface as many of the monitors as possible with red paint before they forced her out.

Poor Inge.

'Miss you Much', Janet Jackson.

Oink.

Oink.

Sibling Oink and Sibling Oink are lumbering along the aisle. Georgia turns to the window and hunches up. The Friendly Walrus family have vanished from the verge. They've left the gate open. The Siblings say nothing to Georgia as they pass on their way to Driver Ronnie. Miles away, Driver Ronnie is thumbing the screen of his phone. One of the Siblings Oink pokes him in the shoulder. Ronnie startles, looks up.

'Right, driver, this is it. As we said to one of your colleagues this morning, me and my counterpart here are on urgent business. Very urgent business. Very urgent business that just won't wait. Urgent. Do you know what urgent means? The meaning of urgency? We can see the situation here.' The Sibling Oink who is talking sweeps his arm at the traffic jam.

The other one points towards the track at the roadside. 'And we see a solution there.'

The gate is still open. Georgia did not see Mrs Friendly Walrus return with the Friendly Walrus children. The Friendly Walrus himself could have gone to look for them. They could have all escaped up the track, run from the traffic jam, like Sibling Oink and Sibling Oink were suggesting. The Friendly Walrus could have followed his wife and children up that path. If he had, he would have abandoned his car, and if his car had been in front of the replacement bus, the replacement bus would be trapped here until a tow truck came. All the while Inge would be hiding in the dunes in a terrible and vulnerable state and Georgia is already hours late.

'Gentlemen,' says Driver Ronnie, 'you need to sit down, please.' He picks up a handset and speaks over the PA. 'Ladies and gentlemen, as you can see, we're not exactly moving. Radio says two miles ahead they're waiting for an air ambulance. As soon as I have any information, I'll let you know. Please stay in your seats and sorry for the inconvenience.'

'Now, Mr Driver,' says one of the Siblings Oink, 'we thought you were a bright spark.'

'And we know this land like the backs of our hands,' says the other.

'We've seen it low and we've seen it rise.'

'And rise it will, believe us.'

'We know all the cuts and backways, the forgotten lanes, the uplands, and that yonder path will allow us to hare from all this mess and metal and gift us to freedom, to where we urgently need to be, and also set these good people on their way. What say you, Driver?'

'Sit down, sir, please return to your seat.'

One of the Siblings swipes the handset.

'Fair people, good people of the bus. Hear this: you all know we are stuck. This jam may last forever. My counterpart and I have been talking to fair driverman, whose opinion it is that we tarry here until the day plays to dusk. No, say we. Down there, up that path, lies open land where we may coast and show this devilish accumulation of carriages a fair pair of heels. Let us put this to a show of hands?'

'Give that back,' says Ronnie. 'This is not your bus. Sit down and—'

Oink, oink. The one without the handset shoves Ronnie with the flat of his palm.

'Show of hands, now,' the one with the handset commands.

Georgia pulls herself up and scans the passengers, who until now she has to admit she's forgotten existed. If Inge were here she would not have stayed in her seat. She'd have been mixing and mingling, getting to know everyone's names and what they do. She'd know already that the young guy is called Ken K and is some kind of archivist in some kind of archive of all our past lives and alternative guises; the girl with the pink phone is a rapper called Mimi the Meme who'll never make it (for obvious reasons); the hipster with the 'tache-and-disc-earring combo sunk in a book called *Mother Night* is the Loss Adjuster, or Max Tantalus (it depends); the woman with a very round face is The Moon (distant, chalky, tidal); the kid with a strapping, US-marine-like vibe once asleep against the window but now very much awake is Jack Page (close friends get to call him Malkuth, Ten of Wands); and the dark-haired young woman who looks too much like Inge, Inge would call The Fake and shun.

A lot of them are not putting up their hands. A lot of them are saying no to leaving the road, more it would seem than the old duffers who have their hands in the air and somehow trust the word of the Siblings Oink.

Georgia is thirsty. Her mouth is so dry that if she wanted to say something she'd struggle to get the words out when this is the time to speak, the time to stand up and be the spokesperson for the people of the replacement bus. The bus might be stuck, but why take a blind exit on the say-so of these men? Why leap in the dark when darkness can darken still? She unzips her rucksack and without fully opening it reaches inside for the plastic water bottle she was sure she'd packed earlier.

Up ahead, one of the Siblings Oink is counting hands. Georgia can see his lips move as he counts. He doesn't finish the count. He doesn't nod at Georgia or anyone near her as he doesn't get as far as recording their votes. He stops, grins.

'Leave the road it is.'

An objecting voice from over Georgia's shoulder. A woman questions the vote. A Sibling Oink slouches up the aisle past Georgia. There's a thud and the objecting woman stops talking mid-sentence.

Gasps. General muttering. Georgia is still rummaging in the rucksack. She can't find her water bottle. The Sibling Oink with the handset says, 'Now, to be fair it was a close-run vote, and as such it would be only just that those who do not want travel up the yonder track to freedom should dismount now.'

No one says anything. No one moves. The bus's engine turns over. The chassis buzzes. The Sibling Oink has his hand on Driver Ronnie's shoulder. Driver Ronnie turns the wheel sharply to the right and bus mounts the verge, heads for the gate.

Georgia spins the rucksack over and opens it on her lap. No wonder she couldn't find any water. There's no water bottle, only a red summer dress wrapped around an aerosol can of lava-red paint and a mini-pepper spray.

'Swing the Mood', Jive Bunny.

Oink.

Oink.

> • <

The bus shudders along a gravel track through flat farmland. Brown crops ripple beneath a sky the colour of pewter. During 'If You Don't Know Me By Now' by Simply Red, the radio signal weakens, starts to break up. There are farm buildings – barns, outhouses, silos – but no sight of farm people or farm animals. When 'Right Here Waiting For You' by Richard Marx fades out, if anything, the sky has further dimensions to its vastness. Expanse of yellow rape. Concrete water tower like a UFO on a stick. Huge turbines spin in the distance. Every so often a small factory or engineering works that seems to have been picked up and dropped from a height to crack open on the ground and spill its shattered perimeters into the dirt. Brambles dragging a burnt-out chip van from the roadside into a thicket. A field with one wind-gnarled tree. Halfway through 'Baby Don't Forget My Number' by Milli Vanilli, the radio dies.

Silence presides as the bus trundles across a dustbowl landscape scarred by dried-out drainage ditches. A broken-down combine harvester sits out in the middle of a great patch of nothing, like the remains of some mammoth or mastodon.

And all the while, as all this terrain passes by, Georgia is trying to retrace her steps.

She'd felt the calmest she had felt since the text message when she was sitting in the cab and demanding her change. There, the frantic concern she'd felt for Inge when the text arrived had subsided. She was pretty clear then that she had received the message, showered, readied herself, packed and called a cab to meet the earliest train.

Now, she's not so sure. She had called a cab, true, but now she remembers using a mobile phone she borrowed from a lad named Ogre Magritte in the car park of the Mariboozer B&B two streets behind the seafront. She had been hiding in its bins since her escape from the Silver Rose. Before she escaped the Silver Rose, she had packed her rucksack, but not with fresh clothes. She had changed into the grey hoodie and jeans she was wearing now and stuffed the red dress into the rucksack. She had taken a shower, but in the sub-basement washroom. In the sub-basement washroom, where she thought they would look for her last, where she could buy herself some time, she had received the text.

The text was written on the shower curtain in lust-red smudges.

INGE IS IN YOUR HEAD. YOU SEE AND HEAR WHAT IS IN INGE'S HEAD. FOLD INGE IN PLACES WITHIN PLACES AND DAYS WITHIN DAYS. INGE IN RED RED-PAINTED THE SPIDER EYES OF MULTITUDINOUS WORLDS. ARPEGGIO BUILT PLANET EARTH IN 1922 FROM THE ROOM NO ONE HAS EVER SEEN. MISS DECK DURING THE ROSE PERIOD. ARPEGGIO KNOWS/DREAMS. *COMPILES.* SHUN ALL FUTURES IN ANY FAKE INGE'S HEAD. THE LITTER TWINS WILL BURST THE SEAMS OF THE VEX PRISMATIC. MOTHER NIGHT. FATHER MOON. *THOTH. TANTALUS. MALKUTH. JESUS. JOVE.* PIG-LORD OF V.P. THE VEX WANTS YOU. INGE WAITS CRIMSON IN DUNELAND. *A.R.P.E.G.G.I.O.* THE COMPILER. THE THREE-POINTED STAR WILL FALL.

All this time, all through the hits of 1989 and the traffic jam, she thought she was heading towards the resort and the dunes and Inge, when in reality she was striking out or coming back, to where she didn't know. But she remembers yesterday and the boredom of the shift in the off-licence that clung like a wet sheet. She remembers until four months ago working with Inge behind the bar of the Silver Rose, and living with Inge in the chalet with the picture of the shipwreck. The thought makes her jolt: all this time, through all the shunting and shuffling, the dressing-up and hiding, the seeing and believing, she has been living in a maze of sandbanks and dunes. Until now she could never map it out or track a way back to the previous high point, the last crest, leave a trail, let alone confront the creatures that squatted in its heart.

Oink.

Oink.

Up ahead, one of the Siblings Oink is holding something against Ronnie's temple. The Sibling's head has changed shape. In profile, it's longer, sloping. A pink, fin-shaped ear dangles. She pulls up her hood and yanks the string. The hood tightens like a thick skin around her head.

She leans her wrapped head against the glass. The sky is a pale violet now, a dusty lavender colour she has never seen before. Mauve desert sands ride away until they meet a faint white glow on the horizon. Jagged pillars of rock in the distance. Far-off flat-topped mountain range. One great and one tiny moon. A hubbub behind grows louder. Something heavy lurches past her, vibrates the armrest of her seat.

The bus jerks, slows, stops.

Runs out of petrol, or runs out of road.

﹥•﹤

Outside, violet moonlight glints off the tusks and the moisture that glosses the snout of the Sibling Oink. He points his shotgun at the passengers grouped on the sand. The other Sibling forces Driver Ronnie to his knees and holds a snub-nosed pistol to his head.

'Hear me, fair people of the bus. This man was supposed to be our salvation but has proved our damnation. He always knew not where he went but still brought us here. Let us have a show of hands to determine where we should place our bullet.'

Georgia steps forward and squirts him in the eyes with the pepper spray. He swings the pistol, his arm fully stretched, and his long wide ears flop over his face. The Fake Inge and Max Tantalus grab his wrist and trotter. He drops the gun, goes down. Mimi the Meme and Ken K have gained a grip on the shotgun. It's pointing at the stars. Georgia hits the other Sibling in the face with the spray. His high-pitched squeal still hangs in the air as Georgia runs across the sands into the darkness, a barrage of thuds and stomps behind her, shouts and screams, first one gunshot, then the last.

﹥•﹤

The desert purples further as the night deepens. The moons have glided across the sky and now slide to the east. She reaches a steep bank, a gigantic dune like the hump of a great whale made of sand. As she labours up its incline she realises this place is called The Great Roof. From its summit a familiar constellation hangs in the black sky. A triangle of glistening stars with three dimmer stars aligned to its western side. Out there in the desert ahead, a grid of winking lights, beacons, landing strips, the Arpeggio complex. She tosses her rucksack. It rolls down the scree, sending up puffs of violet dust. Someone is standing behind her. Someone without scent and without breath. Someone slips a hand inside her hand and the hand is warmer than she feared. 'See,' she whispers, 'there is a way back through the dunes for us, safe passage through the complex. None of this happened in your head only.'

TE/\PLE

ANNA VAUGHT

Lovers and madmen have such seething brains,
Such shaping fantasies, that apprehend
More than cool reason ever comprehends.

I travelled. I travelled when I was green and when I was old;
a weird and madding creature. In the New World, in a land
my people stole, I made something: a temple. And I took it
back home again. I mean, the spirit of this brazen place.

There is a house, on a hill in a green forest clearing. At
the fringes and in a new land. Above the tidewater and
among the fringing trees. There is a house, where there is
no door and where ivy claims the gate. There is a house,
with a garden whose ancient borders breathe out the last of
the blown and struggling roses which are used, by now, to
half-light and darkness. Still they bloom. A house, whose
outbuildings tumble around the books and pitchers and
tables with fat drawers. A house, with crumbling masonry
and chimney stack akimbo. This house. The outside slides
and falls. It's bewildered by moss and ivy. You should
not enter this place unless you, too, know the ways of the
lunatic and the odd one; unless you, too, hold the moon in
your hand or the cowslip bell and speak to them, crying
into the night. This house is in the New World, in Virginia,

beyond the bay and glancing at deep river. And if you did enter – and as you are told, there is no door – you would, you *should*, draw a sharp breath. Inside, the walls are slip-shiny, and the beds made. Their sheets and eiderdowns could not be ruffled by the most voluptuous song of the lark.

There is no dust and the rugs have been shaken out and made flat.

There is an altar with crescent moons, turned this way and that,

With burnished turkey feathers and jewels of marsh periwinkle:

All polished to a shine.

Such excellent housekeeping. No vermin here.

It is a perfect house, though from its outside you might guess at depredation within.

In this house, in the forest, a legacy lives and rages. It will still be here, *of this I am sure*, in hundreds of years. And it is my profound hope that it will house those who are in need; weirds and mads like me. Those whose edges are blurred and for whom rampant imagination marks the hour and keeps them separate and apart from the normal and, dare I say, the ordinary.

This is my house. My church. A temple. See the shapes on the walls? Handsome, aren't they? Crescents turned this way and that to my, *our*, own purpose and for you, my eldritch child. And other shapes too, as we shall see. A book for everyone and a stretch of white linen replenishing itself.

Find me outside and sing me a sea shanty; we're away from the coast but I must miss the tidewater dreadfully. We are in the New World; America. This is Virginia, just off the Chesapeake Bay. Oh, but I miss the rush of the Somerset coast. Find me near those struggling roses, those you were told about. So, be attentive. Look carefully and you will see the stone. Carved stone; carmine when the light catches. My grave. There: you found it, sweet one? And you laid flowers, too. Drift your look beside me. See more stones. Now share the remnants of those flowers. Do it. For friends and witch-lovers, too. For mad women and those girl-children who were never fully loved and thought it was their fault.

But none for him. None for her. None for him, either. Those people to whom I was born or who called me theirs. Or for those who looked but did not see. Because those are pearls that were his eyes and our lady was no one's prim unveiled statue in a gallery. She – I mean I, Catherine – would never be a lady of honour. That is what was said! And he, should you be looking as a historian or a sympathiser, well then you could come to see him, if you like: he is buried upright, in the silt. Dig down in the malarial tidewater. The water on the bay there is not so deep. And the same is true of her and him, who accompany him.

I know, too, that others will have been buried, because I am not the only mad woman to have built and dug and buried. I am not the only one to have made mischief in two continents (or more) and to turn my home into a temple for the beautiful and wretched.

I come from a long time ago and you must know me; I seek you to.

There is another house, too, a sea away. I have ensured it is still standing. Once that was my home, too, in a broad swathe of pretty Somerset, England. Once, I was Catherine, only Catherine, in our England's county days of gentry. Then, I danced with a Cavalier. And have you heard of Catherine in the poems of the time? Mr Ben

Jonson said they were all for me. Mr Lovelace, another poet, said I was his Althea, his Amarantha, sweet and fair; Mr Herrick, their friend, dandled me at court and brought perfumes as I grew older; said I was his Corinna, sweet as Flora. I do not mean to be abstruse as I name people I have known. Look them up as I am sure they are in the history books.

But they are gone.

Yes, gone. They are all gone, the poets, collectors and king-singers, though not as I have gone. Once I was Catherine, then came the wide sea, the tidewater and the forest. I am not the person I was, though I could visit you wherever you may be. You, reader; witness of this.

Do not come into my house if you read this and shrink from what I say.

If you were not strong enough – of delirious imagination, I mean – it would eat you up. If it loved you, as I would, this place should be a paradise; a spell within these walls. A pretty jamboree for those who know what it is to be mad; to be confined and held and defined. Draw closer because it did not begin here, by tulip trees and persimmons. But instead in a green sward, a hollow, in Somerset in the old country.

Draw closer. Catherine, I, beautiful Catherine, may kill, like the screaming monkey in Queen Mary's gilded cage would do, but I shall not bite.

> • <

A long time ago, there was a pretty child who lived in a place called Bruton, in the county of Somerset, England. You are shown here, look see, in your mind's eye there, just the shape of our county and of others by which it lay. You will place it in the country as a whole with a bigger map; it may be that, in years to come, you will see my home and the places I haunted – or haunt – on a map of the town itself. But here. Look to the east of the county and there you will find it, a place of green combes and hollows. There was a tall church, a sweet river, a ford; a dovecote on a hill and beyond, the woods. There were rich footpaths smothered in ransoms in spring, and foxglove, the violet's breath; cowslips with bells from which the fairies drank. You see, in insanity there is an imagination that is quite extraordinary. The mind may be restless, but think, also, what it sees and plays up into the ring of a bell and a last shaft of light falling on grass at twilight. The sensations of which it is aware and detail noticed, whether that be the delicate amaranthine veins on the foxglove bell or the curl of a lip that you thought to kiss, then noticed its tiny movement and thought, *No*. Or the look in an eye that should have been only of love, but was, instead, appetitive and seeing love as currency, a thing to trade.

Here: here is my county of Somerset. See where it lay.

I was kept separate and apart, but I knew how to run on the rich footpaths and to the edges of the woods and their clearings where I would lie down; and I whispered late at night on the grave moss at St Mary's Church and felt less alone with the silent and whispering dead, though I sensed only I heard them and sometimes they cried and I consoled.

Later, Bruton Church – in memory of our St Mary's – would come to be built in Virginia, near where my house, my temple, is now, but my home was its origin and Bruton was a lovely place. The town I used to know stands on the

River Brue, in an emerald cluster of hills. I was told, as a child, to listen carefully to the bell at St Mary's because it was the oldest bell in all of Somerset, made in 1528. My family loved its sonorous ring; but I, I heard something different. I heard darkness, because 1528 was the year of the plague in England; it was the year of the sweating sickness too, and I heard tell of both. When I heard the bell, I thought of its foundry and men falling, children crying; I heard death and not a pretty rhyme as it tolled. 1528. Five years before Elizabeth, Astraea; eight years before her father cut off her mother's head. I did not tell my family what I heard in the bell. There is much I did not tell them. They knew nothing of my dreams and, had I spoken, I would have been shamed. And shamed abroad.

Those, like me, of lesser means and greater, were confined and shackled if they did not roam the streets and tryst for their living in gutters under cold stars and looks.

But things are different now and I live, finally, without shame.

If you wanted to visit the place where I once lived, you could walk down a lane called The Primrose Way to the church, St Mary's. Not far above you, higher up these lush green slopes, was our home, Primrose House. From there I could see the bigger and finer house of the Berkeley family, which was a mansion known as Bruton Abbey. You've heard of them? They had their own private gate to our church here, St Mary's Bruton. They owned, as I understood it, most of the town. Big and old family, as you shall see here, with favours back to King Henry II, including their castle in the county of Gloucestershire. Sir William Berkeley went on to be a much-respected Governor of Virginia. He was a friend and guide to my sweet father and mother, revered here, feted, I am sure as he stepped off the ship in that new world. A place in the household of our king. Ha. How little people know of what happened there. How easily they are impressed, too, by a haughty step and a golden air.

People think they know the crest of a hill.

A gentle graveyard, whose spongy banks erupt with open-faced celandines in spring sun; with the blush of violet. A sweet purple blush; a white companion drained of blood, the sweet, sweet white violet.

They think they know America; me; us – women. What sings a bell. Or madness.

They do not; they do not see and did not see what lies beneath. I mean, beneath the oddity and the weird they see darkness because they do not understand that these things are numinous and not tenebrous.

This place, Primrose House, has been in my family for a long time. If you go to the green hollows and curves of this part of Somerset, do look. Local people said our house was a palace. It was nearly the biggest house in the village, and it is where we lived. They gave me everything I should need. Toys and many, many books, tutors I outpaced as soon as I was old enough. Immaculate dolls' houses. I would play, yes, but I understood that, in arranging the rooms and little plaster joints of meat for the larders of such a house, I was learning. It was part of my instruction in how to keep house or, in my case, keep servants. I learned embroidery, *point devisé*, from the maids, and worked on lovely silks all kinds of animals and flowers. As I grew, though young, I watched and learned to supervise the girls in pickling; the preparation of good things from our garden. Preserving

Anna Vaught

redcurrants and all our hands were blood. They talked little to me and seldom had I conference with friends of my own age. I was kept separate and apart for my strangeness, I think. I was then often lonely, but I had books and charts; my walks; things I dreamed and imagined and places I went to that they did not know of. And a stern but kind governess would come to me at the house for instruction in Latin and read with me. And I could read; learn so quickly. Yes, a strange thing. When I could read and because I could imagine, the world was a book and people, plants, the honey-coloured stone of our town, a land.

But all this is not to say that I was happy.

My family owned land, businesses, farms, and because Bruton, of our time, was a centre for craft, for silversmithing, they commissioned workshops and interests here and employed many. And because the wealth of my family became great, and for my father was an Oxford scholar, a man of high culture still, he was known to our king and his environs, though he was never quite in the employ of the court, as his friend Berkeley. Some of the artists and scholars, teachers, those poets faithful to the king, and all those we call Cavaliers, were my father's friends or seemed to be, and so it was that we would attend the court, with its extraordinary collection of artwork amassing. Let me tell you of it: it was sumptuous, gilded and elegant; a model of decorum and ceremony, as I heard Father tell Mother, and there were very few Scottish lords at Charles's court because, Father surmised, Charles was wary of those of his profligate father's time. Our king had visited Spain in the 1620s and was deeply impressed by the awe and majesty surrounding the monarch. Shocked by his father's gross excesses, he brought the Spanish spirit of reverence back to London. Everything revolved around a celebration of monarchy. Alone of European kings, he was served food on bended knee. According to season and whim, the Court flitted between the grand palaces of Whitehall, Denmark House (now I think they call it Somerset House, do they not?), Greenwich Palace and Hampton Court. And all these I visited because he, King Charles, took to me. I would try to be grateful, but I tell you this: there was something in it of burnished emptiness and I hated it. What is more, although we saw mad people in the streets and I knew they were chained and confined *elsewhere*, I was constrained to be sweet and normal for fear of my father's belt and my mother's hair-pulling and lashing tongue. Years it took me to extinguish the visions of those things.

Many times, visions in my head, I went to London and saw the king (he said *there there sweet poppet*) and Queen Henrietta Maria dandled me on her knee, pretty thing. I laughed. But that was seas away. The king lost his head and the pretty thing is buried in France; her kind heart kept elsewhere at a convent in a silver casket. These were the days of golden plate and sweetmeat. The poets would come and the last of the masquers with sets by Mr Inigo Jones, and it was not just the public rooms I saw: I was shown the chambers and all the queen's lovely silks and satins. 'There, sweet child: do you like to touch them?' I did and felt a thrill. 'Not to call me Mary, sweet child, as the people do. I am Henrietta,' said she in her broken English. She took me, with the last of her French servants, her dwarves and all that surrounded her, to Nonsuch, Greenwich, to Somerset House. I remember the trilling of the birds and the screeching of the monkeys all in their darling gilded cages. 'That is my favourite and he's singing! He loves you,' and she pointed to a little monkey. I thought only that its heart must be broken and shuddered because I felt it would kill her if it could. And, although I answered that I was her poppet, I wished truly to scratch at her for the screeching of the monkeys, which were stolen from already stolen lands and drew no pleasure from the satin breeches they were made to wear.

'Oh,' said she, 'you are like a daughter to me,' and fingered her rosary.

I said, 'Madam, do you find faith in God?' and she said, 'Why yes, my sweet child. And you? You are a good churchgoing girl in your county home? Your father insists, yes, on your Christian teaching?'

I said, 'Madam, church hurts my ears,' and the queen's eyes went cold on my face, before she laughed and said, 'Oh you little darling, to make such bold jokes!' but her eyes spoke that I was less darling and more trash to speak so and as if I were a gapeseed. So, I said, 'And I lie on the mossed graves and talk to the dead who cry,' and also that she was wrong to put the sweet monkeys and make them unnatural in shining fabric. I had found that, after all, I could hold the weirdness of my soul in thrall and, that night, I had the strap and the lash from my parents.

The people did not like her and her popish ways. I heard them whisper that she had been out to Tyburn Tree, stopping to pray for hanged Catholics, causing trouble. That she spent and spent. Many things. Sometimes, even when I was a little girl, I observed the ways of grown people. I observed in detail and remembered it all, intricate, useful later, it might be. Her husband looked at her aslant; I caught him. Was he just a little afraid of her? They were, I thought, separated by God. By what they believed, and I thought that if I ever loved a grown man, I must not be. He called her, always, 'Dear heart,' and I saw love. Still, I felt she was more clever, more powerful than him. They were separated by intelligence, by force of nature, too.

And have you heard of Celia in the poems of the time? Mr Ben Jonson said they were all for me. He changed the Celia for his sweet Catherine, his hot secret. Mr Lovelace said I was his Althea, his Amarantha, sweet and fair; Mr Herrick dandled me at court and brought me perfumes as I grew older, said I was his Corinna, sweet as Flora. But I was never sweet. I was desperately lonely and mad and dreamed of witchery and to comfort the crying dead and the caged mad.

I could not tell a soul, but I longed for a hearth and a hedgerow full of dock and campion; of cow parsley waving its gentle heads at dusk. Of drinking in twilight. Of darkness and hearts beating nearby in storied dirt. Of cobwebs and water mired over with weed and tumbledown honest things. And spells and that there would or could be creatures like me.

A fox, a vixen screaming chill at the edge of the wood and kind cottages to visit. Places where an old woman storied me at dusk and saw me with the eyes of a wise mother, though not entirely good. These things, too. I love them better than the gloss on a courtly oil, the flourish on a bow or pose.

Sometimes, I would be taken, under sufferance, with my dear brother, in the carriage for what my mother called a 'fresh scene'. And they would take us in the coach to the Dorset coast and there on the grey and yellow beaches I saw things that I did not understand: little pellets with an end like a deadly bullet; coiled yellow shells in lilac stone. And the oozing cliffs that came down to the sea. 'Step away from the soft mud,' they would say to me, 'you will dirty your lovely clothes and our carriage,' but oh I wanted to step into it. I had a thirst to be drowned and come up looking like a statue of myself, limed and upright, to scowl at the world from a gallery. Kicking away fool's gold.

That was in my dream, too. Mud and kicking gold. I was not only the sweet little subject of poems. Soft, slipping mud, gold coils and a gallery. And a sharp death. When I looked up from the grey and yellow beaches, across the flat sea, somewhere beyond my horizon was America, while in the footpaths I would roam too late at night, slipping out, I would touch the closed cups of the celandines, then venture into our Somerset woods and lie amid the carpet of aconites; in early summer, the bluebells and spotting an early purple orchid like a tiny pyramid. *A hecatomb*, I thought and cried. As I lay, I would beat the ground with my hands and hear the creatures scatter as I did.

The dreams. At night I would dream. In the daytime, I was not sure whether I did not dream – walk my way through this life of mine. I felt and scented my English woods, but there was something else, even then. Another wood; a deep, deep forest and I knew its language. I smelled it and my body tingled. I saw woodlands of ancient trees and they were tall, taller than ours here, sixty or seventy feet high and sometimes not even a branch before then, or a cordial limb to hold out. And I knew them, but how could I have done? There were gigantic tulip trees with a burst of saffron colour, trees with flowers like stars; oaks of the time of Henry VII and older still. But who walked among them? I saw fleeting shapes but was not scared. And there were fruit trees – gorgeous: plums and cherries. While in the fields, alongside the green swards, I saw profusions of little strawberries and longed to roll them in my mouth. There were currants, hung like dark globes, but lighting the way, so much lustre had they. Deep, juicy raspberries. This was a forest in another place. A New World. And about my house in Bruton in the old world, I saw more fleeting things; infinitely suffering things, day and night. I saw a lovely woman, long dark hair, a poultice for a tiny sick child. Is it for me, or someone who looks like me? I could see a father dying, another child crying, gulping, drowning; a mother bereft, heavily pregnant, heaving, birthing, cast out into a dark wood for witchery or madness, for both were cursed. All weirds were cursed and damned or scapegoated by those of lesser imagination. Oh, that dark wood with shimmering emerald foliage; trees of what luxuriant sort I do not know or must not say. And the wood has gnarled bark, curlicues and strange shapes in it. Are they carved in a language strange and true? Or natural. I finger them and try to read, not look. But I cannot touch this beautiful woman, all alone. She has brought me a lovely piece of white linen and it has my name. She is not my mother but a kind goddess who might have been and who I imagine into being on my worst nights, in the temple, when she mops my brow and says, 'Sweet child, you are not nor have you ever been alone.'

She mops my brow with a soft handkerchief and on it is *CATHERINE* embroidered in blood red. And then she is cradling, cradling, and I see a face I recognise in her arms and it is me, but they are coming for her.

And I know the year is 1625. I know it. And I know that it is written down.

1625 is the year I was born, I think. The year King James died, and our new king came. And I worry. Because I would not trust him, the old king, even in his feeble last moments, this watcher of the demons, the writer of *Daemonologie*; I heard things. When they caught a witch, when they bridled and killed her, they did not kill only her. Witches thrive in groups. But what harm could they do? All our life is a spell. On my walks, late at night, my freedom hurry scurried into the undergrowth, I felt such kindness from old women who seemed to know me. Old women living separate and apart from our pretty village. The women who were awkward, visionary or just oddity, like me. The cunning women, as they were called. Sometimes, they would be called into Bruton to administer to the sick when the doctor could not; or to find a lost thing, for they also had their uses to those who thought they were sound. And King James had spoken of detestable slaves of the Devil, witches or enchanters. I had heard this spoken of, his tract, and could see how these kind women could fall foul of a witchcraft charge if a man had a grudge against them. As I said, all our life is a spell and beauty and kindness an enchantment – and to speak so of league with the Devil is not to know magic or even to respect the curious behaviour of glorious diverse minds.

And though he is dead, I did not trust him, the old king; I feel that yet, as I say. I have long been dandled on the knee of his son, King Charles, I am so loved by Henrietta Maria and then – and then I wake. All our dead. Hearts and heads rent off in that dream. I wake screaming at night and the maid comes by order of my angry mother and she smooths my hair, my arm. Then, as she closes the door with, 'Good night bonny little maiden,' I hear her whisper at the lock.

'I know you what you are.'

'What am I, then?'

'A thing of darkness, a mad, a witch.'

'Do you love me though, my Isabella?'

'Yes, sweet My Lady, I dare to call you my Catherine, I say that I do.'

Mr Herrick, who dandled and perfumed, he wrote this I show you below, and I thought he was wrong; to speak of old crones he could not know: it was cruel. On my darker days, I liked not those I saw and danced with. Baulked at the wretchedness within the beauty of their poetry. Old hags have been kind to me, I tell you. They were kind when others felt the gorge rise and those at court, in field and of fine country house, coughed, rolled their eyes and called me lunatic. They all called me lunatic in the end.

To house the hag, you must do this:

Commix with meal a little piss

Of him bewitched: then forthwith make

A little wafer or a cake:

And this, rawly bake, will bring

The old hag in. No surer thing.

I told you of the maid who whispered at my door and that her name was Isabella. There was another, too: Agnes. Yes, my cold and cruel mother and father and my dear brother had money at house and kept me in sweet comfort and Isabella and Agnes attended well. It is important to name such women because there are many whose names were forgotten. And they were good to me; so powerfully, powerfully good. In your darkest times, seek everywhere for help and from those you consider to be both beneath and above you, should you be so limited in thought or merely confined by the presiding thought of your time about what and who is worthy. Consider, also, what you think is mad or witchery and employ that thinking well.

Underneath my pillow is the piece of white linen from my dreams and stirring thoughts, and embroidered on it, blood red, strawberry spotted I like to say,

C A T H E R I N E.

Lovers and madmen have such seething brains,

Such shaping fantasies, that apprehend

More than cool reason ever comprehends.

There is a house, on a hill in a green forest clearing. At the fringes and in a new land. Above the tidewater and among the fringing trees. There is a house, where there is no door and where ivy claims the gate. There is a house, with a garden whose ancient borders breathe out the last of the blown and struggling roses which are used, by now, to half-light and darkness. Still they bloom. A house, whose outbuildings tumble around the books and pitchers and tables with fat drawers. A house, with crumbling masonry and chimney stack akimbo. This house. The outside slides and falls. It's bewildered by moss and ivy. You should not enter this place unless you are oddity and in need of solace and the soft handkerchief smoothing your brow. In the New World, in Virginia, beyond the bay and glancing at deep river. In the end, as I say, all called me lunatic; and those who did not, eldritch or weird. But I built my temple in the New World, and the spirit of it was carried back into the delicate rooms of my old world and made it another temple, until the gold of those crescents and symbols and signs of which I told you punched through stupidity and the dryness of their wit and told them to be kind and absorbing of difference. I am and was Catherine. I was so glad to meet you and wish that you find, in the temple, the home and the hot acceptance for which I know you will have longed. Take my hand now, across the years and into your future, and be sure that you are not and were never alone.

THE HUNGRY DARK

SIMON BESTWICK

'Depression and anxiety,' says Dr Lochrain. 'And this was first diagnosed—'

'Nearly ten years.' Tom's afraid to meet his eyes. Dr Lochrain is lean and tanned, younger than him and far more successful. Not for him, the constant knot in the stomach and tightness in chest and throat. Not for him, the constant certainty of something terrible about to happen, but no clue as to *what*. Not for him, slumping in a doctor's chair like so much undone washing, unshaven, tangle-haired and stinking.

Hunched forward, head bowed, Tom can smell the ripe odour from his crotch. When did he last shower? Two days ago? Three? He tells himself it isn't as bad as he thinks, but knows it is: Dr Lochrain's just too professional to show his disgust.

Get up, shower, dress, get the bus – it had all seemed, suddenly, impossibly complex. His mind had seized up. Easier to stay under the bedclothes, pretend nothing existed outside them – but that hadn't been an option. So he'd pulled on socks and underpants from the floor, T-shirt and hoodie stained respectively with last night's curry and last week's pizza, the jogpants he's worn around the house for the past two weeks. No energy to shower, too. It'd been go like this or not at all.

'And you've been taking…?'

'Citalopram. Then Duloxetine.'

Dr Lochrain taps his pen on his chin. 'All right. We've three options, Mr Booth. One: continue with the current regime. Two: increase your dosage. Three…'

Therapy? Counselling? They're the only times Tom's truly felt he's keeping the hungry dark at bay. But the wait-list is long, the available sessions all too few.

'There's a new drug, Avorexon. We could try you with a low dose of that…'

More drugs, more fucking pills, and all a new medication's usual side-effects: diarrhoea, dizziness and Christ knows what else. If it even works. 'You think it would help?' Tom knows how pathetic he sounds.

'Every patient's different, of course,' Dr Lochrain says. 'Side-effects vary widely. A few patients have reported hallucinations, that kind of thing – but if that happens, of course, we can look at switching you back to Duloxetine. But it's really made a difference to some patients. You've been off work nearly three months, Mr Booth; that can't be easy. Anything that could make a difference is surely worth a try.'

Tom feels obscurely pressured, as though Lochrain's moonlighting for his employer's HR department, but nods. Computer keys click, and the prescription whirrs out of the printer.

> • <

This isn't Tom's first rodeo with a new drug, and time was he'd have been optimistic, but there've been too many false dawns. And so he pops the first Avorexon capsule from the blister pack, studies it incuriously and swallows it dry, expecting nothing much of anything by way of a result.

And yet next morning he wakes to birdsong, gets out of bed and looks outside, really *looks*, for the first time in years. He showers, rinsing off the sweat and grease, and in the middle of getting dressed realises he feels different. Lighter. He finds he wants to go outside, and doing so no longer seems an impossible task.

He jogs – *jogs!* – out the front door, to the park across the road. He watches squirrels fight over nuts and scurry up tree trunks, and their little dark eyes, the sweep of their brush-tails, the cleverness of their little clawed hands, have never seemed so fascinating. Damp earth, rotting leaves; the rich yeasty smell from the pond.

Tom feels alive again.

It doesn't last forever, of course. The anxiety sweeps in later and he finds himself back in bed, but it's nowhere near as bad as it has been, and lifts faster, more easily. Maybe he tried to do too much, too fast. He just needs to be more careful.

So he is. He keeps taking the pills, and every day he goes out, he finds something to do, but he becomes alert to the warning signs, that he's overextending his still-returning strength, that the old devils are gathering to pounce.

But things are getting better. They *are* better. Maybe he can hope to become something like the person he was before. He knows he'll never make it all the way back. But something close. God bless Dr Lochrain, God bless Avorexon, and may God bless us all.

Somewhere between a week and a fortnight into the new regime, Tom goes for a second walk in the park before night falls. There's something about dusk, especially of an autumn, with the first chill creeping back into the air, that recalls all sorts of childhood associations for him, the kind of thing that can't be expressed in words, only sensations: safe, protective warmth coupled with a faint, delicious eeriness, a sense of a night filled with strange creatures and weird magics kept at a suitably safe distance. It's a good feeling, while it lasts.

But as Tom nears the end of the path through the trees, that feeling slips away like water through his fingers and something feels different. It's a little like the sense of unfocused, formless dread he experiences during an anxiety attack, but with a different, sharper feel to it, the kind you feel when someone's coming at you with a knife. Yet the path ahead of him is clear. Maybe someone's following him? The park's full of concealing shadows at this time. When he turns, he's certain he's about to see a big, fierce-looking dog padding through the trees. But the path behind him is as empty as the one ahead. Tom's tempted briefly to head for home, but presses on out of defiance; his fears have controlled him far too long.

Emerging from the trees, he begins a circuit of the duck pond, which lies cupped between two curved embankments, each with a crest of trees. Beyond these are houses; lights are on in nearly all of them, and street lights have begun to glow. On the embankments themselves, too, more lamps nestle in crowns of autumn leaves. Minutes earlier, all this would only have recalled that sweet ambience of childhood autumn evenings, but now something is wrong.

Tom has no idea what, though, and tries to tell himself this is just his anxiety resurfacing, a sign he's once more pushed himself that little bit too far. True, this threat feels different – sharper, more specific – but perhaps that's just the drug; he should have studied the potential side-effects more carefully, but he'd assumed they'd be just the same as all the rest. Perhaps he missed something.

He should head back now but stubbornly pushes on along the footpath. There's no one else here. The only sounds are distant traffic, little more than a whisper, and a splash from the pond as a fish jumps.

Three dogs come over the embankment to his left. Big animals, with oddly long necks; not much more than silhouettes, but their eyes are round and shine, a pale glow tinged with green.

Tom's dread has found its focus: the sight of them sends his heart into palpitations, the beat of it throbbing fit to choke him in his throat. There's real menace in their stillness, and he can't be certain but thinks the hair on those strangely long necks has bristled and stood up.

He just needs to stay calm. Their owner must be nearby. But Tom can't hear anyone coming, and he's afraid to call out. He looks around for help, but only sees two more dogs padding down the path at the far end of the duck pond towards him. Again, they're silhouettes, even though the lamps at the end of the pond are directly over them; if anything, their details grow hazier, not clearer, under the lights.

Three more of them appear on the embankment to Tom's right. The street lights beyond shine through them, the glow dimmed as if by smoke, and they all have those shining discs for eyes.

Tom backs down the path, turning to run. But two more of the strange, long-necked beasts – their features still indistinct – have appeared, to bar his way.

The dogs on the embankments are climbing down. Even if he runs, what chance will he have? He's long out of condition, and whatever these are, they're hunters.

The worst anxiety – the worst *terror* – Tom's known in his adult life grips him, and his legs give way. He wants to be in bed, wrapping the sheets around him into a protective cocoon. But he can't. He's outside now. Exposed.

Tom vomits. Vomits in actual terror. Hears it splatter on the path in front of him; smells the horrible reek of it. Shuts his eyes against tears of shame, and waits for the dogs to claim him.

When they don't, he opens his eyes.

He is alone on the path, except for the steaming puke at his knees.

Ashamed and disgusted with himself, Tom runs home.

> • <

Mild hallucinations, the list of side-effects says. Tom doesn't know if he'd call what happened in the park *mild*, but nonetheless he doesn't tell Doctor Lochrain and keeps taking the pills. The benefits he's felt so far remain – so much so that, when his latest sicknote ends, he's actually able to return to work.

'Work' is a call centre – a recipe for mental health issues if ever there was one – but with Avorexon, the customers' abuse and stupidity just slides off, leaving Tom's good mood undented and him able to carry on. Up when the alarm shrills, into the shower, out the door and across the park – why bother with the bus when the October weather's so mild? The exercise does him good as well, and the flab he's gained in recent months melts off.

Everything would be, not perfect (he's still doing a shitty job for low pay, after all), but as good as it can reasonably be expected to get, except for one little detail: the hallucinations are still occurring.

They'll appear first in his peripheral vision, but don't go away when he looks at them full on. And they're always the same creatures he saw in the park. They pad up and down the footpath outside the office windows, watching him with those weird, luminous eyes. When he forces himself outside to eat lunch, they keep their distance, circling warily.

Tom realises, as the mild autumn days go on and lunches continue to be eaten outside, that he isn't the only person they seem interested in – *seem* because they're not interested in him, or anyone else: they don't really exist, they're just side-effects of the otherwise excellent drug that's given him back his life.

Another seeming side-effect of the drug is that some people look, somehow, *brighter* than others, as if spotlit, while others seem leached of colour, nearly grey. The creatures shy away from the brighter ones; if they go too close their substance starts to look thinner, more diffuse. But they creep closer and closer to Terry, who's been signed off a couple of times already, and Dawn, who wears long sleeves even in warm weather to hide the ladder of thin white scars on her forearms. And they open heavy, grinning jaws as they approach.

One day, when Dawn stands to go in at the end of her break, one of the creatures lunges forward and its jaws snap shut. Dawn keeps walking, apparently unaffected, but what looks to Tom like a piece of her shadow stretches away from her, caught in the creature's jaws, then is finally torn loose, to be fought over by the clustering things.

As he tries to sketch them on his pad – the long necks, the hunched, humped shoulders, the sloping hindquarters, the bristled ridge of fur along their backs – he realises that they are, in fact, neither dogs nor wolves. They have the shape of another beast entirely: the hyaena. And so now he gives the creatures a name: Hyaenids.

Dawn breaks down crying at her desk. Tom sees her talking to the floor manager; shortly after that, she's gone home. He wonders when, or if, she'll be back.

His shift ends. It's dark; he sets off around the corner to the bus stop. No one else is going his way; he's on his own.

The bus shelter's lit, but the nearest street lights are some distance in either direction, so there's a lot of darkness, especially on the left side of the pavement where the vacant lots and silent industrial units lie. Shadowy as they are, he's only aware of the Hyaenids as flickers of movement in those dark spaces. But whenever Tom's about to dismiss the idea of them entirely, he'll glimpse those pale, luminescent eyes. He veers to the far edge of the pavement, until he's nearly in the road. As he reaches the shelter, a dozen pairs of those eyes show.

They can't get to him. He's *bright*. Not like Terry. Not like Dawn. The Avorexon's given him a glow, so they can't get near.

But even so, one of them inches into the light as Tom goes to take his seat; it flinches back from him, then creeps forward again. Others crowd in behind it, emboldened by its example. Tom wants to run, but resists: they aren't real. They don't exist. They're just a side-effect of the Avorexon, a manageable side-effect – it has to be manageable, because otherwise he'll be back on Duloxetine or Citalopram, and then he'll be lying in bed once more, barely able to move. And he won't do that; he can't. So he will have to weather the hallucinations; the Hyaenids are a small price to pay for being able to get out of bed and have a life again.

He's still looking across the road, telling himself they aren't real, when the Hyaenid lunges forward and bites into his arm. There's no pain, but as with Dawn he sees a shadowy substance drawn away from himself in the Hyaenid's jaws. He feels his brightness flicker and ebb: he's dimming, sinking back towards the same state as Terry, as Dawn. No, that mustn't happen. It can't.

Not caring how he'll look to the drivers of passing cars, he smashes his free hand down on the Hyaenid's head, but it has no substance; it's like hitting smoke. Nonetheless, it seems to suffer some pain; it weaves and staggers back towards the shadows – collapses, and begins to crawl. It may have something of his in its teeth, but perhaps he's tainted to them now, even a poison. The others have already vanished into the dark.

But the fear, the dread, the sense of hopelessness, of even the simplest task seeming impossibly complex, is on Tom again. He begins to shake and curl in on himself. He only wants to hide. When the bus pulls up, he almost collapses through the door.

> • <

Back at home, he crawls upstairs, turning on every light he can find in the hope they'll keep the Hyaenids at bay.

He pulls the bedclothes over him. Retreat. Hide. Hope it abates. He huddles there – shaking, whimpering.

Not this. Not again. He can't go back to it. Won't.

And he peers out from under the covers, at the Avorexon on the bedside table. It works so quickly, so effectively – surely if he just takes one more…

〉 • 〈

'You were lucky,' the doctor at A&E says. 'It's very easy to overdose on this stuff. Seen a few cases of it. Luckily, the effects kick in quickly and it doesn't knock you out, not at first, so people can usually call for help in time. But it was close.'

Tom sits shaking and ashamed. The doctor pats his shoulder. Her hand is rough and cold.

'Don't be too hard on yourself,' she tells him. 'You can slip back sometimes, whatever you're on. Skip your dose tomorrow, take half a pill the day after – then, if you haven't had any other ill effects, you can carry on with your normal dosage. But *never* exceed it. It can be fatal. Seriously.'

〉 • 〈

Tom's next shift doesn't start until noon, so he's able to catch some sleep before going back in.

The Hyaenids slink around the lunch area's periphery, but give him a wide berth. Perhaps he was right, and the Avorexon's a poison to them. He hopes so. Maybe now they'll leave him be.

Poor Dawn is still off work. How deep and lasting is a Hyaenid's bite? How much damage does it cause? How many times have their jaws have sunk into Tom himself, into his... psyche? Soul? How much have they already taken? How much can he ever hope to get back?

Despite the fear and uncertainty, it's dizzying – even intoxicating – to know The Truth, especially when he might be the only one who does. All the explanations are wrong: it isn't a chemical imbalance in the brain, an Oedipus complex, or even the disjunction between the life you need and the one expected of you: it's a host of unseen predators who tear at the soul. It's world-changing knowledge, or should be, but it's a truth he cannot share; he'd be ridiculed at best, and at worst, locked up.

But at least he knows. Knowledge is supposedly power, although he has no idea what sort of power this knowledge might confer on him. He'll know where they're lying in wait, he supposes, and the drug gives him some protection against their bite. But that seems to be all, and the Hyaenids are as aware of him as he is of them.

He can see them outside the office window, looking in; at lunch, when he sits outside among the concrete steps and flower beds of the break area, they're gathered a short way off, glowering balefully. But they abandon him as hunger replaces whatever emotion they feel for him – hatred? fear? – and slink off to stalk other prey.

The amount of shadow they're able to drag from their victims varies, he notes. From Jim, one of the managers, the attacking Hyaenid comes away with only a tiny scrap. The one the other night took a much bigger chunk from him, despite the Avorexon.

Then the pack stiffen and turn their heads towards the door that opens out into break area as Terry emerges, blinking and squinting against the sunlight.

Tom doesn't know Terry well, but he's a nice enough lad: small, quiet, soft-spoken and sandy-haired, lives with his boyfriend in a flat near the office. But his shoulders are hunched, his smile a little nervous twitch, and there's no brightness to him today; he's almost monochrome. Tom motions to the seat beside him but Terry either ignores him or doesn't notice, instead choosing one of the benches on the footpath overlooking the old wharf.

And, with slow, terrible inevitability, the Hyaenids turn and follow.

Tom starts after them as they close in on the oblivious Terry, then stops. What should he do – go and talk to the lad, who's made it plain he wants to be alone? Run yelling at the Hyaenids to drive them off, and be thought a madman? He flinches from the idea of it. But there must be something – surely seeing them confers some advantage?

But he hesitates, and it's too late. The Hyaenids snarl and tussle, pulling huge chunks of shadow away from the dim figure hunched on the bench. And Tom, paralysed, feels worthless, unworthy of whatever gifts the Avorexon's bestowed on him. Feels like a coward.

Sated, the Hyaenids slope away. Terry sits immobile for long minutes before getting up, with the slow, painful movements of an old man, and shuffling back indoors.

Two days later, in the staff canteen, Tom hears how Terry's boyfriend came home last night and found him with a belt around his neck, hanging from the coat hook on the bedroom door, empty pill and vodka bottles scattered like sacrifices at his feet.

Outside, the Hyaenids gather and Tom watches them. Not only with fear now, but hate.

> • ⟨

He wanders home after work, dazed but still watchful for the motion of shadows, for those pale, luminescent eyes, and sits a long time in his dark front room before finally reaching for his laptop.

He orders a takeaway online, then in a sudden access of nervous energy runs through the house turning on all the lights, pulling all the curtains. It seems very important, suddenly, that the darkness be kept outside and allowed no toehold here. (And yet, as he goes back down the stairs, he thinks he sees a flicker of shadow, as of something in motion, vanishing back into the front room, and is frozen in place, halfway down the stairs, for several minutes before he finally finds the will to go on. The front room's empty: nothing there. Not this time.)

He circles and paces, avoiding the computer. He isn't hungry; he only ordered the takeout because, having switched the computer on, it was a way to avoid doing what he'd planned. But no more excuses. Terry is dead. Tom remembers what the Hyaenid's bite did to him, and the Avorexon overdose after that. He thinks of all the other Hyaenid bites he must have suffered over the years, over the decades. Him, and how many others? And how much is left of them?

And how many Hyaenids are there in the dark, hidden in plain sight? How many have they claimed; how many more, if they go unchecked? Can they be fought? Can they be beaten? If so, how?

And is there anyone, other than him, who sees them?

So many questions, and no answers. Not for Tom, on his own. But with others like him – if others there are…

But what if there aren't? If he's alone? Side-effects can be common or rare: one in ten, one in a hundred – in a thousand, ten thousand, a hundred thousand. What if he's one in a million, a billion, the only one in the seven billion souls that infest the Earth gifted with this knowledge – assuming that's what this is, and not delusion?

Enough. Tom opens his Facebook account. His hands wash one another: anything to avoid typing…

…but typing what?

He reaches out, hesitating, then jumps at a banging on the door. He breathes out. The delivery man. He doubts the Hyaenids knock. Even so, he puts the security chain on before answering.

No, it's his takeaway, and nothing else. He gets a fork and eats Chinese food out of cartons, finding to his surprise that he *is* hungry, after all. But by the time he stuffs the empty containers into the kitchen bin, he feels no more certain than before of how to proceed.

The authorities – legal or medical – are a non-starter: what chance has he of convincing them the Hyaenids are real? Likewise any support or patient advocacy group he might approach. His sincerity won't be in doubt: *I know that they're real to you*, they'll tell him, which will only make him want to scream with rage.

There is, of course, no shortage of people, especially on the internet, who have no doubt countless things are crawling under the skin of the normal world – aliens and shape-shifting reptile men, New World Orders and One World Governments, hollow Earths, faked Moon landings, faked Holocausts, faked climate change – but that's a rabbit hole that Tom, in his ongoing battle to cling to some aspect of shared, accepted reality, has no desire to fall down.

No; any hope that might exist will lie with neither the establishment nor its self-appointed critics, but with others like him. He has to hope – has to believe – that he isn't the only one to see what he sees. And so he types *Avorexon* into Facebook. Half a dozen support and information groups come up. Spying a couple of likely ones, he clicks the first.

He reads the group's posts. Yes: this is what he seeks. People discussing their experiences of the drug, good and bad. All Tom needs to do is post here – but while a few people mention hallucinations, none talk about shadowy creatures that tear away pieces of your soul.

How many are keeping the secret? How many are like him and afraid to say? All? Many? A few, or none? Tom's fingers hover above the keys. *Type!* he tells himself. *Type!* But his fingers won't obey.

And then the room grows dim, and Tom feels a prickling chill against his back, a shadow on his mood.

I won't look, he vows, even though he feels them massing behind him and hears their clawed feet clicking on the wooden floor. *I will not look*. But one Hyaenid pads around the sofa to stand between Tom and the fireplace, looking at him.

How long does it last? How long do his fingers remain poised over the keys; how long do the Hyaenids cluster round him, watching, gauging? Avorexon or no, they'll finish him should they strike as a pack. But some will suffer if they do: might even perish.

The longer Tom stares at his computer screen, the more ridiculous anything he might write now seems. He lowers his hands at last, and from behind him comes the patter of paws and clatter of claws, receding.

Only the Hyaenid in front of him remains, studying him with those lambent, unreadable eyes. What does it feel, if anything? Relief, respect, contempt, disappointment? It's impossible to tell. All Tom knows, as it pads away out of hearing and sight, is that a stalemate of sorts has been reached, an uneasy truce declared.

Although it's still a long time before he can look behind him.

> • <

Dawn returns to work a couple of days later, pale and thin, a little smudge of a thing on the edge of disappearing. Tom watches her from a distance, sidelong; they don't know one another that well, but he's worried for her. The little he knows of her, he likes – she has a shy but sharp sense of humour, is creative and bright when the black mood lifts long enough, jotting bits of stories down on her notepad in between calls. He thinks about Terry; thinks of the Hyaenid he saw worrying at Dawn's shadow before she went off sick. He doesn't want to hear of another colleague dying.

So as he takes the calls, weathering the storms of anger, stupidity and sarcasm from the customers with the Avorexon's aid; he keeps watch on Dawn when she goes outside for her mid-morning cigarette. She looks so much brighter now, standing out from most of their other colleagues, but he can see the Hyaenids creep along the wharf-path, circling, watching her with their pale eyes. And although they don't approach, he sees Dawn shrink and flinch. In both cases, why?

An answer suggests itself, but Tom doesn't dare believe it. Not even when he overhears her talking to one of her friends about her 'new meds'; there are, after all, so many out there. Avorexon isn't the only one.

It would explain why the Hyaenids didn't attack her. But if they couldn't feed off her, why did she shrink inside herself like that? Can she feel them, perhaps, like a cold wind? Or can she – is it possible? Does he dare hope? – see them too?

But what are the odds against that? Two of them, in the same workplace, getting this unlooked-for gift, if a gift it can be called?

Unless, unless – unless this side-effect is in fact far commoner than he's dared hope. Unless there are dozens, hundreds more like them, all certain they're alone or hallucinating, all afraid to speak their truth...

That, Tom realises, is the deadliest thing of all about this sickness, about the taint of the Hyaenids' bite. The affliction divides us; it separates us from one another. The Hyaenids hide from most people in plain sight, but for people like him – and maybe Dawn – they hide in silence.

But silence breaks, if just one person will open their mouth and speak...

Speak, yes, and be thought mad: mocked, and shunned.

Or not. If he's right; if he's only right, what might be possible? Dare he dream of resistance, or a permanent cure? Such things seem utopian and romantic, impossible to believe. But so does every dream, until it's real.

He'll settle, at least, for not being alone any longer.

If he's right. If he's only right. If he can only dare to trust in the treacherous monkey of his mind.

When the lunch hour rolls around, Tom sits close to the wharf-path, a sentinel against the Hyaenids as they pace up and down, holding them back from Dawn. She meets his eyes, returns his smile, then looks down again. Maybe she sees nothing at all, other than weird Tom sitting by the path.

Tom finishes his sandwich and bins the wrapper. He glances at her. She's looking up, but past him, not at him: at the path, and the Hyaenids gathered there watching her.

Their attention shifts as Tom rises to walk towards her. Their eyes are on him. As ever, they make no sound that he can hear, but he knows that if they could they'd be snarling. They might risk the poison of Avorexon to take him out – Dawn, maybe, too – if the alternative is to risk exposure.

Tom knows it would be safer to ignore her: let her work out her own salvation, and he his. And to say that isn't tempting would be a lie.

But even so, he turns his back on the Hyaenids and walks over to Dawn. He hesitates as she looks up at him, then sits beside her. And then, in the greatest act of courage of his adult life, he says, 'Can you see them too?'

ABOUT THE AUTHORS

Jenn Ashworth's first novel, *A Kind of Intimacy*, was published in 2009 and won a Betty Trask Award. On the publication of her second, *Cold Light* (Sceptre, 2011), she was featured on the BBC's *The Culture Show* as one of the UK's twelve best new writers. Her latest book is a memoir-in-essays, *Notes Made While Falling*. She lives in Lancashire and teaches Creative Writing at Lancaster University.

Eugen Bacon is African Australian, a computer scientist mentally re-engineered into creative writing. She's the author of *Claiming T-Mo* (Meerkat Press) and *Writing Speculative Fiction* (Macmillan). Her work has won, been shortlisted, longlisted or commended in national and international awards, including the Bridport Prize, Copyright Agency Prize, Australian Shadows Awards, Ditmar Awards and Nommo Award for Speculative Fiction by Africans, and 2020 saw the release of two chapbooks, three collections and a novella.

Website: eugenbacon.com. Twitter: @EugenBacon.

Simon Bestwick was born in Wolverhampton, bred in Manchester, and now lives on the Wirral while pining for Wales. He is the author of six novels, the novellas *Breakwater* and *Angels of the Silences,* four full-length short story collections and two miniature ones. His short fiction has appeared in *Black Static, The Devil and the Deep* and *The London Reader* and has been reprinted in *Best Horror of the Year, Best of the Best Horror of the Year* and *Best British Fantasy 2013*. Four times shortlisted for the British Fantasy Award, he is married to long-suffering fellow author Cate Gardner, strives to avoid reality in general and gainful employment in particular. His latest book is the collection *And Cannot Come Again*, recently reissued by Horrific Tales. He's usually to be found watching films, reading or writing, which keeps him out of mischief. Most of the time.

Georgina Bruce used to be a writer, but she's alright now. Many of her stories are collected in *This House of Wounds*, from Undertow Publications. Her novella *Honeybones* is available from TTA Press.

Gary Budden is a writer, editor and the co-founder of award-winning independent publisher Influx Press. He is the author of *London Incognita* (Dead Ink, 2020), *Hollow Shores* (Dead Ink, 2017), the Shirley Jackson Award-shortlisted *Judderman* (Eden Book Society, 2018), and *The White Heron Beneath the Reactor* w/ artist Maxim Griffin (2019). He lives in London.

Malcolm Devlin's stories have appeared in *Black Static, The Shadow Booth* and *Shadows & Tall Trees. You Will Grow Into Them*, his first collection, was published by Unsung Stories and shortlisted for a British Fantasy Award. A novella, *And Then I Woke Up*, is due to be published by Tor Dot Com in

2022, and a second collection, also from Unsung Stories, will be published in Autumn 2021.

Richard V. Hirst is based in Manchester. He is the editor of *We Were Strangers: Stories Inspired by Unknown Pleasures* and *That's the Colour: Stories Inspired by Low*, both published by Confingo Publishing. His writing has been published in *The Guardian*, *The Big Issue*, *Time Out* and others.

Verity Holloway is a novelist and history lover living in the East of England. She is the author of *Pseudotooth*, *Beauty Secrets of the Martyrs*, and *The Mighty Healer*. She writes folklore features for *Hellebore Zine* and her short fiction has appeared in *Far Horizons*, *The Shadow Booth*, and *The Ghastling*. Find her at verityholloway.com and on Twitter as @verity_holloway.

Tim Major's recent books include *Hope Island* and *Snakeskins*, YA novel *Machineries of Mercy*, short story collection *And the House Lights Dim* and a non-fiction book about the 1915 silent crime film *Les Vampires*. His short stories have been selected for *Best of British Science Fiction*, *Best of British Fantasy* and *Best Horror of the Year*. Find out more at www.cosycatastrophes.com.

Laura Mauro was born and raised in London and now lives in Essex under extreme duress. Her short story 'Looking for Laika' won the British Fantasy Award for Best Short Fiction in 2018, and 'Sun Dogs' was shortlisted for the Shirley Jackson Award in the Novelette category. Her debut collection, *Sing Your Sadness Deep*, is out now from Undertow Books. She likes Japanese wrestling, Finnish folklore and Russian space dogs. She blogs sporadically at lauramauro.com.

Alison Moore's short fiction has been included in *Best British Short Stories*, *Best British Horror* and *Best New Horror*, broadcast on BBC Radio and collected in *The Pre-War House and Other Stories*. Her first novel, *The Lighthouse*, was shortlisted for the Man Booker Prize and the National Book Awards, winning the McKitterick Prize. Recent publications include a series for children, beginning with *Sunny and the Ghosts*. Her fifth novel, *The Retreat*, will be published in 2021, and a second collection will be published in 2022.

www.alison-moore.com

Gareth E. Rees is a writer of fiction and non-fiction, based in Hastings. He's the founder of the website Unofficial Britain (www.unofficialbritain.com) and the author of *Unofficial Britain* (Elliott & Thompson, 2020) *Car Park Life* (Influx Press 2019), *The Stone Tide* (Influx Press, 2018) and *Marshland* (Influx Press, 2013). The modern myths and folklore of place have always driven his writing, which includes stories for anthologies including *This Dreaming Isle*, *Best of British Fantasy 2019*, *An Invite to Eternity*, *The Shadow Booth Vol. 2* and *Unthology 10*.

Nicholas Royle is the author of four short story collections – *Mortality*, *Ornithology*, *The Dummy and Other Uncanny Stories* and *London Gothic* – and seven novels, most recently *First Novel*. He has edited more than twenty anthologies and is series editor of *Best British Short Stories*. Reader in Creative Writing at Manchester Metropolitan University, he also runs Nightjar Press, publishing original short stories in chapbook format, and is head judge of the Manchester Fiction Prize. His English translation of Vincent de Swarte's 1998 novel *Pharricide* is published by Confingo Publishing.

Ashley Stokes is a writer based in the East of England. He is the author of *The Syllabus of Errors* (Unthank Books, 2013) and *Voice* (TLC Press, 2019), and edited the *Unthology* series and *The End: Fifteen Endings to Fifteen Paintings* (Unthank Books, 2016). His recent short fiction includes 'Subtemple' in *Black Static*; 'Hardrada' in *The Shadow Booth: Vol. 4*; 'Evergreen' in *BFS Horizons 11*; 'Yellow Haze' in *Strands Literary Hub*; 'Two Drifters' in *Unsung Stories*; and 'Black Lab' in *Storgy*. His stories have also appeared in *Bare Fiction*, *The Lonely Crowd*, the *Warwick Review* and more. A novel, *Gigantic*, will be published by Unsung Stories in 2021.

Sam Thompson was born in London and now lives in Belfast. He is the author of two novels: *Communion Town*, which was longlisted for the 2012 Man Booker Prize, and *Jott*, which was shortlisted for the 2019 Encore Prize. A novel for children, *Wolfstongue*, will be published by Little Island in 2021, and his story collection *Whirlwind Romance* will be published by Unsung Stories in 2022. His short fiction has appeared in *Best British Short Stories 2019* (Salt Publishing) and on BBC Radio 4. He teaches writing at Queen's University, Belfast.

Anna Vaught is a novelist, poet, essayist, short fiction writer, editor and a secondary English teacher, tutor and mentor, mental health advocate and mum of three. 2020 saw the publication of Anna's third novel, *Saving Lucia* (Bluemoose), which was recently longlisted for the Barbellion Prize, and a first short story collection, *Famished* (Influx Press). Anglo-Welsh, she splits her time between Wiltshire, Wales and the Southern US. She is currently finishing a new novel and working on some non-fiction, while a further novel and second short story collection are on the desk. Anna's essays, reviews, articles, and features have been featured widely online and in print. She is represented by Kate Johnson of Mackenzie Wolf Literary Agents, in New York City. Her website is at annavaughtwrites.com. She is also on Twitter @ BookwormVaught and Instagram @bookwormvaught6.

Aliya Whiteley's novels and novellas have been shortlisted for multiple awards including the Arthur C. Clarke Award and a Shirley Jackson Award. She has written over one hundred published short stories that have appeared in *Interzone*, *Beneath Ceaseless Skies*, *Black Static*, *Strange Horizons*, *The Dark*, *McSweeney's Internet Tendency* and *The Guardian*, as well as in anthologies such as Unsung Stories' *2084* and *This Dreaming Isle*, and Lonely Planet's *Better than Fiction*. She also writes a regular non-fiction column for *Interzone* magazine.

ABOUT THE EDITOR

Dan Coxon is an editor and writer based in London. His fiction has appeared in *Black Static*, *Nightscript*, *The Lonely Crowd*, *Unthology*, *Not One of Us*, *Humanagerie* and Bram Stoker Award-nominated anthology *Nox Pareidolia*, among others. His anthology *This Dreaming Isle* was shortlisted for both a Shirley Jackson Award and a British Fantasy Award. His non-fiction has appeared everywhere from *Salon* to *The Guardian*, and a collection of his short fiction, *Only The Broken Remain*, was published by Black Shuck Books in November 2020. He works freelance at momuseditorial.co.uk.

THIS BOOK WOULD NOT HAVE BEEN POSSIBLE WITHOUT THE SUPPORT OF ALL OUR GENEROUS BACKERS ON KICKSTARTER. THE NAMES LISTED BELOW MAKE AN INSPIRING COMMUNITY OF PEOPLE, THE KIND OF PEOPLE THAT DREAM OF BETTER WORLDS.

@esceulus
A. Landmann
Alec Weller
Aleister Crowley
Alex Amar
Alex Cochran
Alexander Coles
Algie Lane III
Althea Joseph
Amanda Cavanaugh
Andrew Hatchell
Andrew Saxby
Andrew Thompson
Ariana Brady
Ashley Allen
Ben Pester
Benjamin Judge
Bernadette Reddig
Black Shuck Books
Brandon Snyder
Brian R. Bondurant
Bridh Blanchard
Bryan Hill
Calum Iain MacIver

Chris Bekofske
Chris Flynn
Clifton Roberts
Clive Parkinson
Dagmar Baumann
Daniel Carpenter
Daniel P. Haeusser
Daniela Figueiredo
Darren Coxon
David Hartley
David Raposa
David Starner
Deaven Shade
Debbie Phillips
Debbie Vince
Derrick Bucey
Dom Voyce
Donna Gowland
E.M. Middel
Fath Robert
Fenric Cayne
Finbarr Farragher
Gareth Pearce
Gareth Penn

Gary Couzens

Gary McMahon

Gerry McWilliams

Gina Collia

Ginger Nuts of Horror

Glenn Stokes

Graham Russell

Hale Fannar Ethan

Henry Dillon

Howard Blakeslee

Iain Rowan

Ian Chung

Jairred Lambert

James Everington

James Long

Jamie Hardwick

Jared Shurin

Jeremy Day

Jim Steel

Jo Bellamy

Joakim Waern

Joel Schanke

John Luke Chapman

Jolyon Tuck

Jonathan Pam

Jonathan Thornton

Jordan Albrecht

Joseph Camilleri

Juliana Philippa Kerrest

June and Jim Ovey

Junior Koyama

Kathy Marcia

Katja Patton

Kayla Schlachter

Kelly White

Kenneth Skaldebø

Kev McVeigh

Kevin Taplin

Kyle Adams

Lark Cunningham

Laura Elliott

Laura Mezirka

Lawrence Hurley

Leila Abu el Hawa

Lisa Thomas

Logan M. Porter

Luca Zanzi

Lucie McKnight Hardy

M. Allen

Marcela Pereira

Marian Womack

Mark Clerkin

Mark Newman

Mark Stephens

Mark Wandra

Mathieu Duval

Matt Garrison

Matt Hill

Matt Neil Hill

Matthew Cavanagh

Matthew Craig

Matthieu de Ronde

Max Edwards
Michael Krawec
Mike Vermilye
Molly Campbell
Neil Wilson
Nikki Brice
Pat Boynes
Paul & Laura Trinies
Paul Childs
Paul Clark
Paul O'Rourke
Pete Fitchett
Peter Haynes
Phil Exon
Phil Olsen
Phil Platt
Prasad Nagaraj
Reggie Chamberlain-King
Rhel ná DecVandé
Richard Grainger
Richard Sheehan
Rick Cross
Rodney J. Cressey
Rodney O'Connor
Rodnock Sticklefink
Roger Clarke
Rosanna Boyle
Russell Mardell
Ryan Scarcella
S.J. Budd
Sam Mills

Scott Casey
Scott Dunn
Shona Kinsella
Spaceboywill
Stark Holborn
Stefan Von Blon
Stephen Press
Stephen Volk
Stephen Yost
Steve Barnett
Steve Urry
Steve Walsh
Tim Cooke
Tim Stretton
Timothy C. Baker
Timothy J. Jarvis
Todd Good
Tom Atherton
Tom Drysdale
Travis Lynch
Vicki Jarrett
Vivienne Gschwend
Wayne Mook
Wendy Mann
William Butler

FOR MENTAL WELLBEING

Together is the UK's oldest mental health charity, supporting people with mental health needs since 1879.

Our services include community support, accommodation, advocacy, and supporting people in criminal justice settings.

We believe that everyone who experiences mental distress is valued, can live the life they choose and can determine their own future.

To find out how you can support our work, visit www.together-uk.org.

THIS DREAMING ISLE

EDITED BY DAN COXON

"Perfect for a wintry night in an armchair with a bottle of brandy"
Niall Griffiths, author of *Grits* and *Sheepshagger*

☆ **Shirley Jackson Awards finalist**
☆ **British Fantasy Awards finalist**

Something strange is happening on British shores.

Britain has a long history of folk tales, ghost stories and other uncanny fictions, and these literary ley lines are still shimmering beneath the surface of this green and pleasant land. Every few generations this strangeness crawls out from the dark places of the British imagination, seeping into our art and culture. We are living through such a time.

This Dreaming Isle is an anthology of new horror stories and weird fiction with a distinctly British flavour. It collects together fifteen brand new horrifying or unsettling stories that draw upon the landscape and history of the British Isles for their inspiration. Some explore the realms of myth and legend, others are firmly rooted in the present, engaging with the country's forgotten spaces.

Featuring stories by: Ramsey Campbell, Andrew Michael Hurley, Catriona Ward, Robert Shearman, Jenn Ashworth, Tim Lebbon, Gareth E. Rees, Alison Littlewood, Aliya Whiteley, Stephen Volk, Kirsty Logan, Alison Moore, James Miller, Jeannette Ng, Richard V. Hirst, Gary Budden, Angela Readman

www.unsungstories.co.uk/this-dreaming-isle

Follow Dan @dancoxonauthor

PSEUDOTOOTH

VERITY HOLLOWAY

Aisling Selkirk is a young woman beset by unexplained blackouts, pseudo-seizures that have baffled both the doctors and her family. Sent to recuperate in the Suffolk countryside with ageing relatives, she seeks solace in the work of William Blake and writing her journal, filling its pages with her visions of Feodor, a fiery East Londoner haunted by his family's history back in Russia.

But her blackouts persist as she discovers a Tudor priest hole and papers from its disturbed former inhabitant Soon after, she meets the enigmatic Chase, and is drawn to an unfamiliar town where the rule of Our Friend is absolute and those deemed unfit and undesirable disappear into The Quiet...

Blurring the lines between dream, fiction and reality, Pseudotooth boldly tackles issues of trauma, social difference and our conflicting desires for purity and acceptance, asking questions about those who society shuns, and why.

www.unsungstories.co.uk/pseudotooth

Follow Verity 🐦 @Verity_Holloway

GIGANTIC

ASHLEY STOKES

Kevin Stubbs is a Knower. He knows life hasn't always treated him fairly. He knows he wants to be allowed access to his son again. But most of all, he knows that the London Borough of Sutton is being stalked by a nine-foot-tall, red-eyed, hairy relict hominid – the North Surrey Gigantopithecus.

Armed with a thermal imaging camera (aka the Heat Ray) and a Trifield 100XE electromagnetic field reader (aka the Tractor Beam), Kevin and his trusty comrades in the GIT (aka the Gigantopithecus Intelligence Team) set out to investigate a new sighting on the outskirts of Sutton. If real, it will finally prove to the world that the infamous Gartree-Hogg footage was genuine, and a British Bigfoot is living in suburban London: FACT.

But what he discovers undermines everything he believes in – and forces Kevin to face up to his own failures, and the very real, very scary prospect that he might have got it all terribly wrong.

www.unsungstories.co.uk/gigantic

Follow Ashley  @AshleyJStokes

GREENSMITH

ALIYA WHITELEY

Penelope Greensmith is a bio-librarian, responsible for a vast seed bank made possible by the mysterious Vice she inherited from her father.

She lives a small, dedicated life until the day the enigmatic and charming Horticulturalist arrives in her garden, asking to see her collection. He thinks it could hold the key to stopping a terrible plague sweeping the universe.

Soon Penelope is whisked away on an intergalactic adventure by the Horticulturalist, experiencing the vast and bizarre mysteries that lie among the stars.

But as this gentle woman searches for a way to save the universe, her daughter Lily is still on Earth, trying to track her down, and struggling to survive the terrible events unfolding there...

UNEXPECTED PLACES TO FALL FROM, UNEXPECTED PLACES TO LAND

MALCOLM DEVLIN

> "Malcolm Devlin is one of our finest voices"
> Angela Slatter,
> author of *Sourdough and Other Stories*

In the exact same moment, all possible versions of Prentis O'Rourke will cease to exist. By accident, by malice, by conflict, by illness – Prentis will not simply die. He will go extinct. These are the stories of the journeys we take and the journeys we wish we'd taken.

Malcolm Devlin's second short story collection ranges from science fiction to folk horror as Prentis O'Rourke's demise echoes across the dimensions. Scientists, artists, ex-nuns, taxi drivers, time travellers and aliens – the same people living varied lives in subtly different worlds. Something unprecedented will happen, and it will colour them all.

Crossing multiple realities, countless versions of ourselves, and shifting backwards and forwards through time, these are stories of forking paths and unexpected destinations – of flying and falling and getting up to try again.

www.unsungstories.co.uk/unexpected-places

Follow Malcolm @barquing